THE IMMORTALISTS

```
          T T G     A T G
      C C A T G C
      G T   G A A C
          T       C       T
          A   C C T     T
      C A C A A T G
      T T C   G G C
      T T G     A T
      C C A T     C
          T T G     A C
      C T     A     T
      G A C C T A T
      C A C A A   G
      T T     A   G C
      T T     G A T G
      C C   T G
      G T T G A A C
          T G       T T
          A     C T A
          A C A     T
          T C A     G C
          T G G   T G
          C     T   C
          T     G       C
          T             T
```

THE IMMORTALISTS

KYLE MILLS

THOMAS & MERCER

Text copyright ©2011 Kyle Mills

Printed in the United States of America.

Published by Thomas & Mercer
P.O. Box 400818
Las Vegas, NV 89140

ISBN-13: 9781612182162
ISBN-10: 161218216X

PROLOGUE

Cleveland, Ohio
April 2

Annette Chevalier slammed on her brakes and winced as the car lurched forward, nearly hitting the rising garage door. Her husband had threatened to duct tape a mattress to her front bumper if she ever did it again, and there was no reason to believe he was bluffing.

She drummed the steering wheel impatiently, glancing at the broken clock in the dashboard and then at her wrist, which hadn't held a watch in years. They were such insidious little machines—always there to pressure you, to make you fixate on what was next instead of taking pleasure in what was now. To remind you that your time was slowly, inevitably running out.

She gunned the car inside and jumped out, rushing for the door. Her son's recital was tonight, and not only had she promised to be there, she'd gotten testy when he'd given her the skeptical eye roll he'd learned from his father.

The light from the exterior floods bled through the windows in the living room, providing just enough illumination to keep her from bouncing off the furniture as she dashed toward the stairs. When she passed the kitchen, though, the digital numbers glowing from the oven caused her to falter and finally stop.

It was almost over. By the time she changed out of her lab clothes and drove to the school, they would be on their way home.

i

She stood there in the semidarkness, trying to recall how many times she'd allowed this to happen. Jonny's disappointment was turning to cynicism as he reached the age for such attitudes to take hold.

But this would be the last time. She was going to buy a watch tomorrow. One with an alarm. A loud, obnoxious one. Maybe even flashing lights.

She padded quietly to the refrigerator, scowling at the plastic-covered plate of leftovers that her husband had arranged for her. His not-so-subtle way of reminding her that he'd always known she'd miss the recital.

Tomorrow wasn't soon enough, she decided, snatching a chicken wing from the plate and making her way toward the office she kept at the back of the house. She'd order a watch from Amazon tonight and have it FedExed directly to the lab.

The darkness deepened the farther she got from the living room, and she navigated hesitantly, reluctant to use her greasy fingers to flip a switch. Pausing in the doorway, she squinted up at something she couldn't quite make out hanging from the rafters. A moment later, the desk lamp snapped on, causing her to drop the chicken and raise a hand reflexively to protect her eyes.

"I want you to be very quiet, Annette."

The unfamiliar voice was completely calm but carried a weight that choked off the startled scream building in her throat. Her eyes began to adjust to the glare, slowly adding detail to the outline of the man sitting in her chair.

"Who…who are you?"

He didn't react, remaining motionless enough that the ceiling and the thing dangling from it again attracted her eye.

A noose.

"Take what you want," she heard herself say.

"I'm afraid that's you, Annette."

She'd been labeled a genius since the first day of grade school, but her mind still couldn't make sense of what was happening. Based on his accent, dark skin, and European features, the man in front of her was most likely Indian. His suit was impeccably tailored, and his tie looked like it cost more than her entire wardrobe. Not a thief. A rapist?

The thought almost made her laugh. A man obsessed with overweight, middle-aged women who hadn't attracted many glances even in their twenties?

"I don't understand."

He pointed to the noose.

"Are you some kind of psychopath?"

"No."

"Then what are you doing here? You have the wrong person. I'm a biologist. A medical researcher—"

"You have a PhD from Harvard," he said, continuing for her. "You've been married for nineteen years. You have a fourteen-year-old son named Jonathan whose piano recital you're missing as we speak."

Her initial shock faded into nausea-induced terror. The room began to lose focus, and she put a still-greasy hand on the doorjamb to steady herself. "Why would you want to hurt me? I don't *do* anything. I work during the week. On weekends, I stay around the house."

"Everyone has enemies, Annette. And, unfortunately, yours are wealthy and powerful enough to afford me."

He stood, and her body tensed. Moving only her eyes, she followed him as he dragged her chair around the desk and placed it beneath the rope.

"If you would be so kind?" he said, motioning for her to climb up onto the chair.

"No."

He nodded, unsurprised by her reluctance. "I'm going to explain something to you, and I need you to listen very carefully. I'm being paid extremely well to make your death look like a suicide—"

"This is insane!" she blurted. "*You're* insane. No one—"

He put his finger to his lips, and her voice faded back into the silence.

"If I'm not mistaken, your son's performance has already ended. If I'm still here when he and your husband come home, my plan changes."

"What do you mean?"

"I mean that instead of just committing suicide, you'll have a complete mental breakdown. You'll kill them both before turning the gun on yourself."

She opened her mouth to speak, but he ignored her and continued.

"Based on your background, no one will be particularly surprised, will they, Annette? No one will ask questions."

She thought about running but knew she wouldn't make it ten feet before he chased her down. And screaming wouldn't help either. The house was well insulated and separated from their nearest neighbor by more than a hundred yards of hedge-bordered grass that she'd insisted on for Jonny. He'd inherited her sedentary ways, and she'd hoped a yard would encourage him to go outside.

The man pulled a gun from his waistband that she recognized as the one her husband had bought years ago against her wishes. For protection, he'd said.

Still, she didn't move. This couldn't be happening. "Tell me why."

"I wouldn't know. I'm just a man who does unpleasant work for people too cowardly to do it themselves. What I can tell you is this: The people I visit always protest, but deep down they know. They know why I'm here."

"I develop medicines that help people," she protested. "I'm in the PTA, but I miss most of the meetings. I…" She fell silent. There was nothing more to say. That was her whole life.

He pointed to the noose with her husband's gun. "Time's running out."

His eyes were dark, almost black, but not angry or even particularly menacing. All she saw there was certainty. He would do what he said he would. He'd make her watch while he murdered the son she'd spent nowhere near enough time with and the husband who had stood by her even when he shouldn't have. And the world would think she did it.

Annette took a shaky step forward, and the man held out a hand, helping to steady her as she climbed up onto the chair.

The noose was now directly in front of her face, and she found herself paralyzed. "I'm afraid."

"It'll be over soon," he said serenely.

"How do I know you won't hurt them?"

"Why would I? It would be noisy and messy. It would attract the press. My only concerns are that I am paid and that no one knows I was ever here. But the longer we wait…" He didn't finish the sentence. He didn't have to.

She put the noose around her neck, and he reached up, tightening it until the sensation of the rope against her skin overpowered the warm trickle of tears running down her cheeks.

She stared straight forward as he took hold of the chair beneath her feet. It was suddenly all so clear—the unheeded coincidences, the odd questions thoughtlessly answered, the inexplicably emphatic demands of her superiors.

He was right. She knew exactly why he was here.

1

New York, New York
April 7

Richard Draman pressed a button on the remote, creating a deep green glow in the room.

"This is a normal cell nucleus," he said, pointing to the well-defined circle projected on the screen behind him. Another click of the button plunged the room into darkness for a moment before the next slide came up. Instead of being round, the cell it depicted was twisted and deformed—a shape that, despite his years as a scientist, he'd come to associate with evil. A demon's wing. The tattered cape of a vampire.

"This is from a child suffering from Hutchinson-Gilford syndrome—more commonly known as progeria."

The four faces staring out from behind the table in front of him reflected little but the light of the diseased cell, as impassive now as they had been when he arrived.

Maybe he'd pushed too hard for the meeting. Hell, he was almost certain of it. But he didn't have the luxury of being subtle. He hadn't for a long time.

"The disease is caused by a genetic defect that essentially causes its victim to age at a wildly accelerated rate." He clicked to a photo of what at first glance seemed to be a frail old man standing amid a group of towering grade school children. Most of his bald head was hidden by a baseball cap, but his bony arms, patterned with bulging veins, were clearly visible where they emerged from the sleeves of a Green Day T-shirt. His nose was hawklike, protruding from a round, wrinkled face, made even starker by the wide smile full of uneven teeth.

"Jack here lives just outside of Atlanta. He's a great kid with a real aptitude for math and a love for camping and fishing. He's only seven years old."

His audience's expressions shifted subtly, a little less dispassionate as they examined the sick child, trying to imagine what it would be like to be born with such a cruel disease. What wouldn't Jack give to have the things they took for granted—a life that stretched out ahead of them for decades and an imperceptibly slow physical decline that came balanced by wisdom, family, and friendship.

"Children like Jack only show some aspects of aging. They don't suffer from senility, for instance. They also have no predisposition to cancer, like most people do as they get older. The first thing that strikes people is that they're just kids. They get scared and excited and curious about things, just like we all did at that age. What's different, though, is that they have an extremely high risk of hardening of the arteries—which can lead to heart attack and stroke."

"How long can they survive with current medical technology?" one of the people behind the table asked.

Richard took in a slow breath that seemed to get more difficult every time he had to say the number aloud. "Most don't live longer than thirteen years."

Their grave nods made shadows play across their faces in a way that was strangely unnerving, and he chased away the darkness by clicking to a picture of his lab. It was modest by most standards and becoming more so every day. Many of the people bustling around in the photo were gone now, working for government agencies, pharmaceutical companies, and universities on three continents.

"I like to think I run the most cost-effective research facility in the country. We get a lot of volunteer help from the parents of the kids as well as other people who understand the seriousness of the disease. Every dollar we bring in goes directly to finding a cure."

Another press of the button, and a slide of a group of kids suffering from progeria appeared on the screen. Despite their appearance, it was actually easy to forget their illness for a moment. They were holding balloons, clowning around, grinning broadly—doing the things kids should be doing.

"In many ways, we're like a family. We try to get together every few years, and people from all over the world come. The kids have an opportunity to spend time with other children like them, and parents get to talk to each other about things that no one else could possibly understand. A lot of the kids form friendships that go on..." his voice faltered for a moment, "for their entire lives."

Richard stepped partially into the projector's beam, putting himself center stage. It was a position he'd never been comfortable with, despite the fact that he'd been told he cut an imposing figure. His broad shoulders were a holdover from growing up on a farm, and his height and shaggy blond hair were what remained of his mother's Scandinavian ancestors. The beard covering his jaw was more the product of admitting he couldn't remember to shave than a fashion statement. He'd carefully trimmed it before leaving the house, aware that when it got long he tended to look like he was applying for a job as the Minnesota Vikings' mascot.

"I've dedicated my life to eradicating this disease, and as I'm sure you read in the information I sent you, my team has made more progress in the last five years than all the researchers before us combined. So here I am, hoping that your foundation will grant me the twenty-five thousand dollars I need to continue pursuing a cure."

He moved out of the light, allowing his audience to take in the screen full of smiling kids who refused to have their childhood stolen from them without a fight. A fight that two in the photo had already lost.

He clicked over to the next slide and continued. "The disease wasn't well understood until—"

"Please have a seat, Dr. Draman."

He fell silent, acutely aware of the sensation of his saliva suddenly drying up. He'd barely finished his introduction—the full presentation went on for almost forty-five minutes, covering the history of the disease, its biology, and details of his lab's breakthroughs. "Excuse me, but I have—"

"Please, Dr. Draman. Sit."

It had happened before. Sometimes presentations were only a formality and donors had made a decision to give him money based on his written submission. And sometimes not.

There was a quiet hum as the shades at the back of the room began to rise, revealing a skyline of glass towers reflecting a cloudless sky.

Who would have ever thought he'd end up here? He'd almost been held back as a high school sophomore, the same year his friends snuck a page into the yearbook naming him Most Likely to Be Indicted on a Federal Level. For the thousandth time, his hard-working, salt-of-the-earth parents had been beside themselves. But now he was making up for his past, and these soul-crushing meetings were part of his well-deserved penance.

"Can we get you something to drink? A glass of water? Soft drink?"

Richard shook his head. It was the man in the center talking. A plump white executive of about sixty. Nice suit. Shiny shoes.

"Richard…can I call you Richard?"

"Please do," he said, trying to beat back the urge to grab the man by his feet and shake him until the change fell from his pockets. He despised this part of his job—it made him feel like a particularly unattractive union between a mugger and a beggar. A megger. A bugger. A—

"Doctor?"

Richard realized he'd let his face go blank, and he conjured a polite smile as the man began to speak.

"First, let me say that this is a horrible disease that deserves far more financial resources than it gets. Sometimes it's hard for us to believe what money gets spent on—by the average person, by the government. I like to say that every childhood disease in the world could be cured in a matter of a few years if we all just gave up big-screen TVs."

It was hard not to notice that this little speech sounded a bit canned.

"I know I speak for all of us when I say that there should be no limits on the spending for progeria. That we wish *we* didn't have any limits."

Richard kept the smile going, though he suspected that the longer he held it the more he looked like a used car salesman from Southern California.

"Second, let me say that we understand your position, and we sympathize. More than you probably imagine. And, finally, your reputation as a brilliant and responsible scientist precedes you. We would very much like to work with you."

The man fell silent, seeming uncertain how to continue and letting the woman to his right take up the thought.

"Let me ask you a question, Doctor. How many children are suffering from this progeria right now?"

"I don't think it's a question of how many, ma'am…"

"I disagree. What you mean to say is that it *shouldn't* be a matter of how many. Are there fifty worldwide?"

He'd been down this road many times and still had never been able to devise an escape. "Almost."

"Almost," she repeated. "One in eight million children suffer from this syndrome, isn't that correct?"

"Something like that. Yes."

"And there's no real chance of it spreading because—and I'm very sorry for this—these children don't grow old enough to have children of their own."

He nodded, feeling the sweat forming at his hairline. Maybe because the sun streaming through the windows had confused the air conditioner. Or maybe it was the man to the far right who hadn't made so much as a sound yet. He just sat there. Staring.

"You understand that I'm not trying to belittle the plight of these children," she continued. "Of course I'm not. But during your presentation, more children died of malaria than have died of progeria in the history of modern medicine."

The man on the right finally came to life, leaning forward over the table. "And we're talking about a genetic disease that's going to be extraordinarily difficult to cure or even to manage. Isn't that right?"

"That's true," Richard said, deciding it was time for a borderline dishonest change in tactics. Desperate times demanded desperate measures. "But the applications of a progeria cure could be incredibly widespread. It could have a bearing on the general problems associated with aging that affect—"

The man in the center held up a hand, silencing him. "There are other forces involved in that fight, Richard. Our foundation deals exclusively with childhood disease. And every single one deserves our attention and funding. Unfortunately, both of those resources are finite."

2

Outside Baltimore, Maryland
April 8

Richard clutched the platter as his wife piled it with sausages from the rusty grill centered in their backyard. It had been up against the house until a few months ago when they'd noticed the glossy mauve paint exfoliating into their food. He probably should have done a little more prep work before, in a moment of weakness, he'd agreed to let his daughter attack the warped siding with "any color in the whole world."

The sun settled into the horizon, softening the lines of his listing fence, the cracked kitchen window, and the litter blowing around mid-eighties sedans in the street. Not exactly what he'd pictured when he left Stanford with two PhDs in the glove box and a beautiful, talented young woman in the passenger seat.

But it could have been worse. The rent was free—an ongoing gift from a sympathetic man whose son had died of a genetic disease unrelated to progeria. The truth was that one terminal disease wasn't all that different from any other. The result was the same, as were the people forced to watch their loved ones fade away.

His gaze shifted to a towering pile of dog shit on his overgrown lawn. That was a somewhat less benevolent but similarly perpetual gift—this time from his chronically unemployed neighbor's horse-sized pet.

"Richard?" Carly said, flipping another sausage onto the plate. "Stop it."

"What?" he said looking up at her.

"Fixating on the dog poop."

"I wasn't fixating. I was just thinking."

"About?"

"The fact that Susie plays out here. And that maybe a good old-fashioned ass kicking is what Harvey needs to understand that."

She laughed. "I think you may be getting a little long in the tooth for that kind of behavior, Dr. Draman."

"Hey, I'm not even forty yet. And he's—"

"A grossly overweight man with a heart condition and an alcohol problem?"

"Just makes my job easier..."

The smoke twisted up her athletic body, clinging briefly to her red hair before shattering in the breeze. She was wearing the sunflower print apron he'd bought her when she graduated from culinary school, now faded and worn through in places. She told everyone that she kept it for sentimental reasons, and there was truth to that. It wasn't the whole truth, though. Somewhere in her incredibly complex subconscious, money played a part. And he hated that. She deserved more. She deserved everything.

Carly tapped the platter in his hands. "They're your favorite."

"What?"

"Earth to Richard. The sausages. They're the chipotle ones you told me you liked so much."

"Oh, yeah," he said, pretending to remember. "Those things were amazing."

He wasn't sure he'd convinced her, but she loaded the last one and started for the house with him in tow.

"Chris!" she shouted as they stepped inside. "Soup's on! Everyone ready?"

Chris Graden appeared a moment later holding what was undoubtedly the only five-hundred-dollar bottle of wine to ever grace the neighborhood. He'd been a big deal before his retirement, running one of the world's largest and most profitable pharmaceutical companies. Now he spent his time playing golf, sailing, and directing a little foundation that funded medical research—things that kept his seventy-year-old stomach flat and his exuberance level somewhere between the Energizer Bunny and a puppy with a new ball.

"Everything smells fantastic, Carly."

"It's nothing fancy, but I think you'll like it."

"Hell, I'd eat a shoe if you cooked it," he said, dumping some wine in their glasses and plopping expectantly into one of the mismatched chairs surrounding the kitchen table.

"I feel kind of bad, though. I know you work your ass—" He looked around guiltily at the use of the word before continuing. "I know you work hard all day at the restaurant, and I hate that you come home and cook for me. You should have let me take you out."

"I like doing it," she said. "You know, alone in your own kitchen. It's like meditation." She turned toward a low archway that led to the living room. "Susie! Did you hear me, young lady? Dinner!"

"How's the restaurant doing?" Graden asked.

"Great—we've had a terrific year."

Graden stabbed a sausage and dropped it on his plate, knowing that Carly didn't stand on ceremony. She just wanted to see people enjoy what she cooked.

"I didn't see you two at Annette Chevalier's funeral," he said.

Richard reached for his wineglass. "We wanted to go, but last-minute plane tickets are insanely expensive, and it's hard to put Susie in a car seat for a drive that long. Honestly, I hadn't spoken to her in more than a year, and we've never met her family. How are they doing?"

"Crappy. They're doing crappy. Can you imagine finding her like that?"

"She had demons," Richard said.

"So many of the brilliant ones do. Fortunately, you're an exception."

"Maybe. Or maybe it's just that mine are real."

"Susie!" Carly shouted again, obviously not happy with where the conversation was going. "I'm counting to ten!"

Their daughter appeared a moment later, wearing a pink sweat suit they'd found on sale the week before. The top fell unnaturally from her bony shoulders, descending almost to her knees before the baggy pants appeared and piled around her tennis shoes.

It hadn't been long after she was born that Richard noticed her baby fat suspiciously disappearing and veins becoming visible through her skin. At the time, he'd been working in cancer research and hadn't known anything about progeria beyond what he'd read in a few offhand paragraphs during school.

"Go give your Uncle Chris a hug," Carly said.

Graden returned her embrace, looking down at the top of her bald head with an affectionate smile that contained just a hint of discomfort. Neither Carly nor Susie noticed, but Richard had developed radar over six years working with the victims of the disease. There was something about seeing these children turn old that hit people on a fundamental level—mortality distilled to an intensity that made almost everyone want to turn away.

"Where have you been all night?" Graden said. "I haven't heard a peep out of you."

"She finally beat Richard down, and he bought her one of those Nintendos," Carly said, not bothering to hide her disapproval.

"It's an Xbox, Mom!"

"A crack box, more like."

"You're exaggerating," Susie protested. "You haven't even tried it!"

"And that's the way it's going to stay."

"Can I take my dinner in the living room and play?"

"Susie, you're going to rot your eyes out with that thing. Not to mention your brain. You'll be sitting at the table."

"Please, Mom? I'm almost at level ten. I know I can get there before bedtime."

"Ask your father."

Susie looked up at him expectantly, and as always, he caved.

"Level ten? Wow. I'm still stuck on that bridge in level six."

She took that as a yes, filling her plate in less than five seconds and taking an extra helping of vegetables as a peace offering to her mother.

"Medication!" he called as she rushed off, but she'd already disappeared.

"I swear to God," Carly grumbled, chasing after her with the elaborate pillbox containing their daughter's myriad prescriptions.

When she was gone, Richard took a long pull on his wine and watched his friend tear gleefully into the pear salad before moving on to the sausages.

"I've got bills piling up, Chris."

Graden put down his fork and leaned back in his chair. "I wondered to what I owed the honor of this invitation."

"That's not fair, we—"

"It was a joke, Richard. Jesus. Try to relax, OK?"

"I'm sorry. But it's a little hard, you know? We've put everything into the lab—into my research. If it weren't for leftovers from the restaurant, we'd have to stop eating."

Graden grabbed a stalk of asparagus with his fingers and began gnawing thoughtfully on it.

"I had to let a guy go yesterday, Chris. He was a solid scientist, but I just don't have the money to pay him."

"I know you want me to say I'll fix it. But I can't. I'm sorry, but I can't."

"Your foundation gives away millions every year. Don't you think this is a good cause?"

"Come on, Richard. You know damn well I think it's a good cause. Just like you know damn well it's not *my* foundation."

"You run it."

"Don't try to send me on a guilt trip here. We've given you hundreds of thousands of dollars, and every time I go to bat for you with the board, I leave bloodied."

Richard opened his mouth to speak, but Graden jabbed what was left of the asparagus in his direction. "Look, everybody admires what you've managed to build with the Progeria Project. But the foundation I work for isn't focused on just one disease. I understand your position, but how many kids—"

"Don't start, Chris. I got the needs-of-the-many and big-screen-TV crap from the Pearner Foundation yesterday. I *hate* those speeches."

"You hate them because you know there's some truth there."

"Look, I'm not a communist. If someone goes out and makes a billion dollars and they want to spend it on a fleet of private jets stuffed with supermodels, I'm not going to begrudge them. But it's hard not to think about the fact that if everyone in that category settled for five jets and regular models, there wouldn't be a sick kid on the entire planet."

"Let's be realistic, Richard. If Susie didn't have progeria, you'd be happily running some massive cancer program and would never have given these kids a second thought. And that's not because you're an evil or uncaring man. It's because cancer kills millions of people every year."

"What do you want me to do, Chris? Quit? Go back to my old job and buy myself a mansion while Susie..." His voice trailed off for a moment, and he leaned farther over the table. "She's getting weaker, Chris. I can see it happening. Do you have any idea what it's like to go into her room every morning to get her up for school and wonder if this is the morning? The morning she doesn't wake up?"

"No. I don't know. I'll never know."

The silence between them stretched out for almost a minute before Graden finally broke it. "I'm worried about you. Sometimes it seems like this has become a personal battle between you and God. This is hard for me to say, but what if God wins? Have you thought about that?"

"God's not going to win."

Graden flopped back in his chair. "Screw it. I give up."

Richard unfolded a magazine photo and laid it on the table between them. It depicted a decrepit old man in a wheelchair being pushed toward a limousine.

"What about him?" Richard said as a deep frown spread across his friend's face.

"Andreas Xander? You've got to be kidding."

"He just put another two hundred and fifty million dollars into an expansion of his aging research center. That's a quarter of a billion—"

"I know how much two hundred and fifty million is, Richard."

"I should be getting some of that money."

Graden set his wine down on the table and tapped absently on the cheap glass. "I hear you have to include a virgin for him to sacrifice along with your grant proposal."

"I'm serious, Chris."

"So am I. Do you know why Xander's one of the richest men in the world?"

"Because he's a good businessman?"

"No, because he's the nastiest, most ruthless son of a bitch on the planet. If being a mean-spirited snake were an Olympic event, this guy'd be Mark Spitz. Did you know that his mother died in some run-down state nursing home in Alabama, and when they started going through her assets, they found out Xander still owed her the fifteen grand she'd lent him for college? That guy's never given a rat's ass about anything but money and power his whole life. Then, a few years back, he realizes that he has to die, just like all those dirty little poor people he's always hated. So now he's throwing a bunch of money at any researcher willing to tell him they can put a straitjacket on the grim reaper."

"Then tell him I'm in the straitjacket business."

"Me? Why me? I don't know that asshole. And he's impossible to get to. I mean, I've done pretty well in life, but Xander's a whole other level."

"You must know people who have access to him."

"Look, Richard. Let's be serious here. He finances closely controlled research into things that directly benefit him. He'd drink Susie's blood if someone told him it would extend his life ten minutes."

"I need the money."

"Deals with the devil never work out, Richard. It's kind of a cosmic theme, you know?"

"I don't have a lot of alternatives at this point."

Graden sighed quietly and produced a checkbook from his back pocket. "Twenty-five thousand, right? Isn't that what the Pearners turned you down for?"

Richard nodded, unable to tear his eyes from the checkbook. It was hard to believe that such a tiny, common thing could mean so much—to Susie, to the other children.

Graden filled out a check and held it across the table.

"I can't tell you how much I appreciate this, Chris. Please thank the people at the—" He looked down at it and fell silent. "This is a personal check."

"I can't go back to the foundation again for this."

"I don't want your money."

"I think we both know that's bullshit."

Richard just sat there for a few moments, feeling the sensation of the paper between his fingers. When he spoke again, it sounded like someone else talking. "Thank you for this, Chris. But it's not a long-term solution. Help me get to Xander. You know people. You can do it."

3

Outside Baltimore, Maryland
April 10

The silence had become oppressive, and Richard pulled away from the microscope to look around at the cluttered lab.

He'd gotten a good price on the space by taking the whole floor, but the size of it now mocked him with a faint echo accompanying every sound he made. It was hard not to dwell on the days that it had been wall-to-wall with recent graduates anxious to work for him and the kids—talented scientists still clinging to their idealism and willing to work on the cheap. But not cheap enough. Not anymore.

He scanned the stools lined up along cluttered tables and once again thought about subletting some of the space. Without question, it would be smart financially, but it felt like the first step toward admitting defeat. He feared that if he started down that path, the momentum would build until it swept him away.

The phone next to him buzzed, reminding him that there actually was life in the building. It was almost noon, and he assumed it was someone making a plan for lunch. Some pizza and a little mindless small talk in the sun was exactly what he needed. Maybe even half a beer.

"Hello?"

"Dr. Draman?" his receptionist said. "I've got Troy Chevalier here."

It took a couple beats to put meaning to the name. "I'm sorry. Did you say Troy Chevalier? Annette's husband?"

"I don't know who he's married to. Do you want me to ask hi—"

"No!" Richard said immediately. "Don't mention his wife. Just have him wait in my office, please. I'm on my way."

Richard ran from the lab, trying to remember his last conversation with Annette, her son's name, and to come up with even a remote reason that her husband would show up there.

"Troy," Richard said, extending a hand as he strode breathlessly through the door. "How are you? How's Jonny?"

"We're good," he responded. "We're doing good."

It was an obvious lie. His skin was unnaturally pale, and there was a slackness to his face that gave him an air of complete hopelessness.

"I'm sorry about the mess," Richard said, clearing a stack of books from the chair in front of his desk. "Please sit down."

Chevalier did, though it seemed like even that simple act caused him pain.

"I'm so sorry Carly and I couldn't make Annette's funeral. We—"

"I understand. You have your own problems. The flowers you sent were beautiful. We really appreciated them."

Richard sank into his own chair as Chevalier's gaze turned distant. As though he was reliving the image of his wife's coffin sinking into the earth. Or, God forbid, the image of her hanging from their ceiling.

"Troy? Have we met before and I can't remember it? I don't mean to sound abrupt, but I'm really curious why you're here."

"Annette was murdered."

Richard froze for a moment, watching Chevalier's face turn angry.

"But my understanding is that the police—"

"That it was suicide? They don't know what the hell they're talking about."

Richard wasn't sure what to say. He'd been around grieving families for most of his career, but the causes of death in his world were always obvious. This was something he hadn't faced before.

"Troy, Annette was a wonderful woman, and I know that she loved you and Jonny as much as anyone could. But we both know she had problems…"

"I'm not an idiot, Richard."

"I didn't say—"

"Annette would have never done anything to herself where Jonny might find her. Do you understand me? *Never*."

The force of the delivery gave his statement more weight than it probably deserved. The loss of a loved one could do terrible things to people.

"I can only imagine how hard this must be for you, Troy. Have you thought of talking to some—"

"I'm talking to you," he said, pulling a thumb drive from his jacket and sliding it across the desk.

Richard looked down at it but otherwise didn't move. "What is it?"

"The data from a pet project Annette was working on. I think this is why she was killed."

Again, Richard wasn't sure how to respond. Should he humor the man or try to bring him back to reality? In the end, he decided against confrontation. Chevalier had suffered enough, and he just needed time to work through it.

"What pet project?"

"I don't really know—I'm not a scientist. She was excited about it, though, and she told me about it sometimes. I had no idea what she was talking about. You know how it is, right, Richard? When someone you love is passionate about something? You just sit there and listen."

"Sure, but…"

"At first, the pharmaceutical company she worked for just ignored it, but about a year ago they started putting pressure on her to stop spending time on it. I guess it's pretty theoretical and didn't have much potential to make money. She told them she'd be happy to resign if they didn't think they were getting their money's worth out of her. They backed down, but then weird things started to happen."

"What kind of things?"

"Look, I don't want to get into it, OK? And I don't want to get you involved any more than I have to. All I'm asking is that you take a look at what's on that drive and tell me what you think. Tell me if this is why they killed her."

The strange inflection on the word "they" made Richard even more uncomfortable—something he would have bet good money wasn't possible.

"I don't know, Troy. I think when horrible things happen we look for reasons. For someone to blame. But sometimes—"

"Richard, please. Are you going to make me beg? Do you want me to get on my knees?"

"No, I don't want you to get on your knees. Look…Why me? You must know a hell of a lot of biologists."

"Precisely because I don't really know you. I think some of the people Annette worked with and I are being watched. And because Annette thought you were one of the top people in the field. You're one of the few people I'm confident will be able to understand it."

"What makes you think people are watching you, Troy?"

"You think I'm nuts, don't you?"

"No. I think—"

Chevalier pulled a small black box from his jacket and slammed it loudly onto the desk. "Do you know what this is?"

"I don't."

"It's a tracking device. I found it on my car."

Richard ran a hand nervously through his blond beard, and Chevalier misinterpreted the change in his demeanor.

"Don't be scared. I disabled it."

"That's not what I'm worried about, Troy. I—"

"You still think I'm crazy."

"Let me finish my sentence, OK? What I think is that you've suffered an incredible loss and that kind of stress can be really destructive. Listen to me on this, OK? It's something I know about."

Chevalier's eyes turned glassy with tears, but he managed to regain control before they ran down his cheeks. "Just look at the drive, OK? If not for me, for Annette."

4

Outside Baltimore, Maryland
April 10

Richard Draman stayed focused on the computer screen as he reached out and moved a piece on the checkerboard laid out across his desk.

"Are you sure you want to do that, Dad?"

He ignored the plastic click of Susie jumping his pieces and opened another file on the drive Troy Chevalier had given him. Impossibly, it was even more mesmerizing than the last.

While none of the research looked like anything someone would kill over, it was groundbreaking stuff and yet another confirmation of Annette's brilliance. The field of genetics was still in its infancy, and the equipment available sometimes didn't feel much more precise than the stone tools of humanity's ancestors. If you wanted to know what genes contributed to a particular disease, you were still forced to compare the genetic structure of healthy people with sick ones, narrowing down the differences and applying statistics until you found a possible candidate.

What Annette was trying to do was create a Rosetta stone that would allow her to read the currently unfathomable code of life. Her ideas were still in the very early stages, but if they were correct and could be fully developed, they had the potential to revolutionize the field of biology and to cure not only progeria but virtually every genetic disease ever identified.

"Daddy?"

Susie was looking up at him from the chair on the other side of the desk, trying not to let her paper-thin lips curl into a smile.

"What is it, sweetie?"

"I won."

He looked down at the board and frowned. "You must have cheated."

"It's checkers! How can you cheat? I won fair and square, and now you have to come and read to me so I can go to sleep."

"I wish I could, but I have to work."

"But it's nighttime. You don't have to work during the nighttime. And it won't take long. We're reading *Matilda*. The chapters aren't very long."

He let out a long breath. "I know. You're right. But this is really important. Let's make a date for tomorrow. You promised to show me how to use that Kinect thing on your video game, remember?"

"Really?"

"Of course, really. But this time I'm going to beat the pants off you."

She slid off her chair and went for the hallway, her bare feet slapping the cracked wood floor. "I'm gonna go tell Mom. Maybe she'll want to play!"

Richard returned his gaze to the computer screen and Annette Chevalier's ghost. "Ha! Good luck with that."

* * *

Richard jerked upright at the sound of the quiet knock, unsure where he was until he managed to focus on Carly standing in the doorway. She was wearing one of his old college T-shirts, the bottom cutting across the tops of her long legs to reveal a hint of the pink panties beneath.

"It's almost midnight," she said, coming around the desk and settling onto his lap. "When are you coming to bed?"

"Sorry, I must have fallen asleep. I was going through the data Troy gave me."

She pressed a little closer to him, resting her head on his shoulder and letting her long hair fall down his back. "I've been thinking a lot about Annette. I mean, I didn't know her very well, but it's hard not to wonder what was going through her mind. She had so much—a healthy son, a beautiful home, a wonderful husband."

The comparison was obvious and a little depressing. "You've got the last one, though, right?"

She smiled up at him. "A wonderful husband? I don't know…I suppose I could have done worse."

"Did you get Susie off to bed OK?"

"Yeah, but she was disappointed you didn't read to her. You need to play that video game tomorrow."

"I told her I would."

"Yeah, but you also said you'd spend some time with her and *Matilda*."

"You've got to cut me some slack on that," he said, pointing to the screen. "This is something I might be able to use to help her. But going through it and doing the thousand other things I have to do every day isn't a nine-to-five job. It's all gotten really complicated."

She didn't respond, and he knew she was building to something. He'd always been a little jealous of her ability to sink into philosophical calm while he was left to shout at the wind or hide in minute cellular details.

But it also worried him. Was it really a natural talent for monklike fatalism or just a cleverly disguised version of the denial he saw in so many of the other parents?

"I know how busy you are," she said finally. "But you have to remember something really important."

"What's that?"

"She's here now."

He closed his eyes and leaned his head back on the chair, trying unsuccessfully to blank his mind, to keep it from exploring the implications of his wife's words.

They'd met when he was getting his master's. She was studying at a culinary school down the street from his apartment and spent a fair amount of time digging around the grocery store where he shopped. By the end of the semester, he'd written a computer program that calculated the probability of her being in the store at any given time, and he lived his life around those carefully printed schedules and an endless supply of phony grocery lists.

Despite a long history of success in attracting—if not keeping—women, he'd found it impossible to find the courage to talk to her. She, on the other hand, hadn't suffered the same paralysis. It had been near the artichokes that she'd finally stepped in front of him, blocking his path to a shelf of summer squash. He could still remember her first words to him: "You shop a lot, don't you?"

Richard tilted his head forward again, resting his chin on the top of her head. "She's going to be here tomorrow too, Carly."

"But what if you're not?"

"I don't understand."

"You could be driving home from the lab a few days from now, and a drunk driver could cross the center line. I doubt the last thought that would go through your head would be that you spent too much time with your daughter."

"Thanks for the vivid preview of my death. I usually don't think about it with that kind of detail."

"My pleasure."

He reached into a drawer and retrieved a couple of glasses, splashing some scotch into them before handing one to her. She turned and put her feet on the desk, pressing her back into his chest.

They didn't sit and drink together enough anymore. The wild, passionate adventure they'd started together had slowly devolved into something squeezed in between Susie, the restaurant, the lab, and the bills.

"Sometimes when I think about our past it seems more like a movie I once watched than something I did," he said. "I can see us getting drunk in bars and driving piece-of-shit rental cars through third world countries. I remember us trying to have sex in that little bed with the mosquito net in Namibia. It was a hundred and three degrees, and every time one of us bumped up against the net, the bugs attacked."

"I know it really happened because I still have a mark on my butt where those things were chewing on me," she said.

He smiled, and they sat there for a few minutes sipping their drinks. "I have to save her, Carly."

She nodded slowly but didn't turn to look at him. "I know."

5

Northern Pennsylvania
April 12

Richard double-checked the map he'd printed and rolled to a stop in front of an iron gate that was a bit more imposing than he'd anticipated. There was an intercom bolted to a stone pillar, and he leaned out the window to activate it.

The machine-gun-toting guard he half expected didn't materialize, and instead a lightly accented female voice greeted him over the speaker.

"Yes? Can I help you?"

"Hi, this is Richard Draman. I spoke with Dr. Mason yesterday. We have an appointment."

"Of course, Dr. Draman. Welcome."

The gate swung open, and he drove through, starting up a winding private road cut from the trees.

The nervousness that had been growing ever since he left his house quickly transformed into full-grown butterflies tearing around his stomach. And why not? August Mason was both the most gifted and most enigmatic biologist of the last century. His contributions to the field still had people shaking their heads, as did his disappearance shortly after accepting what everyone thought would be only the first of his Nobel Prizes. He'd been gone for more than twenty-five years before suddenly reappearing and buying this property a few years ago.

The house revealed itself as Richard crested a small hill—ten times the size of the one he lived in and plopped in the middle of a piece of land larger than the farm he'd grown up on. The stone façade and dramatic roofline made it look a bit like a failed castle—a romantic illusion reinforced by the beautiful dark-haired woman waving at him from beneath the portico.

"Hello," she said, placing a soft hand into his as he climbed out of the car. "I'm Alexandra Covas, Dr. Mason's assistant."

She looked to be about Carly's age, with impenetrable eyes and an exotic accent that gave her an appealing air of mystery. Not really his type, but it did offer one possibility as to why Mason was almost never seen outside the walls of this compound.

Richard followed her to the library, where she left him standing alone beneath towering bookshelves. He stood motionless in the silence for almost a minute, but the butterflies in his stomach started to attack again, and he decided to try to distract them with a self-guided tour.

Original pencil drawings of various plants and animals hung on the walls—reminders of an elegant time of discovery before modern devices like cameras. He walked deliberately, occasionally pausing to examine a particularly impressive insect collection or well-preserved skull, finally stopping at a first edition of *On the Origin of Species* on display under glass. Standing there in August Mason's study looking at a book that could have been personally thumbed by Charles Darwin wasn't doing much for his sense of calm. Hell, he wasn't even sure what he was doing here. Calling Mason had been a ridiculous Hail Mary. He'd never actually thought the man would agree to a meeting.

"Dr. Draman, I'm sorry to have kept you waiting."

Richard spun and found himself faced with yet another surprise. Mason was no longer the puffy, bespectacled man he'd been when he was working, nor was he the wild-eyed recluse so many had hypothesized.

For certain, he looked every one of his sixty-five years, but those years had settled in kindly. He'd lost at least forty pounds from when he'd disappeared, leaving a solid physique and shoulders that would be considered broad in the less-than-athletic world of academia. His skin was deeply lined around the mouth and eyes, but tan and healthy beneath a head of longish gray hair.

"Dr. Mason?"

His acknowledgment was limited to a polite smile.

"It's incredible to meet you, sir," Richard said, pumping the man's hand with embarrassing energy. He'd actually had a picture of Mason on the wall of his dorm room at school. As he recalled, it had held a place of honor just to the right of his highly collectible poster of Raquel Welch in a fur bikini and just above his seldom-used beer bong.

"I really appreciate you agreeing to see me, sir. I know you don't make it a habit. I'm truly honored to be here."

Mason seemed vaguely amused by his guest's breathless delivery.

"I'm sorry," Richard continued. "I'm babbling. I suppose you get that a lot."

"Not so much anymore." Mason pointed to a pair of chairs, and they sat.

"Last I heard, you were working in cancer, Richard. I seem to remember that there were a lot of people talking about you. The wonder boy from…Oklahoma, was it?"

"I'm from a little town you never heard of in Kansas, actually."

"And how does someone from a little town I've never heard of rise to such eminence in as complicated a field as biology, Richard?"

Richard was embarrassed to feel a little surge of adrenaline at the compliment and the fact that August Mason would show any interest in him at all.

"Well, my high school didn't really have classes that challenged me, and I was lucky enough to get an opportunity to study at an out-of-state private school."

Technically correct but hardly the full story. In truth, he'd felt completely isolated as a child, disconnected from his family, his school, his town. And that had led him to use the intellectual gifts he hadn't yet come to terms with for less than productive activities. It had started with him creating a concoction that, when added to livestock feed, turned cows blue—a vast improvement over the normal Kansas monotony in his mind, but an artistic statement lost on the community at large. What had started as a harmless cat-and-mouse game culminated in an unfortunate incident involving a water tower, his guidance counselor's new car, and the better part of the local fire department.

"So it was at this school you found inspiration?"

Richard shifted awkwardly in his chair, uncomfortable talking about himself in the presence of someone as great as August Mason and finding it hard to continue to lie under his intense stare.

"To be honest, Dr. Mason, it was a military school. When I got there, I was so terrified that I actually made an effort on the placement exam they made me take. At first, they thought I cheated, but when they figured out I didn't, one of the science teachers took me under his wing. I pretty much owe everything to him."

"It's interesting how a random event can change our lives in ways that would be impossible to imagine, isn't it?" He had a way of speaking that made it seem as though he knew more than he possibly could—as if he was talking specifically about that damn water tower. "But I seem to remember hearing that you didn't continue in cancer research. Is that right?"

Richard nodded. "Progeria. My daughter has it."

"I'm sorry."

"Then you're familiar with the disease?"

"Oh, in a very superficial way."

It would be an understatement to say that Mason had been as disliked as he was revered during his career. He had the reputation of being a cold-hearted bastard with a tendency to completely dismiss his intellectual inferiors, which, unfortunately, was just about everyone.

Perhaps worse, he'd also been a strong proponent of eugenics. His ideas on developing a program of abortions based on increasingly sophisticated amniocentesis had lost him the few defenders he had in the liberal academic community—Richard included. If it had been up to Mason, Susie would have never been born.

But it was hard now to see any of that in the man. Certainly, he wasn't effusive and he had a disconcerting way of looking right through you, but he didn't come off as one of Hitler's tennis partners either.

"Now, I have to ask, Richard. What is it that I can do for you?"

"I wanted to talk to you about your research."

"What aspect?"

"The fundamental structures of life."

"Ah, the Great Truths. Not one of my favorite subjects."

"But that was the real focus of your career, wasn't it? Some people might even say your obsession."

"Delusion might be a better word."

Richard opened his mouth to protest, but Mason held up a hand, silencing him.

"I spent years believing that I was on the path to a breakthrough that would transform the way we understand life. That I would be the first person to stare directly into the mind of God. And instead, it turned out to be nothing."

"And so you just went up in smoke," Richard said, not bothering to hide his curiosity.

Mason smiled. "So what's the popular theory these days? That I was living in the subway tunnels of New York? Or is the Syrian monastery hypothesis making a resurgence?"

"I'm sorry. I didn't mean to pry. It's just such a mystery to all of us. You wouldn't believe how many times the subject still comes up when biologists get together and have a few too many drinks."

Mason shifted in his seat, obviously contemplating how much he wanted to say. "Let's just say that God turned out to be more elusive than I thought, so I went to look elsewhere."

"And did you find Him?"

"I'm afraid not. It's up to the next generation. People like you."

"And Annette Chevalier."

Mason frowned. "I heard what happened. Horrible."

"Were you aware she was doing research along a similar line as you were?"

"Yes. She called me a few times. I told her she was heading down a blind alley. But she wouldn't listen. Did you know her?"

Richard nodded.

"Then you understand why I wanted to dissuade her. I knew about her depression problems and the fact that she'd tried to kill herself a few years ago. When I discovered my research was going nowhere, it was devastating enough to walk away from everything I'd ever known. I was concerned that she would..." he paused for a moment, "take it harder."

"Where is all the research you did?"

"I threw it away."

"I'm sorry? What did you say?"

"I was upset. I threw it in the garbage."

"You don't have copies?" Richard said, horrified.

"It's not as cathartic if you keep copies. So, I have to ask again. What is it I can do for you?"

Richard hesitated, knowing that he was on thin legal ice.

"Annette's husband brought me a thumb drive with some of her theories and data on it. I looked it over, and it's incomplete and speculative. But it's also pretty exciting. I know you say it's headed nowhere, but I just can't see the dead end you found."

Mason's expression didn't so much as flicker. "Trust me. It's there."

Richard reached into his jacket and retrieved a copy of Annette's data. "As unlikely as it seems, maybe she found an angle you didn't consider. I know I'm asking a lot, but could you just take a quick look at this and tell me what you think? For reasons I'm sure you understand, I don't have time to run down blind alleys."

He accepted the drive and gazed down at it for a moment. "I'm not going to promise anything, but I'll see what I can do."

6

Outside Baltimore, Maryland
April 12

Susie placed a puzzle piece that clearly didn't fit into Big Bird's midsection and poked at it with a bony finger.

"Can I get you a hammer?" Richard said, eliciting a noisy snicker from his daughter that made him smile. Despite her illness, she'd always been an unusually cheerful kid, willing to do whatever it took to find the silver lining in every cloud. A hell of a talent, as far as he was concerned.

"You know what Amy did today at school?"

"What?"

"A flip. All the way. She landed on her feet and everything."

"Front or back?"

Her expression suggested his question was painfully stupid. "Front! Don't be crazy. Nobody can do one backward and not fall. I'd like to do one someday. I'd like to do a front one."

It was hard not feel his heart stutter in his chest when she said things like that, but today he wasn't going to give in.

"Someday you'll be able to do anything you want."

She picked up another puzzle piece and tested it with similar results.

He was so grateful to her friend Amy and all the other children at the school. Kids could be cruel to people different than them, but none of that cruelty had ever targeted Susie. Partly it might have been her personality, but her young classmates also seemed to be able to understand what she was going through. And they wanted to help.

He glanced up and saw his wife watching them from the doorway. "We could use some help, Carly. The Cookie Monster is proving to be a bit of a challenge."

"Yeah, Mom. Dad said he was too tired from driving all the way to Pennsylvania to play with the Kinect. Come and help us."

She pondered the invitation for a moment and then settled down onto the floor. Richard lay back in the carpet and propped his head against her thigh, stretching his sore spine. The warmth of her spread throughout his body, and he closed his eyes, enjoying the sensation while Susie pawed through the puzzle pieces and pontificated on why sane people shouldn't have to take math.

She'd barely warmed up to the subject when a knock at the door threw off her train of thought. Richard rose on stiff knees and strode across the room, stopping in front of the door and glancing at his watch. Almost nine o' clock.

"Who's there?"

"Detective Timothy Sands with the police. Open up, please."

He frowned as he pulled the door open. This happened from time to time, generally when the couple two doors down had too much gin and started chasing each other around with golf clubs. It really pissed him off that he was forced to raise his daughter in this kind of environment, but Carly pointed out that it was unhealthy to give in to the tendency to surround yourself with people just like you. Seemed like a stretch.

"Are you Richard Draman?"

This cop seemed a little graver than the ones who had come before. The man flanking him was in uniform, but Sands wore a gray suit that looked a size too small for his considerable bulk. Combined with the tightly clamped lips and vaguely military haircut, he gave the impression of a man not to be screwed with.

"Yeah, that's me. But look, we haven't heard anything. We've been in the house all—"

"Could you turn around, please?"

"Excuse me?"

He didn't bother repeating himself, instead nodding toward the uniformed cop, who grabbed Richard by the shoulder.

"What the hell are you doing? Get off—"

His protest was silenced when he was slammed into the wall and his arm was twisted up behind him. He heard his wife and daughter shouting, but for some reason couldn't make out the words over the depressingly familiar sound of handcuffs ratcheting over his wrists.

"Richard Draman, you're under arrest—"

"What are you talking about?" he said as more uniformed cops brushed by. One of them handed Carly a piece of paper as she tried to calm their panicked daughter.

"Search warrant," he said before making a beeline for the small office at the back of the house.

"It's OK," Richard said as Susie started to cry. "This is just a mistake. Everybody makes mistakes. They have me confused with one of the neighbors."

The terror on her face subsided a bit, but her eyes remained fixed on him, ignoring the police passing by.

"What's this about?" Carly demanded, stepping in front of Sands, who ignored her and pointed to a man carrying Richard's laptop.

"Is that the only computer?"

"Yes, sir. At least it's the only one we've found so far."

"Search the entire house. I want every computer, every disk, and every piece of paper right down to the goddamn napkins. That means music CDs and players too."

"Hey!" Carly said, louder this time. "I'm talking to you. What are you doing here? Why have you handcuffed my husband?"

"I think I already established that, didn't I?" he said, giving Carly what was undoubtedly his most intimidating stare. She didn't seem to notice.

"If you had, I wouldn't be asking, would I? *Why* are you arresting my husband?"

Richard had a queasy feeling he already knew the answer to that question.

"And you are?" Sands said.

"Now I'm pretty sure that *has* been established. You know, the thing where I keep calling him my husband?"

Sands seemed to realize that she wasn't going to back down and flipped a hand toward the door. A moment later, Richard found himself being dragged through it and into his front yard where a few of his neighbors had congregated for the show.

He ignored them, craning his neck so that he could see Sands and Carly facing off in the entryway. He was still within earshot when the detective finally answered.

"Industrial espionage."

7

Baltimore, Maryland
April 12

"I have to say, you're not exactly what I expected," Sands said, crossing his arms in front of his chest and tapping out a rhythm on his shoulder holster.

The room was a little more elaborate, but pretty much what Richard remembered from his youth—a claustrophobic box furnished with a wooden table, uncomfortable chairs, and an enormous mirror that reflected the image of him sitting with his hands secured behind his back.

"I didn't expect to find anything on you in the computer, so imagine my surprise when it turns out that you have one of the most interesting rap sheets I've ever had the misfortune to read. What kind of sick little bastard kills his neighbor's livestock?"

"Now just wait a minute," Richard said. "What I gave those cows was completely harmless. It was some idiot vet that said they had to be dest—"

"And then you tried to kill a cop."

"That's bullshit! When we reassembled that car on top of the tower, we screwed up reattaching the emergency brake. It was just bad luck that the police cruiser pulled up right when it rolled off. He didn't have a scratch on him when the fire department finally got him out."

"And then the judge goes soft and lets your parents ship you off to military school. Then, a few months later, they die in a fire. Makes me wonder if you weren't pissed off at being sent away. If you—"

Richard jumped from the chair and lunged toward the cop, but his hands were restrained behind him. A moment later he found himself face down on the floor with the detective's foot on his neck.

"Careful, Doc. I'm not some redneck sheriff with a soft spot for sob stories."

He gave one last painful shove with his wing tip and then walked from the room, locking the door and leaving Richard alone. He just lay there, cursing his stupidity and remembering the look on Susie's face when the police dragged him away. What was she going through now? What was the stress doing to her weakened heart?

He wanted to call her, tell her it was OK, but no one had offered to let him use the phone. He suspected he was being watched through the mirror and wanted to demand his rights from it, but he couldn't find the strength. Instead, he struggled to his feet and fell back into the chair, leaning forward until his forehead rested on the table. He'd really done it this time. Of all his many screwups over the years, this was going to be the one that destroyed him. Him and everyone around him.

The door opened again, and he jerked upright. "Look, I didn't mean to—"

"You didn't mean to what?" Chris Graden said, slamming the door behind him hard enough to vibrate the walls. "You didn't mean to steal a drive full of research performed by a former PharmaTan employee in PharmaTan's labs? Or you didn't mean to take it to August Mason—let me just repeat that: *August fucking Mason*—and make him an accessory?"

"What are you doing here?"

"Trying to save what's left of your ass."

He flipped an empty chair around backward and sat, staring angrily at Richard but saying nothing further.

"I didn't steal the research," Richard said emphatically. "Troy Chevalier brought it to me. He thought it might have something to do with Annette's death, and he wanted me to look at it and see if I could figure anything out. Ask him. He'll tell you."

Graden's expression softened. "You didn't hear?"

"Hear what?"

"Troy was killed in a car accident yesterday. Word is he'd been drinking. A lot, apparently." Graden shook his head miserably. "He missed a curve, went down an embankment, and bled to death before anyone could get to him."

Richard found himself unable to speak—he just sat there thinking about Chevalier's young son and the fact that he'd lost both his parents over the course of a week. That at the age of twelve, he was suddenly alone in the world.

But it wasn't just Jonny. Richard knew that he was alone now too. Without Troy to tell the police what had happened, they would just think he was a run-of-the-mill thief.

"I didn't mean to…" he started, but then fell silent. No one was going to care about his intentions. No one was going to care that he was the only hope Susie and the other kids had. They'd just throw him in prison to rot.

"Was it Mason, Chris? Was he the one who called the police?"

"What choice did he have? Do you have any idea what kind of position you put him in?"

"I guess I didn't really think about it."

"And that's the problem, isn't it? You've become so obsessed with what you're doing, you've lost sight of everything else."

Richard sagged in his chair, feeling the handcuffs pull painfully at his wrists. "Is Carly here?"

"She's out in the lobby. But I didn't come with her. She's not the one who called me."

"Then who?"

"Mason. He knew that you and I were friends, and he's not happy about being the guy who had to burn you on this. Oh, and did I mention that I spent the entire drive over here on the phone with the CEO of PharmaTan trying to convince him not to crucify you?"

"What was I supposed to do?" Richard said. "Throw it in the garbage? Tell Troy I wouldn't help him a few days after he found his wife hanging from the ceiling?"

"Considering your current situation, that doesn't seem like it would have been too bad a choice, does it?"

Richard nodded, but then leaned in as close as he was able, lowering his voice to the point that it was barely audible. "You should see the stuff she was working on, Chris. It has incredible potential. I mean, you could actually see a day that you could put someone's genome into a computer and have it spit out a picture of what they look like, what illnesses they would be susceptible to—hell, maybe even their IQ and personality. Can you imagine what that could mean? If we actually understood what every gene does? How they interact? Do you understand what that could do for kids like Susie?"

"Jesus Christ, Richard. Are you listening to yourself? Do you know where you are?"

"It's just that—"

"How smart is August Mason?"

"What?" Richard said.

"It's a simple question."

"I don't understand what you're—"

"Well then let me make it crystal clear. You're one of the most brilliant biologists alive today. And Annette sure as hell was. But would it be fair to say that Mason's twice as smart as both of you combined?"

"Yeah. I suppose."

"And he said this was a dead end."

"You never know. He could have—"

"Shut up, Richard. Just shut up, OK? If you keep going on like this…" His voice faded for a moment. "You know, I did what you asked. I figured out a way to get to Andreas Xander's people. Do you have any idea how hard that is right now? I hear they had to get the paddles out last week to keep what I generously refer to as his heart beating. What do I do now? How does this make me look?"

He was right, Richard knew. Word of this would spread. Even if he stayed out of jail, he'd become a pariah. He'd never raise another dime as long as he lived.

"You've got to help me fix this, Chris. It just fell into my hands. I wasn't trying to make money off it."

"And that's the only reason *I'm* here instead of PharmaTan's army of lawyers. But Susie's disease isn't a free pass, Richard. You can't do whatever you want and then scream 'sick children' when it bites you in the ass."

"I know. I—"

"Do you have copies?"

"Just the one on my hard drive. But the cops took my computer."

"You're telling me the truth?"

"I swear."

Graden walked to the door and was about to bang on it, but instead turned and looked down at Richard again. "I went to PharmaTan with hat in hand, and they agreed to hold off pressing charges for now as a personal favor to me."

"You mean, you can get me out of here?"

"I don't know. I really don't. Do you have any idea how far out on a limb I am?"

Richard's gaze fell to his feet, and he stared silently at them.

"You've got to pull it together, son. I love you and Carly like family, but if you're dead set on going down in flames, you're going to have to do it without me."

8

Outside Baltimore, Maryland
April 13

Richard Draman used a shaking hand to push open the heavy doors leading into his lab. He stood in the threshold for a moment, unsure whether to sprint inside or just get back in the car and drive away. Carly gave him a gentle nudge from behind, and he walked stiffly forward.

"Richard!" Eric Manning, the Progeria Project's de facto second in command, said, dropping the stool he'd been righting and looking nervously around the room. "The police were here."

Richard felt his wife's hand on his back again, but this time there was no push, just the reassuring pressure of her touch.

The lab looked like a pack of wild animals had been set loose in it. The computers were gone, leaving wires hanging limp and useless from the walls. Filing cabinets had been ransacked, refrigerators were empty, and key pieces of heavy equipment had been dragged away, leaving telltale gouges in the floor.

"I wasn't sure what you knew," Eric said, glancing up at a clock that read three o' clock a.m. "I wanted to be here when you…" His voice trailed off.

"What happened?" Carly asked when Richard didn't speak.

"Some guy named Sands called me and made me come down and let his men in." He waved a hand around the room. "That's who did this. They're responsible for all of it."

Richard pulled away from his wife and walked unsteadily to a stool in the middle of the room. He sat, propping his elbows on his knees and taking long, even breaths.

"What's going on?" Eric said. "The cops had a lot of questions. And I'm not the only one they talked to. I think pretty much everyone has already either gotten a call or a visit."

And it wouldn't be just his employees, Richard knew. By tomorrow, it would be everyone involved in the Progeria Project—the parents, the donors, the press.

"It's nothing," Richard managed to get out. "A misunderstanding."

"They aren't just asking questions," Eric pressed. "They're making threats and talking about us being involved in stealing intellectual property. Everyone's pretty freaked out."

Richard raised his head and looked at Eric, who had backed up against an empty countertop. He seemed to be trying to get as far away as possible. "I'm going to fix this. I swear to you I'm going to fix it."

"Richard, the people working here have reputations and careers to worry about. A lot of us are just starting out. Some of us have families to support." He paused for a moment, obviously choosing his words carefully. "Look, we all care deeply about this project. About the kids. And about you. You're the most talented and dedicated man I've ever met, and you've always treated everyone here like family. But..."

When Richard fixed his stare on the floor again, Carly spoke for him. "But what?"

Silence.

"If you have something to say, Eric, say it."

"OK. You've been laying people off, and a lot of us are already working for less than we'd make in other places, on projects that are just as important. And now this."

Richard pushed himself straight on the stool again. "I told you I'd make it right."

Eric nodded miserably. "I've got another offer, Richard. I didn't go looking. It just landed in my lap a week ago. I'm sorry, but I have to take it."

The sensation of someone jabbing a knife into his chest suddenly flared, and Richard wondered if he was having a heart attack. His vision stayed clear, though, and he was still perched solidly on his stool. The slight twinge of disappointment he felt worried him more than the pain.

"I understand," he heard himself say. "I'm grateful for everything you've done. Good luck."

The concern etched on Eric's face deepened. "I'm so sorry, Richard. I really am."

"I know."

Carly hugged him as he passed, and Richard could see her tears glinting in the harsh fluorescent light.

When they were alone, she crossed the lab and knelt next to him. "Are you all right?"

He wasn't sure how to answer. The unwavering sense of purpose—the hope—that kept him going, was turning to smoke. And now he found himself wondering if that's all it ever was. Smoke.

"I've killed them. Susie. The others. They're the ones who are going to pay for me being so stupid."

"It's not over, Richard. Susie's still with us, and so are the rest of the kids."

"Are you kidding? Look around you. There's nothing left."

"So this is it? You have no problem fighting God, nature, and the laws of physics, but some Baltimore cop in a bad suit is completely insurmountable?"

He laughed bitterly. "I have no equipment, barely any money, no employees… And by this time next week, I'll probably be in jail. You make it sound like we just found a parking ticket on our windshield."

"For God's sake, Richard. When one of your teachers kept you a half hour after school, you reprogrammed the entire town's phones to forward to a sex chat line. This isn't about having to clean a few chalkboards. The kids are relying on you. Your daughter is relying on you. Now take a deep breath and use that famous brain of yours to figure a way out of this."

He stood and began pacing around the ransacked lab, picking up speed as despondency turned to anger. She was right. He hadn't let the cops get the better of him when he was fourteen, and he wasn't going to start now. Screw Sands. And screw PharmaTan.

"You told me the research you got from Troy was mostly theoretical," Carly said. "Why would they even care about it?"

"Because it's theirs. The truth is, it's probably already collecting dust in their basement."

"God forbid they let someone use it to help a man deal with his wife's suicide. Or to cure a bunch of sick kids."

Richard stopped next to an overturned table.

"What?" his wife said.

"You're right. That's all I could do with Annette's work. They know damn well that I could never legally profit from it. Everyone would know exactly where it came from."

"So why go through all this trouble? Why wouldn't they just call you and keep the police out of it?"

"That's the problem—it's not any trouble. They can make their point about intellectual property rights with a bunch of lawyers who are already on their payroll and a bunch of cops who are paid by the state. It's easy, so why *not* hold me up as a warning to others?"

"I'm not following."

"What if we made it so it wasn't easy? What if we made it hurt?"

"Sure, that'd be great. But how do you hurt a huge multinational corporation?"

"Simple. Big companies hate bad publicity. Why can't we go to the papers? It's a great story: Annette tragically commits suicide after devoting her life to a theory that could help a bunch of kids survive a horrible childhood disease."

"But if it's just a bunch of theories, can you really use it?"

"I only got through about a quarter of it before Sands took it, so the answer is maybe. And maybe is plenty for a good headline."

"Sure…" Carly said. "Hell, what if the reason Troy gave it to you wasn't some conspiracy theory? Who's left to call you a liar if you say it was because Annette thought you could use the data to help the kids?"

"It could be that it was her dying wish."

"Yes! That's exactly what it was. Look at you—living in a tiny house, sacrificing everything to cure your daughter and children like her. And what's your reward? Not only does PharmaTan withhold critical research, but they have the police vandalize your lab and run off your people. They might as well have put a gun to a bunch of kids' heads. And over what? A thumb drive full of crap they're not even interested in."

"PharmaTan Dooms Sick Children to Certain Death," he said, imagining the headline.

She nodded approvingly, a malevolent smile spreading across her face. "You tell them to give you all your stuff back including the drive with Annette's research. And while they're at it, tell them you'd appreciate a million-dollar research grant."

"That might be pushing it, Carly..."

"And I think you're selling yourself short. You always have. You're one of the top people in the field. Hell, with Annette gone, you may be *the* top person in the field. Just tell them that they can have the patents on anything you come up with. Why wouldn't they agree?"

He jammed his hands in his pockets and took another look around the devastated lab, feeling his anger slowly transform to hope. She was right. Pharmaceutical companies' decisions revolved entirely around dollars and cents. And based on that, PharmaTan had everything to gain by making a deal and absolutely nothing to lose.

9

Outside Baltimore, Maryland
April 18

It was two in the morning, and the only sound in the street was the rattle of a collapsing gutter on the house next to him. Light was courtesy of a full moon, occasionally supplemented by a street lamp that had escaped being vandalized by the local kids.

It was the second time Richard had run home that week. He was putting in brutal hours at the lab to try to revive his work, and unfortunately they only had one car. Or maybe it wasn't so unfortunate. He'd been a pretty decent athlete in college, and the six miles of lung-searing torture was getting him back in touch with his physical side.

So far the long days and late nights were paying off more than he could have reasonably hoped. He'd managed to recover most of his data from offsite backups, and an embarrassing amount of groveling had allowed him to hold onto about half his staff. Mostly the youngest and least experienced—the ones who didn't care much for authority and still had the luxury of defying it—but all were capable, dedicated people.

He pulled the sleeves of his sweatshirt down to protect his arms from the cold as he cut through a trash-strewn lot a few blocks from his house. He'd promised Carly he'd be home by one thirty, and she tended to worry when he missed his self-imposed curfews.

He'd made his offer to PharmaTan almost a week ago through Chris Graden—everything he and Carly had discussed, plus a sweetener that he hadn't yet told her about: an offer to sign a ten-year employment contract with very few stipulations. Graden thought it amounted to indentured servitude, but there wasn't time to screw around with negotiations.

Despite being an offer that no company in its right mind would refuse, though, there was still no word. What the hell were they waiting for?

The light on his sinking front porch came into view, and Richard picked up his pace to the degree his cramping thighs would allow. No point in courting any more of Carly's wrath than necessary.

His stride faltered when he saw a shadow cross from his neighbor's yard through the large hole in the fence that he'd been meaning to fix for months. He bent at the waist and put his hands on his knees, breathing hard from exertion and a sudden flair of anger.

That was it—the last goddamn time that dog was going to take a horse-sized dump in the grass where his daughter played. No more friendly reminders. No more reasoning. And sure as hell no more pleading. That mutt was going to the pound.

He crept onto the grass, trying to quiet his panting and stay in the shadows. The dog was nearly as old and fat as its owner, but he wasn't exactly Speedy Gonzales either anymore.

The fit was tight, but he managed to get through the hole and slip into his backyard. Empty.

Endless years in school, countless academic awards, two PhDs...and he'd been outsmarted by a dog. Again.

Richard started to skirt the house on the way to the front door but stopped when he noticed the screen from Susie's open window lying in the dirt. Yet another thing that needed fixing.

He padded over and was about to reach for it when he saw something move in his daughter's room. At first, he thought he might have woken her up, but the shadow moving toward her bed was far too big to be either her or Carly.

The windowsill was probably five feet off the ground, and Richard was shocked when his attempt to vault through it succeeded and he found himself slamming down painfully on top of Susie's open toy chest. The loud crash caused the man hovering over her to spin around, an object in his hand glinting briefly in the dim light before it dropped and he reached for something at his side.

Richard rolled gracelessly off the chest, managing to land on his feet and launch himself toward the figure. Susie shrieked as he and the man collided, and Richard felt something impact the top of his skull. The butt of a pistol. He had a gun!

The blow was hard enough to collapse his knees but not hard enough to stop him from swinging a fist upward toward the man's stomach. At the last moment, though, a more effective target presented itself, and he drove his knuckles into the man's groin with the same adrenaline-fueled power that had gotten him through the window.

A satisfying grunt filled the room, but the gun barrel kept swinging inevitably toward his face.

Then he was blind. For a moment, he thought the gun had gone off, but there was no sound. It took another split second to realize that Carly had turned on the lights and that the gun was still coming at him. He got hold of the man's arm but then took a blow to the side of the head that drove him the rest of the way to the ground.

The man was shading his eyes with a gloved hand, so it was impossible to see his features—only his short black hair and wiry build beneath a windbreaker and jeans. What was clear, though, was that this time there was nothing Richard could do about the pistol lining up on him.

He put his hands up reflexively and waited for the impact of the bullet, but it never came. Carly jumped across their screaming daughter's bed and slammed into the man with enough force to spoil his aim but not enough to knock him to the ground. He grabbed her throat and held her suspended as Richard fought to get back to his feet.

It had been a good try, but he realized that all she'd done was delay the inevitable and doom herself too.

Then Richard spotted the object the man had dropped on the carpet. A syringe.

He grabbed it and sunk it into their attacker's khaki-covered thigh, using the last of his strength to push down the plunger.

A surprised yelp rose above his daughter's wails just before Carly's full weight landed on top of him.

Again, the gunshot he anticipated didn't come. The man staggered to the open window and fell through it, landing with a muffled thump in the dirt below.

Richard pushed his dazed wife off him and crawled to a position where he could peek over the sill, spotting the man running unsteadily across the yard, syringe still dangling from his leg. It fell into a patch of weeds just before he squeezed through the hole in the fence and disappeared into the darkness.

Richard slammed the window and shut the curtains, turning to see Carly untangling their trembling daughter from her sheets.

"The police!" he shouted. "Call the police!"

His wife looked back at him, eyes still wide with panic, and then ran from the room.

"Susie!" he said, grabbing his daughter by her delicate shoulders. "Listen to me. Calm down. Are you hurt? Did he stick you with anything?"

10

Outside Baltimore, Maryland
April 18

"Do you mind?" Richard said, leaning out his daughter's bedroom door and eyeing a uniformed cop pawing through the linen closet in the hall. "He wasn't after my pillowcases."

"We're just trying to be thorough," a voice behind him said. "Is there some reason you would have a problem with that? Maybe afraid of what we'll find?"

Richard turned back to see Detective Timothy Sands staring out Susie's bedroom window, his face bathed in the swirling red and blue light of a police cruiser parked in the driveway. He looked even more pissed off than when he'd showed up with an arrest warrant the week before. His short hair was matted, and his clothing was disheveled in a way that suggested he'd been pulled from bed to come there.

"Look, someone climbed through my daughter's window and tried to kill her in her bed. I never graduated from the police academy or anything, but I'm thinking that the critical piece to this mystery isn't in my towels."

"What makes you think he was trying to kill her?"

"Because he was leaning over her with a gun and a syringe?"

"Right," Sands said. "But you told me you emptied the syringe into his leg and he ran away. If it was a weapon, it wasn't a very good one."

"Come on," Richard said angrily. "The dosages to kill a grown man can be very different than what it would take to kill a sick eight-year-old

47

girl. Or it could be slow acting or some kind of biological agent. You know that as well as I do."

"What I'm saying," Sands said, turning away from the window, "is that I seem to be coming here a lot lately. I'm also saying that you have access to syringes. And I'm wondering why neither you, your wife, nor your daughter seem to be able to give me a solid description of a man you were dancing around with for God knows how long in a ten-foot-by-ten-foot room."

Carly walked in and handed her husband a bag of ice to slow the growth of the lump rising on his head. He tried to smile in thanks but only managed a wince as he pressed it to his scalp. Miraculously, his was the most serious injury of the night. Susie was terrified but completely unharmed, and beyond the bruises darkening on her neck, Carly seemed no worse for the wear either.

"You do have access to syringes, don't you, Doctor?"

"You've got to be kidding me," Carly started but fell silent when Richard motioned for calm. She glared at Sands long enough to make the cop look away and then marched back toward the living room where their daughter had started crying again.

"You think I had something to do with this?" Richard said. "What possible motivation could I have?"

"How about this: I hear you're trying to do a deal with PharmaTan where you get off scot-free. Seems like it wouldn't hurt to drum up a little sympathy."

Sands leaned back against the wall, his scowl making it clear that he wasn't a fan of being denied a conviction by a bunch of backroom dealing.

"Christ," Richard said under his breath. "Are we just wasting our time here, Detective? Are you even going to look into this?"

"That's exactly what I'm doing," he responded, jabbing a finger in the air. "Do you have an insurance policy on your daughter's life?"

"What?"

"Must be hard, huh, Doc? Single-handedly trying to cure a disease like this? But if your daughter was dead, it'd be over, wouldn't it? You could go be a plastic surgeon in Hollywood and live the good life."

Richard just stood there blinking, trying to quell the anger rising in him. It was clear that Sands was purposely trying to throw him off balance, but it wasn't going to be that easy.

"Detective, that's one of the stupidest things I've ever heard. If it had been me, I'd have succeeded, and no one would have ever known."

"Maybe your wife came in and surprised you. But she understands the stress you're under and she's trying to protect you. You should just tell me. Get it off your chest. I mean, you don't need any more stress than you've already got, right? That shit'll eat you alive."

Richard kept his expression placid but struggled to unclench his teeth. "I think if you were to actually give that theory any thought, you'd find that it's not all that plausible."

"Oh, I intend to give it some thought. A whole lot of it, in fact."

Another uniformed cop came in and whispered something into Sands's ear and then left them alone again, closing the door behind him. An arrogant smile spread across the detective's face. "No syringe, Doc."

"What are you talking about?"

"My men looked where you said it was, and it's not there. Care to change your story?"

"Bullshit! I saw it drop."

"Well then maybe it sprouted wings and flew away, huh?"

Richard was having a harder and harder time tracking on what had happened that night. It was just another of a hundred things that didn't make any sense. He'd watched the backyard through the edge of the curtains virtually nonstop to make sure the man who had come through the window didn't return. The syringe had still been there when the police arrived. He was sure of it.

"Tell them to look again."

Sands's smile broadened, transforming his expression into an inexplicable one of triumph. The truth seemed to be of no importance to him, and he saw no reason to hide the fact. His only interest seemed to be burning a certain down-and-out biologist.

"No problem," Richard said. "I'll pull some soil samples from where the syringe dropped and tell you exactly what was in it. With a little luck,

I'll also be able to give you the genetic signature of the man it was stuck in."

A bluff, of course. He was pissed off, and it was all he could think of to wipe the obnoxious smirk off the cop's face. And it worked. Maybe a little too well.

Sands charged, jamming his thick forearm into Richard's throat and driving him back against the wall. "There *was no syringe*," he said, enunciating as though he were talking to a slow child. "Do you understand me, you son of a bitch?"

That was about all Richard could take. The confusion, fear, and frustration of the last week suddenly overwhelmed him, and he pushed back. Hard. Sands was lifted off his feet and bounced off a chest of drawers before landing on his ass in the middle of Susie's Sesame Street rug. He leapt immediately to his feet and reached for his gun as Richard put his hands in front of him in a gesture of peace. "Whoa! I'm sorry, OK? It's been a long day."

Of course it would do no good. When you shoved a cop, there was only one outcome. He was heading to lockup with an assault charge added to his long list of sins.

But Sands seemed frozen, crouched on the rug with his hand halfway to his holster. He'd won, but for some reason he seemed unwilling to take his prize. Instead, he just started for the door, pausing for a moment before opening it.

"*There was no fucking syringe.*"

11

**Outside Baltimore, Maryland
April 18**

Carly pulled the blanket from the back of the sofa and placed it over her daughter, tucking it gently around her delicate neck. She'd stopped crying less than a minute ago when exhaustion finally overpowered her terror and sent her into a sudden, comalike sleep.

Carly, on the other hand, wondered if she would ever sleep again. Her heart was still pounding uncomfortably in her chest and adrenaline continued to course through her, keeping her on the edge of panic.

The last police officer had gone fifteen minutes ago, and she could hear Richard banging around at the back of the house but had no idea what he was doing. A few moments later, he strode in with a large duffel thrown over his shoulder and scooped Susie off the sofa. His eyes seemed a little wild as he looked around the room. She thought she'd seen every emotion possible play out on her husband's face over the years, but this one was new and a little frightening.

"Richard, what are you doing? She just got to sleep—"

He put a finger to his lips, then waved an arm around them as if to indicate that someone might be listening.

"We're leaving," he whispered.

"Leaving? To go where?"

But he was already heading for the kitchen. Carly chased, finding him peering through the window at the still darkness beyond. Convinced that the coast was clear, he pushed through the door and started across the backyard.

When she caught up, he had stopped at the edge of their lawn staring down at a wide, shallow hole where the syringe had dropped and at the old shovel lying next to it.

"Richard. Please. Tell me what—"

But he'd set off again, squeezing awkwardly through the hole in their fence and cutting through their neighbor's yard, careful to circumnavigate any light bleeding from windows or beaming from porches.

Carly followed, unsure what else to do. Her husband seemed to have sunk into some kind of paranoid alternate reality as he crossed onto the property of one of the few neighbors they actually knew. Susie remained motionless with her cheek resting on his shoulder as he paused, looking around him with birdlike jerks of his head. Apparently satisfied that there was no army lurking in the shadows, he continued to a pickup that Carly recognized as the one that he occasionally borrowed to haul lab equipment.

Richard opened the driver's door with his free hand, pulling the seat forward and laying Susie in the tiny backseat. Carly circled around the bed as he slipped behind the wheel. After a nervous glance toward the owner's house, she climbed hesitantly into the passenger seat.

"What the hell are we doing?" she said as he grabbed the key from the visor and shoved it into the ignition.

"We're getting out of here."

"We can't just leave. Detective Sands—"

"Sands?" he said, starting the engine and backing along the dirt track that led to the road. "He's in on it."

Carly fell silent, examining the side of his face in the gloom.

On their wedding day he'd been tanned and athletic, with a handsome, clean-shaven face and blue eyes that always hinted at the excitement he felt about the world and the things he could learn from it.

After Susie had been diagnosed, that excitement had dulled, but he'd soldiered on, somehow managing to continue to be all things to all people—to their daughter, to her, to the other kids and parents. The question of what he'd left for himself sometimes kept her awake at night.

She suspected he'd been having periodic panic attacks for at least a year, but he hid them well, and she found herself afraid to bring it up. She knew him better than anyone did, but still had never found a way to gauge how close he was to the edge.

How could she possibly understand what he was going through? She couldn't save Susie—all she could do was love her. But his situation was completely different. He *might* be able to save her. And that glimmer of hope—that unfair responsibility—was slowly tearing him apart.

They dropped off the curb into the road, and he threw the vehicle into drive, accelerating up the empty street, eyes flicking to the rearview mirror every few seconds.

"Do you have your cell on you?" he said.

"No. I—"

He nodded and dug his from his pocket, then threw it out the window.

"That phone had your whole life on it, and we just stole a car," she said, concentrating on keeping her tone serene. Was this it? Was he finally in the throes of the breakdown that anyone else would have collapsed into years ago?

"Joey said I could borrow it anytime I want."

"I don't think he meant in the middle of the night without asking first."

"What do you want me to do?" he said, his voice sounding like a shout in confines of the cab. "They'll be able to track our car. Like they tracked Troy's."

Carly twisted around in her seat and looked down at Susie in the dim light, running the back of her hand gently across her sunken cheek. It wasn't fair that she had to live like this. And that her husband—one of the few truly good people she'd ever met—should be destroyed by it.

"Who's 'they,' Richard?"

He swerved toward an on-ramp, not answering until they were safely on the highway and he was satisfied that the road behind them was empty.

"I know you think I'm crazy. I just need you to give me a chance to explain."

"I'm listening, Richard. I always have been, you know."

He reached over and squeezed her hand. "Yeah, I know."

He fell silent, and she decided not to press.

"I told you that Troy thought Annette's death was related to the data on that drive and that I didn't believe him. That I thought it was just the grief talking."

"But now you're not so sure."

"Troy's dead, I'm on the verge of going to prison, my lab's trashed, someone tried to kill Susie, and the cops seem very interested in making that syringe disappear. It's getting hard to ignore the fact that there are a lot of bad things happening to people who come into contact with that data."

He went silent again, and Carly watched the side of his face for a few moments, unsure what to think. "Can I ask some questions?"

His eyes darted toward her and then back to the windshield. "I'm not having a meltdown, Carly. You don't have to talk to me like I'm about to throw myself off a bridge."

"Are you sure?"

"About the meltdown or the bridge?" He forced a smile, and she relaxed a bit.

"What does Susie have to do with any of this?"

"What if that guy'd succeeded? When we found her in the morning, we'd just think her heart finally gave out."

"But what does that have to do with the research?"

"If there's anything there that can help kids like Susie, there's no lawsuit or criminal charge that's going to keep me from pursuing it. But what if she was gone? With the legal problems, my people run off, the memories…" His voice faded for a moment. "I'd probably just walk away. I don't think I'd have the strength to keep going."

Carly nodded slowly, wondering exactly what he meant by "walk away." It was something she thought about a lot. What would he walk away from? Where would he go? But those were questions for another time.

"What if someone is getting close to a breakthrough along a similar line?" he continued. "Or maybe they're even far enough along to be coming up with usable therapies based on ideas similar to the ones Annette was working on? They might have spent hundreds of millions on research and development. That's a hell of a lot of money, and I doubt they'd be too happy if someone like me or Annette cut their legs out from under them."

"Richard, Sands is going to think you're running. You're going to be a fugitive."

"Sands? It's not Sands."

"What are you talking about?"

"I bounced him off a wall earlier—"

"Jesus, Richard…"

"You know what he did? Nothing. Just sat there looking confused. That's not normal, Carly. If cops know anything, it's what to do when they're attacked. He's taking his orders from somewhere else. I surprised him, and he didn't know what to do."

"Are you—"

"And what about the missing syringe? I told him I could test the area where it fell to figure out what was in it and get DNA from the man who I stabbed with it."

"Maybe that's why he took the dirt. Maybe he's taking it to the lab?"

"So he just had some cop dig it up with a shovel they found in our shed? Come on, Carly. They have crime scene people who do that kind of work. You know that as well as I do."

She nodded and settled back into her seat, watching the glare of the lights speeding by. What else could she do?

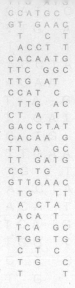

12

Hagerstown, Maryland
April 18

"Are you sure I have an Uncle Burt?"

Susie slid around in the tiny backseat of the truck, testing the unfamiliar sensation of not being strapped into a car seat. She'd bolted awake an hour ago, scared and confused, but had swallowed the story that the events of the night before were nothing more than one of the vivid nightmares she occasionally suffered. And now even that memory had been lost in the excitement of an unannounced road trip into uncharted territory. Despite what the disease had done to her body, she had the same passion for adventure that all children did.

"Well, he's not strictly a *real* uncle," Richard said, twisting around in the passenger seat and looking down at her. "He's kind of like your Uncle Chris."

The sun had cleared the horizon fifteen minutes ago, illuminating neat rows of suburban houses bordered by carefully manicured lawns. Carly followed the advice of their GPS and turned onto a street as still as a photograph.

"How come you never talk about him?"

The device announced that they'd reached their destination in time to save Richard from having to concoct another lie. He faced forward again, examining a small home with the vague feel of a gingerbread house as Carly pulled into the driveway. He hadn't anticipated gun turrets and barbed wire, but the lawn gnomes weren't expected either.

Carly was obviously thinking the same thing, and she looked over at him before turning off the ignition. "Are you sure you got the address right?"

"Yeah. I mean, this is what it said. Maybe it was wrong."

She didn't look happy as they got out, slamming the door a little harder than necessary and speaking across the hood of the truck at a volume that Susie wouldn't be able to hear. "This is crazy."

"If you have a better idea, I'm listening."

"Look, I'm a little scared to go back to the house too. But if Sands finds out you're gone, the top of his head is going to blow off." She thumbed back toward the house. "And you barely know this guy."

"That's the point, remember?"

"When's the last time you talked to him?"

"I don't know. Maybe twelve years ago?"

"Twelve yea—" She fell silent when the front door opened and a man stepped out onto the porch.

"Can I help you?"

They *were* in the right place. A dozen years had deepened the lines across his sun-damaged face, but the muscles were still visible in his forearms where they emerged from the pushed-up sleeves of an olive drab sweater.

"Hi, Burt."

The man cocked his head and came down the steps, favoring his right leg quite a bit more than the last time they'd seen each other. Carly shot a glance back, her expression configured to let him know that she was unimpressed.

"Richard?" the man said in a light Southern drawl. "Richard Draman?"

"It's been a while. This is my wife, Carly. Carly, meet Burt Seeger."

"Of course. But you weren't the wife back then. You were the new girlfriend. The one who gave Richard those wonderful pastries to bring to the hospital."

She smiled uncomfortably, shaking his hand.

"And this," Richard said, tapping the driver's side window where his daughter had her face pressed to the glass, "is Susie."

He opened the door and she stepped out, examining the old man in front of her with obvious suspicion. Richard felt the same nervousness he always felt waiting to see how someone who had never seen Susie would react.

"Well hello, young lady. It's very nice to meet you."

Richard let out the breath he hadn't been aware he was holding. There wasn't anything in Seeger's voice or expression to suggest he saw anything but a little girl.

"I didn't know I had an Uncle Burt," she said.

His brow began to crease, but he caught himself quickly enough that she didn't notice. "You didn't? How could that be? Your parents never told you what a great guy I am?"

She thought for a moment and then stepped forward and opened her arms. A wide smile spread across his face as he knelt to hug her.

"I'm sorry. I'm being rude," he said, scooping Susie up and heading for the house. "Come inside. I made cookies last night. I bet you like cookies, don't you?"

Susie craned her neck and looked back at her mother. "Can I?"

"OK," Carly said, staying close as Seeger teetered up the steps, Susie's less-than-considerable weight taking its toll on his damaged leg. "But only one. And one isn't two, right? And it's definitely not three."

They followed Seeger inside, Carly pausing as they passed a half-finished quilt in the living room. "If his wife's dead, who's working on that?"

"Maybe he got remarried."

"Then wouldn't his wife be the one making the cookies?"

"Give him a chance, Carly. You wouldn't believe the stuff I heard about him fighting the Russians in Afghanistan."

"Maybe he was exaggerating."

"Actually, he never talked about it. Some of the guys he fought with would come to the hospital every now and then. That's who I heard the stories from."

She nodded noncommittally and followed her daughter's voice into the kitchen with him close behind.

"Do you have an Xbox?" Susie was asking through a full mouth as they entered.

"Susie! Why on earth would Burt have an Xbox? And do we talk with our mouth crammed full or do we keep it shut and chew?"

"Sorry, Mom."

"Your mother's right," Seeger said gravely and then broke into a grin. "But I do have a Wii. With all the best games. Do you know how to fly a fighter jet?"

"No," Susie said, wide eyed.

"You don't? Well, in my opinion, all young ladies should be able to fly a fighter jet. You never know when it might come up. If you play your cards right, maybe I'll teach you later. But for now, why don't you head back there and watch a little TV. Your parents and I have some catching up to do."

She rushed off before there could be any protests from her mother about watching TV when the sun was shining.

"I stayed in touch with people from the hospital for a few years, and one of them told me your daughter was ill," Seeger said, taking a seat at the kitchen table and indicating for them to do the same. "I'm sorry. I know what it's like when someone you love is sick."

"Burt's wife had cancer," Richard explained. "She was part of that clinical trial I was involved in."

"No one ever talked to us. They treated her like a piece of meat," Seeger said and then pointed to Richard. "All except the new kid, who showed us real kindness and friendship. Richard always had time to explain what was happening and make sure our questions were answered. We both appreciated that. More than you can imagine."

"I'm sorry we couldn't save her, Burt."

"I know you are. But it wasn't your fault. People die."

"So did you remarry?" Carly said, obviously still concerned about the quilt.

"Never found the right woman. Not yet." He glanced at a picture of his wife hanging next to the refrigerator, and his face slackened noticeably. "Now, I don't mean to be rude for the second time today, but my curiosity is killing me. I assume you didn't show up on ol' Uncle Burt's doorstep to reminisce."

"No," Richard admitted. "You once said you owed me a favor. Did you mean it?"

"I never say things I don't mean. It's a disgusting habit."

"Well, then get comfortable. We've got a little story for you."

13

Hagerstown, Maryland
April 18

Burt Seeger rummaged around in a kitchen cabinet for a teabag and dropped it into the pot on the stove. According to the clock on the wall, they'd finished telling him everything that had happened more than two minutes ago. Since then the only sounds in the tiny house had come from the living room where Susie had figured out how to get the Wii running.

Spoken aloud, their story seemed even more dubious. In all likelihood, the old soldier would throw them out of the house and call the cops. It was undoubtedly the smart move.

"Maybe we could go to the FBI," Carly said, obviously unable to bear the silence anymore.

Seeger turned and leaned against the counter, crossing his arms across his chest. "With what? It sounds like the police have a pretty strong case against Richard, and this Sands guy will sure as hell tell them that he thinks you staged the attack on Susie. There's a serious credibility gap here—more like a credibility canyon—and you're on the wrong side of it."

"What about the press? It's a good story, and they don't seem to demand all that much in the way of proof anymore."

"Yeah, but they demand *something*. This sounds more like something from one of those tabloids my wife used to read. I'm still waiting for you to tell me how Elvis fits in."

"So you don't believe us," Richard said.

"Don't take it personally, son. The years I spent working in intelligence left me not believing anything."

Richard let out a long breath. Coming here had been a stupid idea. Like Carly said, he hadn't been in touch with Burt Seeger in more than a decade. What had he expected the man to do? Breathlessly accept everything they said before risking everything he had to help?

And the truth was that Seeger wasn't the only skeptic. Carly was far from convinced and most likely just humoring him because she thought he was in the midst of a nervous breakdown. If there was one thing he'd learned from his years as a scientist, it was that when people you respected started lining up against you, you might be wrong. Maybe it finally all *had* come crashing down on him. Maybe he was losing it. And if that was the case—or even if it wasn't—what now?

"Listen," Seeger said, clearly concerned by the sudden hopelessness of Richard's expression. "You helped me out once, and I take that debt seriously. I also don't want to see you living in your car jumping at shadows. Particularly with a sick little girl in tow. On the other hand, I don't know how deeply I want to get dragged into this."

"I understand. We—"

"Let me finish. I'm going to put you up for a few days and see if I can help you figure this thing out. But we're going to do this by the numbers. No one is ever going to know you were here. And if for some reason they do find out, you never told me any of this. You're just some old friends who dropped by on a road trip, right?"

"Agreed," Richard said. "Thank you, Burt. I can't—"

The old soldier waved a hand irritably. "You can thank me by doing everything I tell you exactly like I tell you. First, we're going to get that stolen truck the hell out of my driveway. And while you're at it, you're going to get some prepaid cell phones. Remember, though, that they can be traced to the cell tower that they're connected to, so don't use them if you're somewhere you don't want anyone to know about—most importantly, here. You're also going to buy a satellite phone—it's possible to listen in on those, but it's impossible to track their location with enough accuracy to make the information useful. Now what are you doing for money?"

Richard shrugged.

"No debit cards, no ATMs, and no credit cards. You're going to need to go to a bank branch far away from here and pull out all your savings in cash. How much do you have?"

"Not much," Carly said. "We put everything into research."

"Do you have access to your organization's accounts?"

"Sure," Richard said. "But most of that is donations. We can't—"

"Being on the run isn't cheap," Seeger said. "If you think this is for real, now isn't the time to get squeamish about a little embezzlement."

Richard's nod was a little hesitant. That was the burning question. Was it real? How far was he willing to take this? And how far was Carly willing to follow?

"Most important of all, though, is to think," Seeger continued. "Do it hard and do it often. Because I can tell you from experience that one mistake is all it takes to kill you."

14

Near Seneca Rocks, West Virginia
April 18

Darkness had descended almost an hour ago but didn't bring with it the peace or perspective Richard hoped for. He glanced over at his wife and saw her watching impassively as the trees flashed by in the old U-Haul's headlights. She'd hardly said a word on the drive, and as much as he wanted to ask her what she was thinking, he wasn't sure he wanted to know.

A sweeping turn loomed in front of them and he slowed, struggling with the wheel as the trailer they were towing pushed at the back end.

"There," he said, pointing at what looked like a reasonably well-maintained dirt road to the right. "That looks like it'll work."

Carly nodded, and he eased into it, bouncing along at barely a walking pace as the biting air washed through his open window. At Seeger's insistence, they'd crossed into West Virginia and headed for the mountains, staying on secondary roads and leaving Hagerstown far behind.

When Richard was certain they were invisible from the main road, he set the brake and jumped out. There was a light fog clinging to everything, magnifying the cold and causing the air to shimmer in the headlights.

He climbed up on the trailer and threw the cloth cover off his neighbor's pickup, sliding into the driver's seat as Carly pulled down a set of steel ramps. The vehicle rolled to the damp ground with no sound other than the soft scrunch of rubber against dirt.

Confirming that the keys were in the visor, he got out and looked around them again. Based on the number of tire tracks and the sharpness of the tread patterns, it was obvious that the road saw a fair amount of use. It wouldn't be long before people noticed the abandoned vehicle with Maryland plates and called the police, who would return it unharmed to his neighbor. Hopefully with an explanation that involved joy-riding teenagers and not a certain biologist fleeing justice.

Carly was using Windex and a roll of paper towels to wipe away prints and other evidence like Seeger had shown her, and Richard walked back to the U-Haul's cab to retrieve a plastic shopping bag. He rummaged through the prepaid cells it contained, finally locating a satellite phone at the bottom.

The more time that passed, the hazier the events of last night became. Other explanations forced themselves into his mind, melting away the panic he'd felt when he was in the moment. Maybe Sands was just a dim, violent jackass pissed off at being woken up in the middle of the night. Richard had to admit that he tended to bestow more brains on people than they deserved—seeing careful intent when, nine times out of ten, all he was looking at was incompetence and self-absorption.

And what about the attack on Susie? The truth was that people had all kinds of reactions to her. The man in her room could have just been some kind of delusional nut. It wasn't like the world wasn't full of them.

The bottom line was that he needed a third opinion. Had he lost it his mind? Was he endangering himself, his family, and Seeger over nothing but a series of coincidences blown out of proportion by stress and confirmation bias? And if so, what was the most effective—and least humiliating—way to go crawling back?

He dialed a number from memory and held the unfamiliar phone to his ear.

"Hello?"

"Hi, Chris."

"Richard! Where the hell have you been? The cops called me looking for you. They're talking like you're on the run or something. They said you told them someone attacked Susie."

"It's a long story."

"So it's true?"

"Yeah."

"They weren't exactly polite, you know what I mean? I'm starting to think this Sands guy has it in for you."

"Shit," Richard said quietly. "What the hell's going on with PharmaTan, Chris? Why aren't they dropping the charges?"

"The CEO's being a hard-ass. The guy's a complete prick, if you ask me. Says he feels like he's being blackmailed. I don't know how to say this other than to just say it, but he's dead set on pressing charges. I'm trying to go over his head to the board, but I don't know what's going to happen."

Richard lowered himself unsteadily onto the truck's running board as Carly approached, just a disturbance in the thickening fog until she sat next to him. There was a strange moment's hesitation, but then she reached out and put an arm around his shoulders.

"I can't go to jail, Chris. Susie doesn't have that much time and neither do the other kids. We have to make this work."

"I know. Look, I'm not promising anything, but I think the board will be more receptive. It's not going to be tomorrow, though, right? And all this shit isn't going to make my job any easier."

"You think I wanted someone to break into my daughter's room with a syringe and a gun?"

"Is that what happened? Jesus. Look, I'm not trying to place blame here. I'm just saying it doesn't look that great, you know?"

"Doesn't look that great? Do you have any idea—"

"Richard! Could you try being just a little less touchy? You've got to admit that it's a pretty big coincidence. This thing with Annette's research happens and then suddenly some psycho shows up at your house and tries to kill your daughter?"

Richard let out a long breath, trying to regain his calm. "I'm not a hundred percent sure he was a psycho, Chris."

"What are you talking about?"

"What if all this is connected? I mean, first Annette, then Troy, and now Susie? What if someone's trying to stop anyone from continuing her research? You ran a pharmaceutical company. You know the kind of money that could be at stake."

"It's a cutthroat business, Richard, but we don't go around killing people."

"Are you sure?"

There was a long silence before Graden spoke again. "No. I'm not sure. The business has changed since I was in the middle of it. The Russians and the Chinese are getting involved, and I wouldn't put anything past those assholes."

"Really?" Richard said, trying not to sound surprised. He was getting so used to people thinking he was crazy, it was a little disorienting to have someone take him seriously.

"Yeah. I'll tell you what. Let me talk to some people and see what I can dig up."

"You'd do that?"

"For God's sake, Richard. How long have we been friends? Of course I'd do that. I mean, I think it's all pretty far-fetched, but I agree that things are getting a little weird. There's no point in taking chances."

"Thanks, Chris. I can't tell you how much I appreciate everything you're doing for us. It seems like everyone else…" His voice faded for a moment. "Well, let's just say we don't feel like we've got a lot of friends right now."

"Don't worry about it. Look, I'm at my place in St. Bart's right now. Why don't I send my jet for the three of you? It'll be a good spot to lay low while we try to figure things out."

"I don't want to drag you into this, Chris."

"A little late to start worrying about that. You know what they say: in for a penny, in for a pound."

15

Pittsburgh, Pennsylvania
April 19

"Dr. Draman!" the pilot shouted, descending from the small jet and rushing across the tarmac to relieve him of the duffel he was carrying. "I'm James, Chris Graden's pilot."

"Good to meet you. This is my wife, Carly."

"I was told there would be three of you," he said as he shook Carly's hand.

"We decided to leave our daughter with a friend."

The man nodded and started toward the plane with them close behind. Richard glanced over at his wife and saw that she still looked vaguely ill.

"It's going to be OK," he said, squeezing her hand.

They hadn't been separated from Susie since the day she was born, and leaving her with a near stranger was one of the hardest things they'd ever done. But there had been little choice—while Richard had stuffed his and Carly's passports in his duffel before they'd fled their home, Susie didn't have one. And while there had been more than a few tears when they'd left, they hadn't been Susie's. She'd taken immediately to Seeger and was already planning a host of parental-supervision-free activities that he seemed genuinely excited to be involved in.

Richard took the seat across from his wife and waited for the pilot to return to the cockpit before leaning forward and putting a hand on her knee. "Did you see her waving from the porch when we were leaving? She

68

didn't even look upset. In fact, I think she's enjoying the adventure of it all."

"I know, but—"

"She's going to be fine, Carly. With everything she's been through, she's stronger than either you or I ever will be."

"Maybe we should call. I'm not sure I was completely clear on all her medications. Burt—"

"You wrote a dissertation on it."

"I didn't—"

"Carly. Seriously. I saw it. There were diagrams."

She actually managed a thin smile at that.

"We're only going to be gone for a few days. Long enough to talk this through with Chris and figure some things out."

She nodded, turning her attention to the window as the plane accelerated down the runway. She continued to stare into the glare outside, as though she could steal one last glimpse of their daughter before they broke through the clouds.

He resisted the same urge, closing his eyes and listening to the white noise fill the otherwise empty plane. He hadn't been able to sleep more than two hours straight since the night he'd been arrested, and right now all he could do was try to rest enough to regain his ability to think straight. He pictured snowcapped mountains reflected in the still water of a lake— a stress-reduction technique he'd learned from a magazine in his dentist's waiting room. The serene image was broken almost immediately by the partially hidden face of the man who had tried to kill Susie, then the syringe, and finally by the strangled cries of his daughter as she fought desperately to untangle herself from her sheets. What if the killer found Seeger's address somehow? What if her heart finally gave out? What if she needed them and they weren't there?

He shook his head subtly, trying to drive away the panic rising in him. Since the mountain lake wasn't going to work, he turned his attention to what he could do to figure out what the hell was happening to him and his family. Was there some way to track the man who was in Susie's room?

Maybe his neighbors had seen something—a vehicle or what direction he'd run. What about the deaths of Annette and Troy? Was there some way he could get information on the investigations and look for discrepancies or things that the police had missed? What about asking around about pharmaceutical companies looking into things similar to Annette's work? Or even individual researchers…

His eyes popped open and he looked at his wife, who was still staring out the window. "Carly! Do you remember Ray Blane?"

She turned to him, but it took a few moments for her to track on what he'd said. "He worked at Cal Tech, right? We went to a party at his house a few years ago. Why?"

"A while back, I heard he was working on something roughly along the lines of the stuff on Annette's drive."

"So?"

"So, I was wondering if he's still pursuing it. If he is, maybe he'd know if any big companies are working on anything similar. Or he could have had problems too—Troy told me that weird things were happening but that at the time he just dismissed them."

"Can you call him?"

"I don't see why not."

Richard used his sat phone to call information and then went through the switchboard at Cal Tech to get to Blane's office. It was a little late to expect him to be in the office, but he picked up almost immediately.

"Ray? This is Richard Draman. How are you?"

"Richard? Hi. I'm fine. How are *you*?"

The inflection was a little too pronounced, suggesting that the story about his trouble with PharmaTan had already made its rounds.

"I'm good. I had a quick question for you, though. A while back, I heard you were doing some theoretical work on the human genome. Are you still involved in that?"

"No. I gave up on that years ago."

"Do you mind if I ask why? Did it turn out to be a dead end?"

"I don't know about the dead end. August Mason seems to think it's there, and it's hard to argue with the guy, but I can't say I ever found it."

"Then why did you stop?"

"It wasn't a scientific decision. I got a huge grant, and they wanted me to focus on other things. I would have liked to have kept dabbling, but they were adamant that it was a waste of time and they weren't paying me to screw around. Why do you ask?"

Richard ignored the question. "Could you tell me specifically who wanted it killed?"

"Chris Graden put together the grant."

Richard felt his breath catch in his chest.

"Richard? Hello? Are you still there?"

"I'm here."

"Yeah, Chris was hell-bent on me walking away from that research, and based on the number of zeros on the check he got me, I wasn't really in a position to argue, you know? Shit, it was probably a waste of time anyway. If Mason couldn't figure it out, what were my chances? Hey, how's Susie doing? Last time we—"

"Good," Richard said, cutting him off. "She's good. Look, I appreciate the information, but I've got to run, OK?"

"Sure. I understand. Good luck, Richard. I hope things turn out OK for you."

He hung up the phone and stared down at it, trying to put what he'd just heard into some kind of context.

"Richard?" Carly said. "Are you all right?"

"It was Chris."

"What?"

He didn't answer, and Carly grabbed his hand. "Richard, you're starting to scare me. What did he say?"

"It was Chris," he repeated, glancing toward the cockpit to confirm that the pilots couldn't overhear their conversation. "He's the one who killed Ray's project."

She released him and pulled back a little. "What are you saying? You think Chris is involved in this? You know that's crazy, right? We've been friends for years. He's done nothing but help us ever since we met him."

Richard looked out the window at the endless ocean below. He had no idea where they were except that it was a hell of a long way from home. A long way from Susie.

"Has he really?"

"Helped us?" she replied. "Hell yes. He just gave you a check for twenty-five thousand dollars out of his own pocket, remember?"

He didn't respond, just staring out the window.

"Richard?" she said, her fear starting to turn to wariness.

"Another way to think about it is that he's never given me enough money to move my work forward in any real way," Richard said, finally meeting her eye. "He gives me just enough to make sure I tell him everything I'm doing in hopes of getting more funding."

"You're saying that he's just been spying on you all these years?"

"Look, I know how it sounds, Carly. But he's the constant in all this, isn't he? He's known us since the very beginning of the Progeria Project, and he's known Annette even longer. He killed Ray's research. He miraculously appears at the police station an hour after I get arrested—"

"Richard…"

"When did that guy show up in Susie's room?" he said, ignoring her. "A few days after we told Chris we were going to go to the mat with PharmaTan and force them to give me back Annette's data."

"Richard! Enough. OK? Enough. Chris is our closest friend in the world, and you're criticizing him for giving you money and getting you out of jail."

Richard shook his head, an overwhelming sense of anger and betrayal building in his gut. "And now he tells me to put my entire family on a plane out of the country."

"Are you actually suggesting that Chris would hurt us? Would hurt Susie?"

He reached for his seat belt and flipped open the clasp. "All I know right now is that we're getting the hell off this plane."

16

Over the Atlantic Ocean
April 19

Richard yanked back the curtain separating the jet's cabin from the cockpit, his panicked expression only partially feigned. "We have to land! Now!"

Both pilots twisted around in their seats, one nearly spilling coffee on himself.

"What is it?" asked the one who had introduced himself only as James. "What's wrong?"

"It's my wife. She's lost consciousness."

James jumped to his feet and looked to the back of the plane as the copilot took over the controls. Carly was hanging unnaturally over the arm of her seat, held in place only by her seat belt. Despite her reluctance, she was playing the part with real artistry.

"She has a history of seizures brought on by altitude, but they've always been mild," Richard said. "I don't know why this time is different, but we have to get down."

"We're over the ocean, Doctor. The—"

"Please. You have to do something. It's rare, but people have died from her condition. There must be somewhere we can land."

The pilot chewed on his lip and looked back again at Carly's still form. "There are islands. We'll find the closest one with an airstrip that can accommodate us. Go back and take care of your wife. We'll get her down as soon as we can."

Richard thanked him profusely and then rushed to the back of the plane, making a show of gently straightening Carly in her seat before sitting down across from her and taking her hand.

She opened one eye slightly. "Are we landing?"

"I don't know. We'll see."

Less than five minutes passed before the pilot started down the aisle toward them, though the gun and roll of duct tape Richard half expected was nowhere in sight.

"How is she, Doctor?"

Either he was a hell of an actor, or he was genuinely concerned. It made sense, Richard supposed. In the unlikely event that Chris really was involved in all this, there was no reason to believe his pilots would be complicit.

"I don't know. I can't get her to respond."

"We've found a strip and called in a medical emergency. Strap in. We're going to start down in just a few minutes."

The sensation of the wheels hitting the ground wasn't as reassuring as Richard had hoped. The descent had been long enough for the initial shock of Ray's revelation to wear off and reality to set in. If he walked off this plane, he would be turning his back on the only person who actually had the power to help them.

He slipped out of his seat and leaned close to his wife as he unbuckled her belt. "I think it's time for you to start feeling a little better."

After throwing their duffel over his shoulder, he pulled her to her feet, supporting her as she hobbled unsteadily up the aisle.

"You're back with us," the pilot said, sounding sincerely relieved. "Are you feeling better?"

Carly smiled weakly and mumbled an unintelligible answer as he opened the door and helped guide her down the steps.

The sun was headed toward a cloudless horizon, and Richard put a hand up to shade his eyes. There wasn't much to see—a beat-up airstrip, scrub brush trying to take hold in sandy soil, a single building that looked abandoned.

The only thing that didn't look like it was in the process of being reclaimed by nature was a tiny blue pickup with a fabric canopy shading the bed. A tall black man unfolded himself from the driver's seat and jogged up to them.

"I'm Henry," he said in a pleasant island drawl before taking Carly's elbow and leading her toward the truck. "I've called the clinic, and they're waiting for you."

Richard turned back to the pilot and offered his hand. "It was just the altitude. She's going to be fine. I can't thank you enough for finding a place to land so fast. I'm not sure what would have happened if you hadn't."

"It was no problem, Dr. Draman. It's what we get paid for. Do you want me to come with you to the clinic?"

"Thanks, but no. We'll manage. I'm not putting her on another plane—not for a while at least. We'll figure something out ourselves."

The pilot seemed confused. "You're saying you want us to leave you here?"

"We'll be fine. Tell Chris that I'll call him in the next day or so to make a plan. Maybe we could hire a boat or something."

He clapped the pilot on the shoulder and then headed for the truck. The driver was already behind the wheel, and Carly was lying on a stretcher in the bed. He climbed in next to her and waved to the baffled pilot as the vehicle started up a rutted dirt road.

They rode in silence for a few minutes, Carly watching the tops of the scrubby trees flash by and him watching the road to make sure no one was following.

"Happy now?" she said, finally.

"Look, I know you feel like I overreacted—"

"Overreacted? You think? I mean, all you did was have me pretend to be in a coma so we could get off a jet owned by one of our only friends, only to be stranded…" Her voice faded for a moment. "Where the hell are we?"

It was a question he'd been too preoccupied to consider. Steadying himself on the top of the cab, he leaned out toward the driver's open window.

"Excuse me. What island is this?"

"Mayaguana," the man shouted over the sound of the wind.

"Where's that?"

"Near Acklins."

Neither place rang a bell. "How many people live here?"

"I don't really know. Maybe three hundred?"

Richard pulled back and looked down at his wife. "Mayaguana."

"Great," she said, the frustration she'd undoubtedly felt since they left home now overpowering her ability to hide it. "I've been planning a vacation here for years."

"No reason to be sarcastic. I just—"

The sound of an explosion filled Richard's ears, and he instinctively threw himself over his wife as the truck jerked hard to the right. Jesus, was someone shooting at them? Was their driver hit?

She tried to squirm out from beneath him as the truck slowed, but he kept her pinned down. When he dared peek over the truck's bed to see if there was sufficient cover for them to run, Carly was finally able to get the leverage to push him off.

"Tire," she said over what he now realized was the flapping of shredded rubber. "It's just one of the guy's rotted old tires, Richard."

By the time they climbed over the gate, the driver already had the jack out and Richard was starting to feel fairly stupid.

"Do you need help?" Carly said.

"I can manage," the man said. "You seem much better. I'm happy to see it."

"Thanks. I feel better."

Richard scanned the low dunes around them and then the road behind. Was the tire blowing at that moment just another of a long line of coincidences or had someone caused it to happen?

Carly seemed to read his mind and clasped a sweaty hand on his shoulder before pointed at Chris's jet heading out over the ocean. "There goes our ride."

"Carly, I—"

She ignored him and started up the road the way they'd come, dragging him along with her.

"I'm really starting to worry about you," she said when they were out of earshot of the driver.

"I know this seems…" His voice faded for a moment. "Annette and Troy. What happened to Susie. I just can't chalk this all up to chance."

"You've taken on so much, Richard. Work, blame, responsibility. I'll never understand how you handled it for this long. Anyone else in the world would have thrown themselves off that bridge you were talking about. But you need to think about the possibility that you've become… overwhelmed. No one could blame you if you finally just needed to escape. Maybe this is your way of—"

"Don't psychoanalyze me, Carly."

"All I'm saying is that after everything that's happened, we left our sick daughter with a man we barely know. And now you believe that our best friend is trying to kill us based on a thirty-second phone conversation with a guy you haven't talked to in years."

"I assume you have a point?" he said, the defensiveness in his voice sounding pathetic even to him.

"I was willing to go along with this," she responded, watching Chris's plane fade into the horizon. "I love you and I'm more grateful than you could ever know for what you've done—what you've sacrificed—for Susie. But this is a bridge too far. I'm not going to stand here and watch you destroy yourself and every chance she and the other kids have over a—"

Her words caught in her throat, and she jerked to a stop, eyes still fixed on the horizon.

By the time he looked up, the dull thump of a distant explosion had reached them, vibrating the humid air in a way that penetrated deep into his chest.

A tiny yellow smear was visible where Chris's jet had been a few moments before. Richard squinted at it, unable to fully comprehend what he was seeing until a black streak of smoke began arcing downward.

They stood there in silent shock, unable to speak as they watched the plane spiral into the ocean.

17

1,800 Miles East of Australia
April 19

The obsession with secrecy seemed to grow daily. At one time, the group had held its rare meetings isolated in the forests of Latvia. When that had been deemed too public, they had tried communicating remotely over heavily encrypted lines. And now, it had come to this.

Chris Graden followed the armed man over a trail cut through thick tropical foliage. The island had been purchased two years ago through the customary maze of offshore corporations and partnerships, but beyond that, he knew nothing—not even its general location. A plane picked him up at a private airport near his home and landed many hours later on a cleverly disguised airstrip. Shades were drawn, and electronics were banned for the entire trip.

Karl cherished anonymity and isolation above all things and avoided gathering the group unless it was absolutely necessary. On the rare occasion meetings did happen, it was usually to disseminate bad news or allocate blame. And if the purpose was the latter, it was certain that the accused would never be seen again.

A stone building that faded in and out of an overgrown cliff became visible ahead, but only because Graden had been there before. Like everything else relating to the group, it was camouflaged to the point that it almost seemed a figment of the imagination. A mirage brought on by heat and fear.

The guard opened a steel door and pointed Graden down a familiar corridor. The walls were stone—damp with humidity and crisscrossed
with live vines. He tried to keep his breathing even as he walked, reluctant
to reveal his anxiety to the inevitable concealed cameras.

He finally pushed through the door at the corridor's end, leaving the
dripping ceiling and buzzing insects for an elegant, climate-controlled
conference room that wasn't much different than the one in his old corporate headquarters. The nine men sitting around the table greeted him
with polite nods, but their eyes didn't linger as he sat.

He could put identities to only two of them. On his right was Henry
Parador, a powerful American senator whose family had made a fortune
in tobacco. Directly across from him was Ivo Ljujic, a former Bosnian general who now controlled an Eastern European business empire that Graden
carefully avoided reading anything about. Curiosity was strongly frowned
upon and had been severely punished on at least one occasion that he knew
about.

Everyone at the table was fit and healthy—nothing less would be tol-
erated—and he assumed that all were extremely wealthy based on the two
men he recognized and the fact that his own initiation had cost well into
nine figures.

It was there that the similarities ended, though. Ages ranged from
mid thirties to early seventies, skin color from white to black, and accents
from familiar to nearly unintelligible.

"Now that we're all here," Karl said with enunciation precise enough
to obscure his place of birth, "I see no reason that we can't start."

Despite being one of the youngest men in the room, Karl was clearly in
command. For some reason, his toned body, thick dark hair, and unlined
face didn't project inexperience—only virility and strength. Graden
always felt just a little slower and more infirm in his presence.

"After a long period of calm, there are now a number of issues that
demand discussion. First, for those of you who haven't heard, Annette Chevalier is dead. Our efforts to block her research through pressure from her
superiors proved ineffective, and we were forced to move more tangibly.

As of today, the investigation into her death has been closed, and it's been deemed a suicide."

The men around the table nodded gravely as Karl watched in the strangely motionless way he always did. There was something about him that was inhumanly exact. Nothing was wasted—not emotion, not movement, and certainly not words.

"Unfortunately, there's been a complication. Her husband went to Richard Draman after her death and gave him a copy of her research."

Concerned murmurs erupted from the group as Karl turned to Graden. "We aren't able to determine exactly what was said in that meeting because we didn't have sufficient capability."

Graden had been prepared for the charge, but that preparation didn't prevent his mouth from going dry as he responded.

"It's been our policy to use as little surveillance as possible because of the risks involved. I knew Richard Draman extremely well, and I'm one of his main sources of funding. It was in his best interest to tell me everything he was doing, and based on our evaluations, his research hasn't gone in a direction that could be a threat to us. Also, it's unlikely that he would have continued in this field for more than a few years—I expected him to move on when his daughter died."

It was a dangerous tightrope. He couldn't afford to be seen as making excuses, but also couldn't afford to appear incompetent.

"In any event, the problem has been resolved," Karl said. "Draman and his family went down in a private jet earlier today."

An Asian man to Graden's left spoke up. "This is very close to us. And the deaths of multiple biologists in such a short time could draw attention."

Karl leaned forward and placed his palms on the table. "It needed to be done quickly. Draman went to see August Mason to discuss Chevalier's research."

"Still," the Asian persisted, "there are quieter ways to deal with this, are there not?"

"Normally, yes. We used a man that we'd cultivated in the local police force, but it wasn't as effective as we'd hoped. Because of Draman's daughter's illness, he isn't easy to deter."

"Perhaps it would have been wiser to deal with the daughter, then?" another man said.

Karl leaned back again, his statue-like demeanor slipping slightly. "We concluded the same thing. Unfortunately, our man was interrupted by Draman in the process."

That elicited audible groans from the group.

"But we are certain that they are all dead now?" the Asian said.

Karl nodded toward a man Graden had never seen before. He was probably in his early sixties with distinctively Eastern European features and gray hair that had thinned in a vaguely unnatural pattern.

"I'd like to introduce Oleg. This is his area of expertise, and I'm going to let him answer that question."

The man shuffled some papers as Graden tried unsuccessfully not to speculate on his background. He'd long suspected that the members of the group were chosen for their particular skills and spheres of influence: him, for his knowledge of the pharmaceutical industry and bioresearch; this man, perhaps because of a background in intelligence.

"Susan Draman did not get on the plane," Oleg said with an unmistakable Russian accent.

Graden tensed, and it took a moment for him to find his voice. "Are you certain of your information? Richard never said anything about her not coming, and as long as I've known them, they've never been separated from Susie."

"My information is correct," he responded dismissively. "We've already looked into family and close friends but have yet to locate her."

"Then you haven't found all their close friends and family," Senator Parador said. "People are pretty damn selective about who they leave their sick kids with. Wouldn't you agree?"

Oleg was clearly unimpressed by the politician. "In fact, we *have* identified them all. Based on the suspicions that Draman expressed and the attempt on his daughter's life, we're working under the theory that he wanted to avoid leaving her somewhere she could be easily found."

Karl broke in, obviously not interested in letting the back-and-forth escalate. "Everything possible is being done, and we'll be calling on everyone here to help us minimize the public impact of the Dramans' deaths as well as to help us find their daughter."

"And what happens when we do find her?" Parador asked.

Karl scanned the faces around the table for a moment. "We're still exploring our options, but it seems likely that she and the people she's with will have to be eliminated."

18

400 Miles East of Cuba
April 20

The darkness around Richard Draman was deep enough to rob him of his balance, and he stumbled toward the bow of the boat, groping for solid surfaces and listening to the waves lapping against the wood hull.

As he passed by the open-air bridge, he could see the face of the man at the wheel, his dark skin faded corpse green by the glow of the instruments. He didn't acknowledge Richard's presence at all, instead staring into the inky blackness as though he could see something in it.

Henry, the man who had picked them up at the airstrip, had introduced them to the still unnamed boat captain—a scarred and sun-blackened man with the requisite barrel chest and faded tattoos. Fortunately, he'd been amenable to smuggling two Americans back into their own country as long as a suitable price could be negotiated. Payment details were a bit complicated since Henry had put a serious dent in the cash they'd brought in return for his promise to tell anyone who might come asking that they'd gotten back on the plane after a brief stop to let Carly's air sickness subside. But fear and capitalism were powerful motivators, and the captain had finally agreed that Carly's engagement ring would suffice.

Richard continued forward, finally dropping to his knees and crawling to keep the rolling deck from pitching him into a cache of fishing gear. A moment later, a hand closed around his shoulder. "I'm here."

He settled into the pile of life jackets they'd arranged on the bow, feeling the misty ocean spray against his face as his wife pressed against him for warmth.

"This is about all we have, isn't it, Richard?"

"What do you mean?"

"We call our families once a year during the holidays after putting it off as long as we can. We don't have many friends because of work and because we want to spend as much time as we can with Susie…"

"Are you trying to cheer me up? Because it's not going so well."

"I was thinking about Chris. About the fact that we're probably closer to him than anyone else in the world."

"So do you still think I'm paranoid?" he said. "That I'm having a breakdown?"

He could smell her sweat and shampoo as she shook her head in the darkness. "I don't know what to think anymore. Like you said, one coincidence is easy to ignore. Two can happen. Maybe even three. But this…"

"Yeah," he said, leaning back in the life jackets and wrapping an arm around her.

"I keep wondering if those pilots had families," Carly continued. "If they had little girls waiting for them to get home too. And I keep wondering why all this has happened."

"It's what we talked about before. Some foreign pharmaceutical company is on the verge of a breakthrough that will make them billions."

"But why Chris?" she interrupted. "He's already rich, and so is everyone else who would be involved in something like this. They fly around on their jets and drive around in their Rolls-Royces while Susie and kids like her die. Isn't that enough?"

Above, the clouds were beginning to part, exposing a narrow streak of stars. "You have to understand that the cost of doing this kind of research is astronomical, Carly. If I had to guess, I'd say that Chris and a bunch of other investors bet the farm on this thing. And if it goes south, they'll be looking at trading in those jets and Rolls-Royces for double-wides and bicycles."

"So where does that leave us, Richard? I'm a chef. You're a biologist. How do we fight people who are willing to blow up a plane full of innocent people? People who would send a man to murder a child?"

It was a question he'd been obsessing over since he'd watched Chris Graden's jet plummet into the sea. So far, epiphanies were proving elusive.

"If they think we're dead, it gives us some breathing room," he said.

"What if they don't think that? What if they know we got off?"

"Fugitives can sometimes stay ahead of the FBI for years. Chris, for all his money, isn't the FBI."

"And we're not fugitives, Richard. We don't know the first thing about being on the run, and we have a sick daughter to think about. We haven't done anything wrong. They have. They're the ones who should be running. They're the ones whose lives should be torn apart."

She laid her head against his chest while he watched the blackness in front of them.

"At least we know one thing," he said.

"We do?"

"Yeah. We know that Chris is involved. That's enough to get started."

"Started on what?"

"Exposing him and whoever he's involved with. Maybe to the police. Maybe to the press. I don't know. But they aren't going to stop otherwise. Even if they think we're dead, they might know that Susie isn't. They'll come for her if we don't stop them."

"What about August Mason?" Carly said. "How does he fit in?"

"I don't know if he does. Other than the fact that Annette and Ray were working on research based on ideas he abandoned."

"He turned you in to the police."

"Yeah, but the truth is that he didn't have much choice after I brought him that drive."

"Shouldn't he be dead?"

"What do you mean?"

"That's how everyone who's been involved with Annette's research ends up. Why would he be the exception? I mean, wouldn't he be the last person in the world a pharma company on the verge of a breakthrough would want looking at that stuff?"

She was right. With everything that was happening, he hadn't given August Mason a second thought.

"Shit!" he said, pushing Carly off him and making his way back to the captain as quickly as he could without falling overboard.

"Do you have a phone?" he asked. In the commotion on the plane, he'd forgotten to put his sat phone back in his duffel, and it was now at the bottom of the ocean.

"A phone?" the man said. "Is that a joke?"

"Let me use the radio, then. I have to contact someone on shore."

"You're not contacting anybody."

"Look, this is life or death," Richard said, reaching past him for a hand mic hanging next to the throttle.

The darkness, combined with the man's surprising speed, made it impossible for Richard to react. He was driven back against the railing, and a gleaming blade stopped its arc less than an inch from his right eye.

Carly's scream was barely audible, swallowed by the black hole they were floating in. The captain's words, though, were extraordinarily clear.

"If you do anything that makes me even *think* it could get me caught, I'll weigh both of you down and throw you overboard. Do you understand?"

Richard stared at the knife. He had no doubt the man was serious, but for some reason he wasn't afraid. Maybe it was exhaustion. Or maybe it was because the threat wasn't a patchwork of conjecture and suspicion lurking just out of sight. It was right there. It had a face. It had a weapon.

The boat hit a wave, rocking it hard enough to cause the smuggler to stagger backward. Before he knew what he was doing, Richard grabbed the man's wrist and swung an elbow up under his chin. It connected full force, and they both toppled into a pile of ropes coiled on the deck.

The strange sense of calm he'd felt only a few moments ago disappeared, replaced by the rage and frustration that he'd been swallowing for nearly a decade. The dazed smuggler was suddenly transformed into everything he'd come to associate with evil—Susie's attacker, Sands, his best friend Chris. But mostly the disease.

He slammed a fist into the man's face, and the sense of release was so overwhelming that he did it again. And then again. The smuggler dropped the knife and used his thick forearms to try to deflect the blows. Richard heard the clatter of the metal against the deck and groped blindly for the weapon, getting hold of it just before an arm wrapped around his neck from behind.

"Richard!"

He recognized the voice as his wife's, but it seemed so far away.

"Richard! That's enough!"

He faltered, dropping the blade and falling backward as his mind slowly came back on line. Carly kept hold of him, and he could feel her breath as it mixed with the breeze coming off the water.

He'd have done it. He was sure of it. He would have stabbed the man if she hadn't stopped him.

Her grip loosened and she leaned in, examining his face in the starlight. "Are you OK?"

He swallowed hard and nodded, unable to speak. A numbness crept over him that he hadn't felt since the Pabst-Blue-Ribbon-fueled brawls of his youth. He'd thought that part of him—the part that had broken the jaw of a rival school's star linebacker and pitched a friend's abusive father through a sliding glass door—was long gone. But maybe it had just been hiding.

Carly used a foot to kick the knife out of reach and crawled around him to check on the semiconscious sailor. "If he doesn't come around soon, I hope you know which way North America is."

19

Near Cutler Bay, Florida
April 22

He didn't hear the wave until it hit, knocking him off his feet and pulling him into the impenetrable darkness. He rolled and slammed into something that felt like a submerged log, confused for a moment as to which way was up.

"That son of a bitch!" Richard Draman said when he finally managed to surface and expel brackish water from his lungs.

"You did almost stab him to death," Carly pointed out, grabbing hold of him for stability as another set of waves hit. "I don't think you should have been looking for any favors."

The smuggler had given them two badly patched inner tubes and dropped them off about a quarter mile from shore, assuring them that if they just followed the glow of electric light, it would be a straight shot to a beach.

When the clouds parted, though, a three-quarter moon illuminated not the glow of white sand but the shadow of a mangrove swamp. From their position, a thick tangle of roots was visible for about fifty feet before going completely black beneath an unbroken canopy. If they went in and lost their sense of direction, they could end up wandering around for days. And even if they got through, did the road they'd been told about really exist?

"Toto, I've got a feeling we're not in Kansas anymore," Carly said in an attempt to lighten his mood. The strain was clearly audible in her voice, but there wasn't even a hint of accusation. Not that it mattered. He was doing a perfectly fine job allocating blame without her help.

Why the hell hadn't he just let that asshole wave his knife around and make as many threats as he wanted? All he had to say was "yes, sir," do a little cowering, and they'd have been strolling past the pool at the Hilton right now. But no. He'd had to pick that moment to lose it.

"Are there alligators in here?" Carly said, looking around as they started forward again.

"How should I know?"

"You're a biologist."

"*Micro*biologist. If there's anything in the world that's not micro, it's a goddamn alligator."

He let out a long, frustrated breath, chastising himself for snapping at her. Precisely none of this was her fault. "I'm sorry, Carly. I think the water here might be too salty for them."

"Might be?"

"That's the best I can do. But look on the bright side. Based on our luck, the snakes will get us first."

* * *

"This is stupid," Richard said, grabbing his wife by the arm and pulling her to a stop. "We're just going in circles."

They'd been wandering around the swamp for an hour now, following what little moonlight could penetrate the tangle of trees. Where they were in relation to the coast, how far they'd gone, and what they were even looking for were all a mystery. At least they were still in one piece, though. So far, the largest reptile they'd seen was only about a foot long.

"Giving up isn't really an option at this point," Carly said. "I'm not looking to take up permanent residence—"

"Look, I know, OK? I know. But this isn't getting us anywhere. Remember what Burt said—the most important thing is to think. And we're not doing that."

"We've got to get back to Susie," she said, sounding increasingly desperate. "I have to know if she's all right."

He understood how she felt. He was dead tired, scared, and fairly certain that they were attracting a fair number of leeches—something his wife thankfully hadn't yet noticed. Much worse, though, were thoughts of Susie. The not knowing.

"Take it easy, Carly. She's got Burt with her, and I've gone over this in my head a hundred times. There's no way anyone can track her to him without basically going though every person I've ever met."

"You don't know that, Richard. Someone could have seen the truck. They could—"

He reached out and put a hand over her mouth, cocking his head at something barely audible over the buzz of the swamp. "Shhh. What's that?"

"I don't hear—"

She fell silent as the periodic thump grew louder—too rhythmic and deep to be natural.

"Wait," she said excitedly. "I do hear it. Is it…is it music?"

They dodged roots and clambered over tiny patches of dry land for another miserable half hour, sometimes in areas so dark they had to navigate entirely by touch. But it *was* music. In fact, it was a Grateful Dead bootleg that he himself had owned since college.

They were able to move faster as they got closer, following the flickering light of a campfire past a canoe tied to a tiny island no more than fifty feet wide. On its high point were two people sitting in lawn chairs—a man and a woman staring into the flames as they passed an oversized joint back and forth. Both looked to be in their early twenties, with matching dreadlocks and bare feet sticking out from the bottom of dirty jeans.

Richard climbed onto the spit of land, looking down at himself and saying a silent prayer of thanks that the leeches had just been a figment of his imagination.

"Hello!"

The woman started, staring wide-eyed at him and trying to hide the joint behind her back.

"Who are you?" her companion said, standing to an impressive height but losing some intimidation points with his Winnie the Pooh T-shirt.

"Police," Richard responded, using the obvious opportunity that the marijuana presented.

"You've got to be kidding," the young man said, watching Carly emerge from the water. "They've got you wading around all night in the swamp to find people camping illegally? What, did you get caught screwing your boss's daughter, 'cause—"

"We work narcotics, actually."

The young woman's eyes became even rounder, and she began slowly retreating with the joint still behind her back.

"Come on, dude. It's a little pot. I'm not Tony Montana, here."

"Do you have a phone?" Richard said.

"What?"

"We had to bail off a boat about a half a mile offshore, and mine's full of water."

"Yeah, I've got one."

"Tell you what. If you let me use it and give us a ride out of here, I'll forget we ever met."

Knowing a good deal when he saw one, the kid dropped to his knees and retrieved an iPhone from his pack. Richard took It and flashed Carly a relieved smile as he walked to the far corner of the island, dialing from shaky memory what he hoped was August Mason's number.

"Come on…" he said, listening to the phone on the other end ring. "Pick up. Pick up the—"

"Hello?"

A woman's voice. Groggy, with a familiar Spanish accent.

"May I speak to Dr. Mason, please?"

"Who is this? Do you realize it's two in the morning?"

"This is detective Anderson from the Baltimore police. I'm sorry about the hour, but it's urgent."

"I'm sorry. I thought you would have known. Dr. Mason passed away."

Despite the warm temperatures and humidity, Richard suddenly felt a chill.

"I'm very sorry to hear that," he said, trying to keep his tone matter-of-fact. "May I ask how?"

"Of course. He was on a private aircraft that crashed."

20

Hagerstown, Maryland
April 23

The windows of the surrounding homes were uniformly black as they hurried across Burt Seeger's lawn and into the impenetrable shadow of his front porch.

Carly knocked, quietly at first, and then more insistently. Nothing. She rang the bell a few times with a similar result.

"Where are they?" she said, the panic starting to build in her voice. "Where would they be at this hour?"

"Calm down," Richard whispered. "He's an old guy and his hearing probably isn—"

The blow to the back of his head seemed to come from thin air, bouncing him off the door and buckling his knees. His vision swam sickeningly, and he heard Carly grunt through what sounded like a hand clamped over her mouth.

He flipped onto his stomach and was trying to get to his feet when he felt the cold metal of a gun barrel press against the back of his head.

"Stop! Don't shoot!" Carly shouted.

"What the hell…"

The voice was unmistakable. Burt Seeger wasn't as old and deaf as Richard had thought.

"Get up," the retired soldier said, already starting down the steps to the lawn. "Follow me around back."

Richard was still dazed from the blow to the head, and Carly threw his arm around her shoulders, supporting as much of his weight as she could as they hurried along the side of the house.

"Is Susie all right?" Carly said as Seeger motioned them through the open door leading to the kitchen. "Is everything OK?"

"She's sleeping upstairs," Seeger responded, taking one last look out the door before closing it. "But you're not supposed to be. You're dead. I read it on CNN."

"Did you tell Susie?" Carly said. "Has she—"

"No, thank God. I've been putting it off and keeping her away from the TV and computer until I could figure out what to do."

"We got off the plane before it went down," Richard said, lowering himself into a chair at the kitchen table. He touched the back of his head and pulled back fingers wet with blood.

"I figured that. How about some details?"

Carly pressed a dishtowel to his wound, and he winced, ducking away from the pain. "Whatever's going on, our best friend, Chris Graden, is involved. We were going to call you but weren't sure it was safe."

Seeger leaned back against the wall, gun still hanging from his hand. He'd always been skeptical, but now he looked downright suspicious.

That wasn't all that had changed, though. He also seemed a little tanner. A little straighter.

"When you got here, the police wanted you for peeking at some research that wasn't yours, and you had a pickup that you could argue you borrowed," he said. "You told me you were innocent, that someone had tried to hurt Susie. Fine. But now there's a body count. I figure two pilots and one Nobel Prize winner."

"Mason…" Richard said.

"They're reporting that he was on that flight with you."

"It's not true."

Seeger took a seat across from Richard, laying his pistol on the table in front of him.

"Are you planning on shooting us?" Carly said, looking down at it.

He didn't answer for long enough that it became unnerving.

"I know better than to believe anything the press tells me. Hell, they said Susie was with you too. And I was there when you tried to save my wife. I feel like I know a little bit about you. But even I'm starting to have my doubts."

"That sounds like an accusation," Richard said.

The older man shrugged. "Could somebody be after you? Sure, anything's possible. But it seems like you're doing pretty well, and the people around you are the ones dropping like flies."

"You think we did something to that plane?" Carly said. "That we killed those people?"

"You've got a daughter to save, and maybe you think someone has information that could help you. I've only known Susie for a few days, and if saving her meant bumping off a couple pilots and a biologist, I might give it some thought."

"Everything we've told you is a hundred percent true," Richard said, the throbbing in his head adding to the challenge of remaining calm. "We're not evil people. We're not killers."

Seeger smiled and ran a hand over the gun. "You make it sound like those are the same things."

They fell silent for a few moments, and Richard rose, taking the bloody towel from his wife's hand and laying it on the table. "I'm sorry you don't believe us, Burt. But it doesn't really matter. Carly and I have talked about this, and we both agree that we had no right to get you involved. Give us an hour to wake Susie up and get our stuff together and you'll never see us again."

"Now, hold on," Seeger said, suddenly looking a little alarmed. "We're just talking here. I didn't say anything about throwing you out."

"This has gotten too dangerous for you," Carly said. "Whatever debt you felt you owed Richard, it's been paid. We don't want to be responsible for you ending up dead or in jail for something that's not your problem."

Seeger toyed with the gun for a few more seconds before responding. "You know what I've been needing for a long time, Carly?"

"No."

"A goddamn problem. I sit here all day alone in this house waiting for my pension checks. Other than a few old bullet holes, the docs tell me there isn't a thing wrong with me. That I could live to be a hundred. Can you believe that? A hundred. I used to make life-and-death decisions ten times a day. Now I melt down if two TV shows I want to watch are on at the same time." He pointed toward the living room. "I took up quilting to meet women. That's what I've come to. Quilting."

She actually smiled at that. One of those broad, toothy grins that dented her cheeks. Richard looked on, suddenly pulled back to the first time he'd seen that smile.

Seeger slid the gun off the table and tucked it into his pants—a peace offering. "So if we assume you're telling the truth—and I'm willing to go down that road a mile or two—then your main problem is that you have people trying to kill you. In the scheme of things, that's not all that complicated."

"It's not?" Carly said.

"Nope. There are only two ways to make that particular issue go away, and they're both permanent: You kill them first or you die."

She pondered that for a moment. "I vote for the first one."

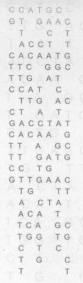

21

Hagerstown, Maryland
April 24

Richard rolled the office chair into a narrow beam of sunlight filtering through the window and flipped through the passports drying there. Burt Seeger's basement was a bit short on creature comforts—not much more than a concrete box lined with exposed pipes—but it felt safe. For now.

He closed his eyes and felt the warmth penetrate his skin. A space heater would have been nice, but money was tight. They'd stuffed just over twenty thousand dollars into a series of shoeboxes that were now perched on top of some old camping equipment in the corner. A lot of money by most standards, but not so much when facing a life on the run. Unless, of course, that life turned out to be extraordinarily short.

The sunlight faltered for a moment, and a wheelbarrow appeared at the top of the window well, followed by Seeger's and Susie's sneaker-covered feet. Carly rose and leaned into the glass, peering up into the backyard.

Her long red hair was short and brown now, and her eyes were framed by a pair of wire-rimmed glasses. Completing the surprisingly effective disguise were a pair of unflattering jeans and a sweater calculated to make her look twenty pounds heavier.

"Susie loves spending time with him," she said. "And have you looked at Burt since she got here? He seems ten years younger."

"No, Carly."

"What?"

"I know what you're thinking. We can't leave her here if something happens to us."

"Where else would she go? My sister's a lunatic, and they'd find her there. Why shouldn't—"

"Because he's already been through this with his wife. It's not fair to him. No one should have to do that twice."

"They've made a lot of progress on the garden," she said, seeming not to hear. "I wish we had a place where we could grow food. When I was a kid, I loved planting things. Watching them come up was a little like magic."

He knew that look, and before she could lose herself in the past he pointed to the cheap laptop they'd bought. "How are you doing on Chris?"

"What?" she said, turning to look down at him.

"Chris. What have you found out about him?"

"Oh," she said, sitting back down in front of the computer. "It's funny, isn't it? We've been friends for years, and I never really thought about the fact that we don't know all that much about him—who his other good friends are, if he was close to his family, what other kinds of research the foundation he ran supported."

"And now?"

"Not much better. I mean, I don't know the first thing about investigating someone, but I don't think that can explain how little I'm finding on Chris. His life was pretty public when he was a CEO, but after that the amount of information really drops off."

"Seems like you'd expect that. It was a pretty public job."

"Yeah, but the contrast is really stark. Since he retired, he seems to actively avoid the limelight and personal relationships. Not that there's any crime in that, but it's pretty unusual for someone with his background— particularly when you consider the fact that he runs a charity."

"What about that? What about the foundation?"

"They don't even have a Website. I can't find so much as a set of guidelines on how you'd submit a grant proposal. Do know who any of the other board members are?"

Richard shook his head. "I talked to Chris about meeting them and doing a presentation, but he always came out against it—said I was better off just letting him to do the legwork."

She put a hand to her face and rubbed her lower lip nervously. "What now, then?"

He shrugged. "It sounds like Chris is a dead end, and the Chevaliers are dead and buried. I've looked through all the scientific literature and haven't found anything even close to what Annette was looking into. We have no way of finding the son of a bitch who attacked Susie, and the Baltimore police are completely focused on me. Or in somebody's pocket."

"As near as I can tell," Carly said, "that only leaves us one path."

"Mason," he agreed. "Someone's got him, and it's a pretty fair bet that they're the same people who are after us. Find him and we've got something real—something people can't ignore. Without him, though, I'm just an industrial spy on the run."

22

1,800 Miles East of Australia
April 24

Oleg Nazarov grimaced as he sat—at the pain in his back, at the worsening arthritis in his left knee, and at the loss of control over his life. No, it wasn't a loss. He'd given it away.

The windows to his left rose from floor to ceiling, holding back the jungle beyond. Everything was the same green—impenetrable, hazy with heat and humidity, home to endless parasites and biting insects. He was a long way from his birthplace in northern Russia, a land of deep cold and open spaces, of horse-drawn carts and wind blowing through stunted crops.

Perhaps he should have spent his life there like his father had. Instead, he'd left as a teenager to attend school in Moscow, become a member of the communist party, and eventually join the KGB. Despite—or perhaps because of—his success in those organizations, there had always been someone beneath him who coveted his position or someone above him blocking his path. He had never again experienced the freedom and contentment of his youth.

It had been the memory of his childhood more than anything else that had prompted him to return to the remote regions of his country after the collapse of the Soviet Union. The derelict oil fields and cash-starved soldiers with arms to sell had been just a happy circumstance, as had the hundreds of millions of euros he'd amassed selling them.

But now everything had changed. Much of his wealth had been siphoned off by the group, and he was back to leading investigations and paramilitary operations—something he hadn't done in almost a quarter century. And once again, he found himself trapped in a luxurious prison. This time by a man who, as far as the world was concerned, didn't exist.

Nazarov watched a brightly colored bird settle on a tree branch outside and wondered if Karl had spent his youth in such a place. If that's why he was so comfortable on the island. But it was dangerous to think of such things.

He turned to his computer and decrypted the most recent e-mail, running a hand over his balding scalp as he read through it. Nothing of use. Nothing new.

He had learned yesterday that the plane carrying Richard and Carly Draman had crashed miles from its expected course. His inquiries had uncovered a disastrous chain of events: The pilot reporting a medical emergency. A brief stopover in Mayaguana. The bomb they'd planted going off while the jet was still within view of people on the ground.

There was no record of the Dramans ever arriving at the clinic, and the ambulance driver had initially insisted that they'd returned to the plane before it left. More persistent questioning—questioning that had ended with the man's body at the bottom of the ocean—laid bare a much more alarming story.

As Nazarov reread the useless e-mail, he felt a burning it the pit of his stomach that he hadn't experienced since his years with Soviet intelligence. Though the development of this plan had been necessarily rushed, he'd signed off on every detail. It had been *his* operation, and it had ended with the entire Draman family falling off the face of the earth.

Explaining to Karl that a medical researcher and his chef wife had outmaneuvered him wasn't something Nazarov was anxious to do. In fact, it wasn't something he was certain he'd survive.

He deleted the e-mail and opened a file containing information on his investigation into the Dramans. Richard was proving to be a much more formidable opponent than anyone would have guessed. Was this the result of an IQ well into the 170s and a youth spent playing cat and mouse with the police? The counsel of an unseen ally? Perhaps both?

The obvious avenues—credit card, ATM, and phone usage—had quickly proved to be dead ends and would undoubtedly continue to be so. According to his information, their personal accounts and those of the Progeria Project had been drained from a number of bank branches in Maryland and Virginia, leaving them with just over twenty thousand dollars in cash. It seemed likely that they'd been dropped off somewhere in southern Florida by a Bahamian smuggler, whom they had yet to locate. This hypothesis was supported by a phone call to August Mason made from a phone connected to a tower near Cutler Bay, Florida.

It was there that the situation became more murky. They would be unable to rent a car without a credit card, and there was no record of them buying a plane ticket. Most likely, they'd used buses—a mode of transportation that still provided an irritating level of anonymity to those willing to take even a few rudimentary precautions.

It was possible that they would run to the federal authorities, and he was actively strengthening his already considerable network at those organizations—particularly the FBI. But he was convinced that it was young Susie who would prove to be her parents' undoing, and it was on that weak link that he would concentrate the majority of his resources.

Speakers attached to his computer began to ring, and he clicked an icon to bring up a secure satellite link.

"Yes."

"We're through the second-tier contacts."

"And?"

"Nothing."

Nazarov leaned back in his chair and fixed his stare on the rock wall across from him. They'd started with immediate family and close friends, concentrating on people within practical proximity to the Dramans' home. The second tier of relationships encompassed family down to cousins and work colleagues.

"Do we have a list of former friends and past coworkers?"

"Not an exhaustive one but enough to start with," the voice replied. "Obviously, when we hit this level there's not much depth but a lot of breadth. Our manpower—"

"Is what it is," Nazarov said, cutting him off.

They were now talking about hundreds of potential contacts, all of whom had to be physically surveilled if they were going to find Susie Draman. It was a task for an army of well-trained men, and he had barely a handful. One of the many drawbacks of being forced to work from the center of a black hole.

"Prioritize as best you can," he said before hanging up and opening a research file on progeria. It was a fascinating, terrifying disease that created victims with special—almost unique—needs. And that distinctness made them vulnerable.

23

Northern Pennsylvania
April 27

The Dramans stepped out of the cab and started up the quiet street's gravel shoulder, stopping when they were out of earshot of the driver.

"I don't know about this, Carly. I'm still thinking that I should go."

She ran a hand down his freshly shaven cheek. "You were here a couple weeks ago, and losing the beard isn't going to fool anyone. Quit worrying. What could possibly go wrong?"

His mouth hung open for a moment, not recognizing the joke until she smiled. The stress of sending his wife on this particular errand was actually making his stomach churn painfully. Even with everything he'd been carrying around for the last eight years, his stomach had always been bulletproof. Until now.

"OK. You're right. I'll wait here for you. You've got the cell, right? If anything happens, just hit—"

"I know how to dial a phone, Richard. Relax. It's going to be fine."

She gave him a quick kiss on the cheek and then made her way to a gate surrounded by mature trees. After pushing the call button, she turned and watched her husband jog hesitantly back to the cab.

"Hello?"

"Hi. Ms. Covas? This is Caroline Bates from the *Washington Post*. We have an appointment."

"Of course. Please come in."

The gate swung open and she started up the long driveway, trying to ignore the intimidating clang as the gate closed behind her. The house came into view when she crested a small rise—every bit as impressive as Richard had described. Beneath the portico, a tall woman in jeans greeted her with a wave. Also as impressive as Richard had described.

"Hello!" Carly called when she was close enough that she didn't have to shout. "Ms. Covas?"

"Alexandra," she said, extending a hand, "Dr. Mason's executive assistant."

"It's nice to meet you. Thanks for taking the time. I know how busy you must be."

"I've gotten a lot of calls from the press since Dr. Mason passed away. But I have to say that yours were the most tenacious."

Carly gave an apologetic smile. "You don't get anywhere in this business without a little elbow grease, you know? So how long have you been with Dr. Mason?"

"About five years."

"Since he got back from…well, wherever it was he went."

She gave a short nod that made it clear she wasn't going to allow herself to be led into a discussion of that particular subject.

"The family isn't keeping the house?" Carly said, watching two men carry a sofa toward a moving truck parked in the driveway.

"Dr. Mason didn't have any family. His assets are being liquidated in accordance with his will."

"Who did he leave the money to?"

"A group supporting healthcare initiatives in Africa."

"I wasn't aware he was involved in charitable work."

"He wasn't. As far as I know, he felt nothing but disdain for the disadvantaged."

"Really?" Carly said, surprised that the woman wouldn't be more guarded in what she said about her former employer.

"Dr. Mason was an analytical man who lived mostly inside his own mind. He didn't give much thought to the people around him beyond demanding they immediately and unquestioningly follow his instructions."

"And yet you stayed with him for five years."

She shrugged. "He paid well and was very helpful in getting me a green card."

"Could you tell me the charity he left his estate to?"

"The Africa AIDS Initiative."

Carly jotted the name down on an official-looking pad she'd purchased, but still wasn't exactly sure what she was looking for. August Mason wasn't a particularly good lead. He was the only lead.

"Did he still work?"

"No. He mostly pursued his hobbies. Fitness, reading, music."

"Doesn't seem like he'd need a personal assistant."

"He didn't like to be bothered with things he felt were beneath him—interacting with the staff that upkeeps the property, fielding requests for his time…"

"Requests for his time?"

"As you can imagine, he had a lot of offers for consulting work. Even though he never accepted, some people making the offers could be extremely persistent."

"You make it sound like there was someone in particular."

She let out an irritated breath. "Andreas Xander."

"Xander? Really? I would think he'd be a hard guy to say no to."

"You have no idea. He used to call personally. Eventually, Dr. Mason refused to talk to him, and I had to do it. Xander is an incredibly rude and vulgar man…" She fell silent for a moment, obviously regretting her statement. "I'd appreciate it if you didn't quote me on that if he's still alive when you print your article. He's also a vindictive and powerful man."

"No problem. What about Chris Graden? What was his relationship to Dr. Mason?"

Her brow furrowed for a moment. "None that I'm aware of. In fact, I'd never heard the name until I was driving him to the airport to get on Mr. Graden's plane."

Carly didn't respond immediately, trying to process what she'd just heard. "You *personally* drove Mason to the airport?"

"Of course."

"Could you tell me what time that was?"

She seemed a bit perplexed by the question, but evidently saw no harm in answering. "About two hours before the flight left. Something like that."

24

Pittsburgh, Pennsylvania
April 27

"This is fine right here," Richard said.

The cab driver pointed through the windshield. "The entrance is up a little farther. I can take you all the way."

Richard peeled a hundred-dollar bill from a roll of cash in his hand and held it over the seats. "No. This is good. We won't be long. Would you mind waiting?"

Carly followed him onto the sidewalk running in front of the private airport's main building and then into the shadow of a tall bush.

"What the hell are we doing, Richard? People saw us when we flew out of here. We're supposed to be dead."

"If Mason's assistant told you that she drove him to the airport two hours before the plane took off, I want to know what happened to him. You talked to the guy at the counter, but I just got a cup of coffee and sat down. No one's going to remember me."

"Don't you think we should—"

He gave her a reassuring smile and hurried toward the front door, feeling his heart rate notch up as he entered the lobby.

"Hi, I'm Richard Grace with the *Washington Post*."

"Fred Terrance," the man behind the desk responded without even a hint of recognition. "What can I do for you?"

"I'm doing a story on August Mason, and I was wondering if I could ask you a few questions."

"Sure. But I can't say that I ever really met the guy. I mean, he was here for a couple minutes and then went out and got on the plane." Terrance shook his head. "Bad luck. You know, a new jet with professional pilots. That's a pretty safe way to travel normally."

Richard looked out the windows that led to the tarmac. From where he was standing, he could see one plane and a small piece of the runway. He walked closer, widening the angle of his view, and saw four other planes, two with open doors and steps leading into them.

"Did you actually see him get on the plane?" he asked, returning to the counter.

"What do you mean?"

"He walked out that door, right? You saw him."

"Yeah."

"Then what?"

"Are you asking if I actually stood here and watched him get on the jet? No. Why would I?"

"Then he could have just wandered off for all you know."

"What paper did you say you were from again?"

"The *Post*."

He looked skeptical. "Seems kind of unlikely that he wandered off. There's a fence surrounding the area, and you need the code to get in and out. If he decided he wanted to leave, he'd have come through here, and I'd have seen him. Besides, if he was still alive, wouldn't he have mentioned it to someone?"

"What if he got on the wrong plane?"

Terrance laughed. "These aren't seven forty-sevens, man. You'd notice if someone you didn't know was sitting next to you grazing on your cheese plate."

"Still, I get paid to be thorough. Could you tell me what other planes flew out around that time?"

He just stood there, trying to decide how much effort he wanted to put into this. Finally, he let out a long, irritated breath and reached beneath the counter for a notebook.

"OK," he said, leafing through it. "Four flights went out around the time he was here."

"Can you tell me anything about them?"

"Like what?"

"I don't know. Who was on them? Where they were going?"

He tapped the page with his finger. "Two were going to New York. One went to Aspen. The other was headed to Argentina. One of the ones that went to New York was a local businessman who flies out of here two or three times a week. The one that went to Aspen was a family going to their vacation house. The other New York flight was a NetJet. I've met the pilot a few times, but I don't remember who the passengers were."

"And the Argentina fight?"

He shrugged. "Don't know anything about it."

* * *

"Come on!" Richard said, holding a hand out as he passed by the bush he'd left his wife in. She took it, and they headed toward the cab waiting by the curb.

"According to the guy in there, Mason was here, and he went out to the planes and never came back."

"You think he got on one?"

"There was someone going to Argentina. How hard would it have been to snatch him? You'd just walk up and say, 'Hi, I'm Chris Graden's pilot. Hop on.' The question, though, is who. Obviously, Chris had to be involved, but I don't believe that this is his show. Someone's pulling his strings."

Carly stopped short. "Xander."

"What?"

"Andreas Xander," she repeated, staring up at him. "Alexandra said that Mason got a lot of calls to do consulting work. But she also said that the most persistent ones were from Xander. He apparently didn't like being turned down and got pretty nasty."

"Xander?" Richard said. "When I asked Chris to get in touch with him for me, he said that he didn't know him."

"He lied," Carly said. "About everything."

Richard started walking again, turning what she'd told him over in his mind. "It actually makes sense. Think about it. Xander's been pumping money into medical research for years—trying to come up with something that'll keep him alive. But maybe it's also something he thinks he can make a billion dollars off of."

"So he has Chris watching people who are working in related fields," Carly said, continuing his thought. "Not only to make sure they aren't getting ahead, but probably to steal ideas that Xander can use. But why take Mason? Why risk it?"

"Xander must be close to something. But he has a problem—something his people can't figure out," Richard said. "Even at half speed, August Mason has twice the mental horsepower of anyone else alive. So Chris uses Mason's guilt about turning me in to lure him to the airport. Then Xander's people grab him and get him out of the country. I'd bet every dime we have left that Mason's sitting in a lab right now with a gun pointed at him." Richard shook his head in disbelief. "Andreas Xander…shit. We're screwed, Carly. Completely screwed. Do you have any idea how much money and power that son of a bitch has? And doing something like this…he's obviously gone insane."

Carly shook her head. "It's worse than that. He just doesn't have anything left to lose."

25

Hagerstown, Maryland
April 28

"Oh, no. Not again," Susie said, looking up from her coloring book. "That guy is *so* boring."

Richard was sitting at a makeshift desk working on the laptop they'd bought. In the corner of the screen, a YouTube feed of August Mason speaking at MIT was playing. Despite the video being almost thirty years old, the man still sounded ahead of his time.

"Boring?" he said. "Are you kidding? He's one of the smartest people of all time. He's like Newton or Darwin."

"Who's Newton Darwin?"

"For God's sake, Susie…do they teach you anything in school? Anything at all?"

The veins crisscrossing her enlarged forehead seemed to deepen in color as she negotiated some particularly tight lines on Harry Potter's face. "Sure. But not stuff about that guy. We'd all be in comas or something."

Richard sighed quietly as his wife came in with a tray of food. Susie rose from the floor long enough to snatch a ham sandwich and squint disapprovingly at her mother's short, dark hair.

"What have you found out?" Carly said, sliding a chair up next to the computer.

"Not much. The plane landed at a private airport in a rural part of Argentina—mostly farmland and a few small towns. Based on the tail number, I found the corporation that owns the jet, but beyond the fact that they're based in Slovenia, I can't get anything else. I don't even know what they do. It's like the company exists just to own that plane."

They'd spent the day researching everything even remotely related to what was happening to them, hoping to find some rational explanation—to find a way to write it all off to paranoia and coincidence. What little they'd turned up, though, pointed to the possibility that they weren't being paranoid enough.

He lowered his voice so that Susie couldn't hear. "The only subject that there's less about on the Internet than the company that owns that plane is us and Mason. I mean there were a few stories right after it happened, but now it's like we never existed. Even the links I bookmarked a few days ago are going dead. That's not normal. Things don't just disappear from the Internet like that."

He clicked on a picture of Xander, expanding it to fill the screen. The old man was sitting in his ubiquitous wheelchair, skeletal legs covered with a plaid blanket and blotched, loose-fitting face shadowed by a fedora. "It wouldn't be hard for him to quiet things down. Hell, he owns about half the media—and what he doesn't own outright, he's got stock in or a seat on the board. It's hard to believe a man who fought in World War II could still have the kind of power he does."

"Maybe that's how long it takes to get your tentacles into everything on the planet," Carly said.

It conjured a depressing but accurate mental picture. There was nothing beyond Xander's reach. He controlled billions of dollars, countless companies, and probably a significant number of America's elected officials. In contrast, they had an aging former soldier who didn't trust them, a gingerbread house hideout, and a stockpile of cash that would barely cover a decent used car. Overall, a fairly lopsided playing field.

Burt Seeger appeared in the doorway and looked down at Susie. "I think you've been lying on that cold floor long enough, sweetheart. Why don't you run upstairs and get ready to go for a walk. It's too pretty a day to be inside."

She pushed herself to her feet, still nibbling on the sandwich. "We should go to a park. Maybe there would be some kids playing soccer or something. We could watch."

Seeger smiled, but the strain was clearly visible in his face as Susie started up the stairs.

"What is it?" Carly said. "Has something happened?"

He crossed the room and laid a sheet of paper next to the computer. It was an article about two missing college students printed from the Internet. Richard scanned it but didn't track on the meaning until he reached their names.

His head sank into his hand while Carly pored over the text, eyes widening in horror. "We...we just got them to take us out of the swamp. They had a boat..."

"No," Richard said. "This is my fault. I called Mason from their phone. How could I have been so stupid?"

Seeger had retreated to the doorway and was leaning against the jamb with his arms crossed in front of him. "You two seem to be very dangerous to be around."

Carly looked up from the article. "You can't think we had something to do with this. That we hurt these kids."

"No," the old soldier said. "They were last seen two days ago. And you were here two days ago."

Richard finally found the strength to raise his head. "Maybe they're all right. Maybe they—"

Seeger shook his head. "I don't know who it is you've pissed off, but based on the fact that everything you've told me now seems to be true, I think we can be pretty confident that no one is ever going to see those two again."

"They...they couldn't have been much more than twenty years old," he stammered. "And I killed them."

"No," Seeger said. "You didn't kill them. Someone else did. And we need to figure out who before anyone else dies."

Richard looked into his wife's eyes and saw his own feelings reflected there. This had gone far enough. Annette and Troy. The pilots on Chris's plane. And now two innocent kids. It had to stop.

"We have to turn ourselves in," he said. "We can't let anyone else get hurt because of us."

Seeger let out a long breath. "With someone as connected as Xander involved, I don't think just walking into some government office and announcing who you are is all that good an idea. You have no idea how far this thing goes."

"What then?" Carly said. "Richard's right, we can't just stand by while everyone around us is murdered. They all had people who loved them too—who loved them just as much as we love Susie."

"Look, I have a friend I served with in Afghanistan who's an FBI agent now—he's the special agent in charge of the Louisville, Kentucky, office. Why don't I have him very quietly look into what's happened—your friend Annette, the investigation into you, the plane, these kids. Then we'll set up an out-of-the way meeting and talk about what we're going to do. How does that sound?"

"I don't know if we want to get you any deeper into this thing, Burt. People aren't—"

Seeger waved a hand dismissively. "I'd trust this guy with my life—in fact, I have on more than one occasion. I can also tell you he's one of the smartest, sneakiest sons of bitches I've ever met. I don't think there's any drawback to hearing what he has to say."

26

Near Sutton, West Virginia
April 30

The intensity of the rain had been increasing for the last hour, and now the wipers were creating waves that crashed spectacularly across the Ford Explorer's windshield. Burt Seeger was huddled over the wheel, concentrating on the road in the glare of the headlights while Richard twisted around to look in the backseat.

Carly glanced up from the DVD she and Susie were watching, flashing him a weak smile. The storm, with its hazy bursts of lightning and their deafening aftermath, was right out of a bad horror flick. But, in a way, it was also vaguely comforting. God himself couldn't track them in this.

"How are we doing on time?" Seeger asked, and Richard faced forward again, checking the GPS stuck to the dash.

"We're about fifteen minutes behind schedule."

"Maybe we should have toned down all this clandestine garbage and met at a diner somewhere. We'll be lucky if the road we're looking for isn't at the bottom of a lake."

They were on their way to meet Seeger's FBI friend in a sparsely populated section of eastern Kentucky, and despite the fact that they had another hour of driving, Richard could already feel the adrenaline leaking into his body. Would the agent have learned anything useful? Would he believe their story and agree to help them? Would he be waiting with a set of handcuffs and an arrest warrant? Or, based on their experience so far, a silenced pistol and a shovel?

Seeger's phone started to ring, and Richard grabbed it to check the incoming number. "It's him."

"Put it on speaker."

He did, adjusting the volume so they could hear over the rain pounding the vehicle.

"Larry?" Seeger said. "We're running a little—"

"Hey, Burt!" he interrupted. "I hate to call you at the eleventh hour like this, but something came up at work, and I'm stuck here. There's no way I'm going to be able to make dinner tonight."

Seeger's face went slack. "I'm sorry to hear that, buddy. I was looking forward to catching up."

"Me too. Getting your call brought back a lot of memories. Remember that Nurestan operation? Man, it's hard to believe I was ever that young."

"I know exactly what you mean. I hope the thing at work isn't serious—that everything's all right."

"Everything's fine. Nothing to worry about. Next time you come through Louisville, give me a call. We'll make it work."

"You got it, Larry. Take it easy." He reached up and shut off the phone before making a U-turn in the middle of the road and heading back the way they'd come.

"What the hell was that all about?" Richard demanded. "Dinner? We—"

"Daddy?" Susie said from the back. "Does this mean we're not—"

He spun violently in his chair. "The adults are talking!"

Her lack of eyebrows had a way of highlighting the emotions playing across her face, and he cursed himself for the hurt he saw there. Cramming her frail body into a car seat for hours on end caused her a great deal of physical pain, and keeping her up to all hours of the night created unnecessary stress on her weak heart. Topping that off by screaming at her like a madman wasn't helpful.

Carly immediately laid an arm around her bony shoulders. "It's all right, honey. Why don't we turn off the DVD for a while, and you can take a little nap? I'll wake you up when we see a place we can get some ice cream, okay?"

Richard turned around again, pushing back the guilt he felt. It was something he'd have to deal with later. "What just happened, Burt?"

The old soldier seemed reluctant to answer, instead continuing to concentrate on the road.

"Burt?"

"The Nurestan operation was something Larry and I were involved in that went south in a very big way."

"Then that's what he was trying to tell you? That he looked into this thing and it's as bad as we thought?"

Seeger shook his head. "When it all hit the fan, we called for an extraction, and they told us that it was too hot—that there was no way they could get to us. What Larry was telling us is that we're on our own."

Richard leaned back in the seat and stared up at the water washing across the moonroof. "He obviously didn't feel comfortable talking freely. Maybe they know about him. About you."

"He was just being cautious. He said everything was all right, and if Larry says he's secure, he's secure. The FBI, though, apparently isn't."

"This is crazy," Carly said, leaning up through the seats. "If they can get to the FBI, what chance do we have?"

"As long as you're breathing, there's always a chance," Seeger said. "I've faced some pretty long odds in my life, and I'm still here."

"This long?" she said.

He didn't answer.

Richard suddenly felt like something was pressing down on his chest, trying to suffocate him. He refused to give in, though. He had a family to think about. It was his responsibility to protect them.

"We have two leads," he said, his voice providing a surprisingly realistic facsimile of confidence. "Chris and Argentina. The way I see it, Argentina is the less risky of the two to go after."

"You're saying we should go to South America?" Carly said. "We'd have to show our passports and buy plane tickets."

"Yeah," Seeger agreed. "But the truth is that the wheels of the airlines and the government don't turn all that fast. Even if they've got ears there, they still have to deal with the bureaucracy. If you buy tickets at the counter right before the flight and get a nonstop, you might be faster than their network."

"Might be?" Carly said.

He shrugged and eased around a submerged section of road. "Under the circumstances, I think that's the best you can hope for."

27

Western Argentina
May 4

Carly eased the struggling car to a stop at a T in the empty road and turned off the engine to let it cool. Outside the open windows, green farmland rolled out in every direction, interrupted only by the occasional stand of leafy trees. The sky was an unbroken blue that promised another day of temperatures over ninety.

"Which way?" she asked.

Richard concentrated on the hand-drawn map in his lap, trying to decipher the directions scrawled in Spanish at the bottom.

They'd arrived in Argentina three days before, buying a flashy but mechanically disastrous BMW on the cheap and setting out for the airport where August Mason had landed. Since then, they'd been posing as wealthy Americans looking for an estate that fit the criteria they'd developed: secure, private, and with a house or outbuildings large enough to contain a lab. They told the local real estate agents that the property didn't have to be for sale—that money was no object, and they'd offer whatever was necessary for the right opportunity.

It had been a futile exercise in old wineries and estancias until that morning when they heard about a three-thousand-acre property situated more than fifty miles from the nearest town. Foreign contractors had built it, and a corporation chartered in Poland owned it, but beyond that, no one knew anything about it.

"Actually, I think this is it," Richard said, finally. "The other side of this crossroad is the northern edge of the property."

Carly started the engine again and drove until she found a pullout surrounded by bushes large enough to make the car invisible from the road.

"I don't see a fence," she said as they stepped out into the dust.

Richard jumped into an empty wash and started to climb the steep bank on the other side. "There's no rule that says you have to put fences on your property line. If I was trying to keep a low profile, I'd hide it in the trees."

"Where are you going?"

"To see if I'm right about the fence. And if I am, to climb over it. Stay with the car. I'll be back in a few minutes."

Instead, she jumped in after him, clambering up the bank with enough irritation to catch him before he cleared the lip. "No way. You're the one who should be staying with the car."

"Carly…"

"We've been through this fifty times, Richard. Even without the beard, people will recognize you a mile away. I can play the lost tourist and get away with it."

He opened his mouth to protest, but she broke into a run on the open ground, forcing him to chase.

"Slow down!" he said, coming up behind her, but she just put her head down and ran harder. He was forced to slow when she penetrated the tree line, his bulk making him less efficient at dodging through the tight branches and fallen logs.

When he finally caught up, she was bent at the waist, gulping air with a wide grin on her face.

"You're not as fast as you used to be," she gasped and then thumbed behind her at a tall wire barrier painted green, "but you were right about the fence."

He was going to yell at her for being so careless, but instead, he pulled her to him and kissed her. She backed up against the fence, hooking one of her legs behind his, rubbing up and down his calf. When they were finally forced to come up for air, he brushed the hair from her face. "I can't imagine my life without you, Carly. I don't know what I'd do if you weren't with me."

"Don't worry. It wasn't just luck that we found each other. And I believe that whatever it was that brought us together will keep us that way."

He wasn't sure whether to laugh or cry at that. For some reason, he'd never told her about the elaborate system he'd developed to meet her. That what brought them together wasn't fate so much as a carefully designed computer algorithm and a filing cabinet full of bogus grocery lists.

He gave her one last peck on the lips and then started pulling his shirt over his head.

"Richard? What are you doing?"

"Barbed wire," he said, throwing her the sweaty shirt and pointing to the top of the fence. "Fold that up and put it over the top. You'll need about five layers with that kind of fabric."

"The voice of experience?"

"Let's just say I climbed a fence or two when I was a kid."

She tossed the shirt over her shoulder and started climbing.

"Now, be careful. Those things can poke through and—"

"Relax, already. I used to be a rock climber, remember?"

"It was a weekend corporate retreat, Carly. And it was six years ago."

When she got to the top, she held on with one hand and used the other to wind the shirt around the wire. It gave her just enough space to throw a leg over, and she eased across it before working her way down the other side.

When she got to the bottom, she put a palm against the links. He did the same, pressing his damp hand into hers and chewing his lower lip.

"Impressed?" she said.

"Maybe this is a bad idea. Maybe..."

She shook her head. "Our other choice is to stand around and wait for these people to find us. And to find Susie. Don't worry—what are the chances that this is anything but some rich Polish guy's bachelor pad?"

He looked at his watch. "Don't screw around, OK, Carly? You're probably right, but if this *is* the place they're keeping Mason, they're going to have security. We're just trying to see if there could be a lab on the property. So get the lay of the land and be back here in no more than forty-five minutes."

"Quit being such an old lady," she said, poking playfully at his hand. "I'm going to be fine."

28

Western Argentina
May 4

When Carly looked back, the trees had swallowed up the fence, her husband, and everything else.

This all seemed like some kind of drug-induced nightmare. How could any of it be real? How could they have gone from the routine desperation their lives had become to being hunted and officially dead? To slinking across international borders a thousand miles from their daughter and climbing barbed wire fences?

Strangely, though, those weren't the things causing her hands to shake and her heart to pound.

Over the last eight years, she'd had no choice but to wrap herself in her own helplessness, to accept what the world had given her. What it had done to her. But now she could feel a little bit of what Richard had been living with for so long—the crush of responsibility, the gravity of hope. The belief, no matter how small, that she actually could *do* something for their daughter. And with that, the paralyzing fear that she could fail.

The trees around her thinned as she came to the edge of a pond full of flamingos. The angle of the sun had turned the water into a mirror that reflected their pink feathers, and she watched them as she skirted the water, trying her best to stay in the shadows.

It took another ten minutes to reach the small dock on the far shore, and she followed a trail up a gradual slope, hoping that it would lead her to the house. Everything was so still and beautiful, it was hard to stay vigilant. To believe there was anything here that could hurt her.

When she crested the rise, she raised a hand to shade her eyes from the sun and then stopped short when she saw the man sitting motionless at the edge of the trail. He was no more than fifteen feet away, and she felt a burst of adrenaline when she realized that she hadn't thought about what she would do if this happened. Should she say something? In English? In Spanish? Should she just run?

He looked to be in his early forties despite longish hair that was completely silver. His eyes were red rimmed and stood out against unnaturally pale skin, suggesting illness or exhaustion or both. Despite all this, there was something familiar about him—the intensity of his stare, the nose that was a little too long and straight for his face. When he raised a hand to point at her, she saw that each of his fingers was tipped in gauze.

"Who are you?" he said in English. "What are you doing here?"

Her breath caught at the sound of his voice, and she couldn't seem to get it started again. He began lurching toward her, and she wanted to run but found herself transfixed by his face as it gained detail.

"This is private property!" he said, wincing as his damaged fingers closed around her arm.

"I..." she stammered, "I didn't know."

"How did you get in here? Tell me!"

She blinked hard and gave her head a violent shake, clearing her mind enough to jerk her arm from his feeble grip.

"Stop!" he shouted when she began to run. The crunch of his footfalls started on the trail behind her, but when she finally dared to glance back, he was on one knee, fumbling with a phone.

She slowed and finally stopped, once again mesmerized by the man, but not so much so that she forgot the digital camera in her pocket. He was intent enough on dialing that he didn't look up until she was centering his image in the viewfinder. The shutter closed just as he was throwing an arm up in front of his face.

* * *

125

"Richard!" Carly shouted as she burst from the trees and saw him pacing along the fence line.

He took a startled step backward when she slammed into the chain link and began climbing. "What? What the hell happened?"

"Run!"

"I'm not going to just leave—"

"Get the car started, damnit! *Go!*"

He hesitated for a moment, but by the time she made it to the barbed wire, he had disappeared into the forest.

Her climb was less graceful this time, and she caught her leg on a barb before falling over the top. Already on the verge of throwing up from exertion, she didn't look down at her leg, instead clamping a hand over the gash and hobbling toward the open field they'd come across on their way in.

Richard was nearly to the ditch at the edge of the road when she heard the roar of an engine. In her peripheral vision, she saw an open Jeep with two men in it barreling across the field toward her. Letting go of her wound, she began to sprint, the burning in her lungs quickly overpowering the pain in her leg.

The Jeep was coming fast, but she stayed on course toward the pullout where they'd left the car. They wouldn't catch her. Not now. She wouldn't let them.

The sound of the motor spiked as the driver downshifted and skidded around the ruts and boulders she was stumbling through. Dust and gravel billowed over her, and she shot a glance backward, seeing that the Jeep's bumper was only a few feet behind. They were going to run her down.

And then she was falling—tumbling into the ditch just before the Jeep sailed over her head and slammed into the far bank.

She lay there dazed, staring up at the bottom of the vehicle that was now suspended directly above her. Fuel was draining from the tank in a thick gush, forming a stream that was making its way toward her and filling her nostrils with its stench. She tried to get to her feet but collapsed, waiting for the inevitable spark and the explosion that would engulf her.

Instead, a pair of hands grabbed her under the arms and began pulling her away. She flailed weakly against them, trying to escape.

"Carly! It's me! Stop fighting."

She relaxed at the sound of her husband's voice, allowing herself to be dragged from the Jeep's shadow.

Inside the open vehicle, the man who had been in the passenger seat was now lying halfway through the windshield. The skin on his face was shredded, and he'd been nearly cut in half at the waist by the glass. The driver was in better condition, staring groggily at them as he clawed for the gun in his shoulder holster.

Richard released her to climb out of the ditch and then dangled a hand down. She pedaled her feet against the loose dirt as he pulled her up, waiting for the crack of the man's pistol and the bullet that would not only end her own life but rob Susie of a future that suddenly seemed possible.

She made it over the edge, and Richard kept pulling, dragging her across the rocky soil as she tried to regain her footing. The gun finally sounded, raising a spray of dust from the edge of the ditch, but by then Richard had shoved her into the car and was sliding back across the hood. Once behind the wheel, he slammed the accelerator to the floor and fishtailed out onto the asphalt.

A second shot drowned out the echo of the first, and he pushed her down in her seat as he fought to keep control of the vehicle. Bullets kept coming, but none found their mark, and soon the terrifying ring of them faded into the grinding of the transmission and the wind coming through the open windows.

"Are you all right?" he said. "Carly? Talk to me! Are you hurt?"

"No," she said, trying to sit straight, but then just crumpling against the door.

"Your leg. Were you shot?"

She shook her head, and he grabbed a sweatshirt from the back, pressing it against her thigh.

"Hang on, OK? We have to turn around and get you to a—"

"No!" she said, grabbing the wheel and holding it steady. "Keep going!"

"But—"

"I'm all right. Just keep going."

Carly released the wheel and leaned forward, trying to control the wave of nausea washing over her. "Oh my God," she said quietly. "Oh my God."

29

Near the Border of Chile
May 4

Richard Draman twisted around in the bed of the pickup and squinted through its back window into the cab. The two men inside were having an animated conversation, laughing and jabbing at each other as the vehicle sped along the dark road. They seemed to have completely forgotten the two American hitchhikers they'd rescued from the side of the road an hour earlier.

Satisfied they weren't being watched, Richard turned back to the computer on his lap. Carly was pressed up against him despite the fact that the heat of the day still lingered in the wind.

"I'm right," she said. "You know I am."

He focused again on the photograph filling the screen. With the exception of the man's hand, which had blurred as he tried to cover his face, the image was surprisingly sharp. Richard examined every detail—the wavy gray hair, the pale skin, the unique slope of the nose.

"Maybe it's a relative. A cousin or something."

"So they kidnapped his cousin too?"

He didn't answer, instead clicking on the video they'd downloaded of August Mason making a speech in the mid eighties. To say that the resemblance was uncanny would be a gross understatement. It was staggering.

"See how his fingers look white in the picture?" she said, raising her voice to overcome the sound of the driver accelerating around a farm truck.

"Yeah. Why?"

"They're bandages."

It took a moment to put meaning to her words. "Altered fingerprints?"

"How else would you injure every fingertip on both hands without hurting anything else?"

"No," he said, turning away from the computer and staring into the dark landscape rushing by. "There has to be another explanation."

"He spoke to me, Richard. It was his voice—the voice of the man on the video. I'm telling you, it's him. It's him, and he's younger now."

"I can't—"

"Are you telling me it's scientifically impossible?"

"Yes!" he blurted, but then thought better of it. "No. It's not impossible. It's just that—"

"So it could be done," Carly pressed. "It's feasible."

He thought about it, sorting through everything he knew about the biology of aging, which was more than just about anyone on the planet. Or so he'd thought.

"Yesterday, I would have said that we were a hundred years from reversing the aging process. Now, I'm not sure."

"But you were working on curing Susie. You didn't think you were a hundred years from that."

"She only has one genetically driven aspect of aging, Carly. That's why kids like her don't suffer from things like osteoarthritis and dementia. I wanted to fix the genetic defect that causes her symptoms, but that's a million miles away from reversing the aging process."

"Because some other aspect of aging would eventually kill her like it does everybody else," Carly said, picking up his thought.

"Exactly. Most people don't know it, but not all animals get old. Lobsters for instance. Barring accidents or predators or disease, they seem to just keep going. But we *do* age—all mammals do."

"Why? What benefit is it to get old and die? How does that serve evolution's purpose?"

"The most important thing to remember about evolution is that it doesn't *have* a purpose. It's just about passing on more genes than your competitors at any given moment. Mammals first cropped up during the time of the dinosaurs. They were small and stuck on the bottom of the food chain. So, it was best for them to reproduce young—before they got eaten, or stepped on, or whatever. Having the ability to live a long time wasn't under strong selection because something else was going to kill them anyway. That was true of humans too. It wasn't long ago that living to be thirty-five was the exception, not the rule."

"But some mammals live a long time, don't they?"

"Sure. Whales are an example. They might live as long as two hundred years, but their lives have been extended by small, incremental changes that take into account they aren't likely to die from other causes like our common ancestors. Mortality is still there, though. It's programmed into all mammals on a fundamental level."

"Maybe not so fundamental," Carly said.

He didn't answer, mentally ticking off the myriad causes of aging and trying to come up with a feasible method to not only solve them but reverse their course.

"I know what I saw, Richard. That was August Mason, and he's not much older than we are now."

He leaned his head back against the cab and stared up at the unfamiliar stars for a long time before speaking again. "Most biologists are like me, Carly. They're detail people. But not Mason. He was looking at the big picture. Not to sound melodramatic, but he was looking for the secret of life. Something new, something fundamental that no one had thought of before."

He felt increasingly short of breath as his mind grappled with the enormity of Mason's discovery. Richard remembered telling his daughter that Mason was like Newton or Darwin. But he'd been wrong. While they may have seen into the mind of God, Mason had figured out a way to step into God's shoes.

"What do we do now?" Carly said.

"I...I don't know. Do you understand what this means? What's at stake here? We're talking a paradigm shift on the same order as the invention of agriculture. I mean, if it's possible—"

"We should assume that he's going to figure out who I am," she said in an obvious attempt to keep him focused on the here and now. "If they didn't already know we're alive, they will soon."

Richard barely heard her. "He did it, Carly. He translated the language of life. He must be able to model the genome in a way that allows him to make changes and see what the outcome is. Can he engineer something completely new? Something that nature has never even considered? Jesus—can he *create* life? What—"

"Richard!" she said, grabbing hold of his shoulder and giving him a shake. "There'll be time to think about all that later. Right now, we need to figure out how we're going to stay ahead of one of the most brilliant men who ever lived and one of the richest and most powerful. We need to find a phone. Call Burt. Warn—"

"It's not Xander," he said, cutting her off.

"What?"

"Think about it, Carly. He's got one foot in the grave. Why would he be rolling around in his wheelchair funding aging research and pestering Mason's assistant? No, if he had access to this, he'd have disappeared and would be well on his way to youth again."

She thought about that for a moment. "OK, it's not Xander. But it's somebody. And based on what we've seen, they're just as powerful. We need to figure out how we're going to stay ahead of them."

He shook his head. "We can't run anymore."

"What? You're not suggesting we just give up. There—"

"You don't understand," he said, turning to her. "He's reversed aging, Carly. *All aspects* of aging. Including the one killing Susie."

"Are you telling me that this could help her? That it could cure her?"

He nodded, eyes glowing with reflected light. "I'm never going to be able to do research again—if the cops don't get me, these people will. *This* is Susie's chance. Her only chance. I don't care who these people are. I don't care how powerful they are. I don't care how violent they are. We're going to get on a plane back to the States, and we're going to hunt them down. We're going to *make* them help her."

30

North of Baltimore, Maryland
May 6

Richard eased the car Seeger had rented for them along the winding drive-way, glancing over at his wife as she nervously scanned the dense trees lining it. The only things keeping her going at this point were adrenaline and determination. He'd stitched up the gash in her leg, and it was beginning to heal, but the long flight back to the U.S. had been incredibly painful for her. Dark circles were distinct beneath her eyes despite the sunburn she'd suffered in Argentina.

Chris Graden's house emerged as they crested a small hill, and Richard reflected on the time they'd spent there over the years—dinners, backyard barbeques, late-night drinking sessions. Now all he could think about was how similar the secluded location and over-the-top security were to August Mason's home—as though they had been designed with the same goals in mind. Ironically, it was their phony, toxic friendship with Graden that had defeated all those defenses. They still had the gate code.

Richard rolled to a stop beneath the portico and turned the engine off. "Showtime."

Carly stepped from the car and walked up to the door, pausing while he pressed himself against the house's stone façade in an effort to stay out of sight.

What was on the other side? Coming there was an act of desperation, and they both knew it. Mason would be a thousand miles from

Argentina by now, and their realization that Xander wasn't involved left Chris Graden as the only thread left for them to pull.

Richard tensed when the door began to swing open, but it was only Chris, wearing a pair of jeans and an old Penn State sweatshirt. For a moment, it felt like none of this had ever happened. Like they were there for lunch.

He seemed confused for a moment, but then recognition registered on his face. "Oh my God! Carly, you're alive!"

He opened his arms to throw them around her, but before he could, Richard stepped out and shoved him back hard enough that he nearly fell to the floor of his foyer.

They entered, and Carly slammed the door shut before taking a position by a window with an unobstructed view of the driveway.

"Jesus," Graden said. "Where the hell have you two been? Everybody thinks you're dead."

Richard slipped one of Burt Seeger's pistols from his waistband and aimed it at his old friend. The regret and nostalgia he'd worried would paralyze him didn't materialize. In fact, the idea of pulling the trigger had a certain undeniable appeal.

"*I'm* asking the questions."

"What are you doing? It's me. Chris. We've been—"

"Shut the hell up," Richard said. "Is anyone working here today?"

"What? No. It's Sunday."

Richard motioned with the pistol. "Go."

"Where?"

"The den."

"Put the gun away, Richard."

"If you don't turn around and start walking, I'm going to shoot you. I'm planning to start with your leg and work my way up."

Graden just stared at him for a moment but then started obediently toward the back of the house. Richard glanced back at Carly as he followed, and she rewarded him with a weak smile. It looked like it was about all she had left.

"Seriously, Richard. Put the gun down. You're acting crazy."

The den was just the way he remembered it—a dusty explosion of books, old newspapers, and antique furniture. Strangely, most of the photos on the walls depicted Graden alone, but a few included what appeared to be friends. Richard wondered if he was spying on them too. If he would send someone for their children one day.

"Where have you been all this time?" his old friend said, keeping his eye on the pistol.

"You tried to kill us," Richard responded.

"What are you talking about? The jet? That was—"

"I called Ray Blane. He was looking into some of the same things Annette and I were. You stopped his research too."

"Ray Blane? I got him a huge grant. The people supplying the money wanted him to concentrate. And what do you mean 'too'? I *supported* your research, remember? Shit, I wrote you a personal check for it and then got you out of jail."

It was an incredibly convincing performance, made stronger by their long history together. But it was too little too late.

"You've been trickling in just enough money to keep your eye on me— to make sure I was staying focused on progeria and not looking into anything broader. Then I ended up with Annette's research notes, and you got worried. Worried enough to try to kill my daughter. *My daughter*, Chris."

"Kill Susie?" he stammered. "Are you listening to yourself, Richard? For God's sake—"

"Where's August Mason, Chris?"

"What?"

"The papers say he was on your plane when it went down. But we both know that isn't true."

"I…I don't know."

"Really? I do. We tracked him down in Argentina. And South America must really agree with him. He looks great."

"You're babbling," Graden said, sweat beginning to glisten on his upper lip.

Richard tossed a hard copy of the photo Carly had taken onto a side table, and Graden looked down at it, his face melting into an emotionless mask.

"Don't move!" Richard said, holding the gun out in front of him as his old friend started toward a wet bar in the corner.

Graden ignored him and poured himself a scotch. "Can I get you one? For old time's sake?"

Richard suddenly felt a little weak. He'd come there blind with anger and tormented by hope, but somewhere deep in the back of his mind he'd expected Graden to have an explanation. A series of unlikely but plausible coincidences that they'd missed. Something that didn't involve their best friend being a spy and a genetic therapy that could reverse millions of years of evolution.

But it was clear that no explanation was forthcoming. This wasn't a paranoid delusion dreamed up by a desperate mind. It was real.

31

1,800 Miles East of Australia
May 6

Oleg Nazarov opened the door and stepped through, stopping short when Karl held a hand up. The room was windowless and expansive to the point of being nonfunctional.

Almost a hundred feet in length, it looked more like an art gallery than an office. Sculptures of various sizes dotted the floor, and original masterworks hung on the stone walls. Karl was sitting behind a glass-topped desk flanked by two tall cabinets that appeared to be made of wood, but were, in fact, elegantly disguised safes. The acoustics were abysmal, perhaps purposefully so, and from his position near the door Nazarov couldn't make out anything Karl was saying into the phone.

It was hard not to wonder about the man. Who was he? How old had he been when he'd taken the therapy? What would it be like to feel yourself becoming young again?

In theory, it wouldn't be long before he would be able to answer that last question. With the help of the group's contacts, his possessions and investments were being reconfigured, liquidated, and transferred in ways carefully calculated to make them untraceable. When it was all done, he would have a painstakingly choreographed accident in which his body would never be found.

And then he would begin his life again—a new identity, an opportunity to leverage what he'd achieved and learned into so much more than he'd ever imagined. This time the incessant ticking of the clock would be silenced. This time it would be forever.

Karl hung up, and Nazarov started forward, reminding himself how quickly it could all end. His power and money were of no value at all on this island. There was only Karl. His decisions were final, and people followed his orders without question. Maybe it would have been wiser just to learn to enjoy old age.

"You have good news for me?" Karl said.

There were no chairs in front of his desk, and so Nazarov stood, clutching a leather portfolio with nothing of importance in it.

"I'm sorry to say that I do not."

"Then what?"

"A trespasser was discovered on the property in Argentina."

"This is important? See that security is tightened."

"They saw Mason."

Karl leaned back in his chair, staring up at him. Despite the unlined face and youthful body, there was still something in his eyes that hinted at his real age. Nazarov wondered if they were all like that—all the ones who had been transformed.

"How clearly? His condition is still intermediate isn't it?"

Nazarov had rehearsed this conversation in his mind a hundred times before arriving at Karl's door. There was no way to soften what he had to say. And no way to protect himself from the fallout.

"I believe that the trespasser was Carly Draman."

Karl froze in the corpselike way he always did when he received bad news, and Nazarov decided to keep talking. The questions were obvious enough that they didn't need to be said aloud.

"She took a photograph and ran. One of our people was killed trying to stop her, and another was severely injured. She and a man who fits her husband's general description escaped."

Karl rose slowly from behind his desk. He was at least four inches taller than Nazarov, with broad shoulders and a narrow waist that were the gift of his newfound youth and obsessive workout schedule.

The Russian found himself experiencing a sensation extremely rare for him: inferiority. He was nothing but an increasingly decrepit old man standing in front of something completely new. Something that even God had never contemplated.

"Where are they now?"

"They managed to get to Santiago, Chile, probably by hitchhiking. There's a record of them flying to New York, where we have security video of them getting into a cab. According to the company, they were dropped off at a bus station. We haven't been able to trace them any farther than that."

"You lost them?" Karl said. The volume of his voice rose for the first time in their short relationship. "You lost them *again*?"

"There are practical limitations on how quickly we can get information from the airline computers, and those delays are even longer in South America. Their flight was an eleven-hour direct paid for with cash at the counter."

"Did she recognize Mason? How did they track him to Argentina?"

The questions had a rhetorical feel, so Nazarov decided to try to redirect the conversation down a more favorable path.

"We've shut down everything relating to Mason's new identity, and he's been moved. The house has been burned. There's nothing left—"

"Nothing left?" Karl shouted. "All your expertise, all our money and planning isn't worth anything. A poverty-stricken biologist and his wife have outsmarted you over and over again! And now they know. They know what we've done."

"We're doing everything we can. We—"

"I'm not interested in you doing everything you can," Karl said, slamming a palm down on the desk. When he raised it again, Nazarov could see the sweaty outline left on the glass. "I'm telling you to *get* them. Bring them in alive and find out who they've talked to. Do it *now*."

"Yes, sir. I understand."

"Do you? Are you certain? If this goes much further, it could become impossible to contain. And then I'm not sure what use you'll be to us."

Nazarov was trying to formulate an appropriate response when the satellite phone in his pocket began to ring. He checked the number and then immediately picked up.

"Yes?"

"We've had activity at Chris Graden's house," the voice on the other end said.

Nazarov let out a long breath, and the pounding of his heart slowed a fraction. "Are you moving?"

"Our ETA is less than five minutes."

32

North of Baltimore, Maryland
May 6

"Mason found what he was looking for," Richard Draman said. "He found his fundamental truth."

Chris Graden finished pouring his drink and stared silently into it.

"Say something, you son of a bitch!"

"Like what? Yes, Mason found what he was looking for and turned it into...well, you know what he turned it into."

"How does it work?"

Graden smiled. "Why would they tell me?"

"They?"

He didn't respond. It was probably true that he didn't know. His rise through the ranks of the pharmaceutical industry had been based on his Harvard MBA and uncanny business acumen—not his grasp of biology.

"OK," Richard said. "Then tell me something else, Chris. Tell me why."

"Why what?"

"Why all this? Mason makes what may be the most important discovery in the history of our species, and instead of patenting it, getting another Nobel, and making a hundred billion dollars on patents, he disappears for twenty years to turn it into a therapy that he keeps to himself."

"Are you sure I can't get you a drink?"

Richard lifted the gun higher, aiming directly at Graden's face. "Answer the question, Chris."

"You already know the answer. The world isn't ready for this."

"What?"

"Come on, Richard. More than half of people in the U.S. don't even believe in evolution. They think a carpenter from Nazareth created the universe. And now you want Mason to roll this one out? To take his little petri dish on TV and show everybody how to create life? That's not playing God, Richard. That's replacing God."

"You expect me to believe that all this—killing Annette, coming after me and my family, spying on anyone doing research in this area—is about the fact that you don't want to offend people's religious sensibilities? Aging kills a hundred thousand people a day. It creates unbelievable human suffering. It costs more than every other disease combined."

"But it's *not* a disease, Richard. Are you sure people want it cured? You know how hard it is to get money for aging research—you've spent the last six years squeezing blood out of that stone. If old age kills so many people, why isn't the money there?"

"Because people don't understand. They—"

"And who's going to make them understand? You? Can you imagine how this would divide the country and the world? What if, in the end, the politicians didn't approve the therapy? Then people who use and supply it would be criminals. And the people who don't would fade and die."

Richard opened his mouth to speak, but Graden cut him off. "And what if it *were* approved? We're talking about a change like our species has never experienced. But human nature isn't going to change. Our government isn't going to suddenly become responsible and thoughtful. How would we pay for it? My understanding is that there's no way to make this therapy cheap, even on a large scale. Would only rich people get it? But what if we did make it cheap? What about overpopulation? And what about the million issues you've never even considered? How would you punish criminals? Would you put them in prison for a thousand years? Because ten isn't going to matter anymore. And worse, how would you tell bad candidates that they can't have it? That they have chronic diseases that we can't afford to maintain forever or genetic defects that we can't have passed on to the twenty-five children they'll eventually have."

"What gives you the—"

"No, no, Richard. I'm not finished. Are you sure that people have the psychological capacity for immortality? Is there some mental clock that Mason hasn't considered? Will our brains get full? Will—"

"So we should all thank you. Is that what you're saying? We should be grateful to you for being willing to play the guinea pig? What a load of shit. Why do *you* get to choose? What makes a man who would murder his friends—who would murder children—so deserving?"

Graden swirled the drink in his hand. "Who said anything about deserving? I know I'm not deserving. What I am is expedient. For now, it's all about fitting the profile. I have money and the right contacts. I don't have a wife or children—"

"What about us, Chris?"

He sighed quietly. "My affection for you and your family wasn't a lie, Richard. I had—"

"I want the data. I want to be able to make it."

"I'm sure you do. But I don't have it."

"Then you're going to help me get it."

He laughed. "You're a genius in every sense of the word, and I've always admired your devotion to your daughter. But you have no idea what you've gotten yourself involved in."

"Then why don't you tell me?"

"OK, I will. Other than Mason, I don't really even know who the people involved are. I mean, I've met some of them, but I don't know their names or where they come from. What I *can* tell you, though, is that combined they have more money and power than an average European country. They know…"

Graden's voice faded when the muffled sound of a car engine became audible through the open door. Carly's panicked shout rang out a moment later.

"You think you're the only one who was being watched?" Graden said, indicating around the room. "They watch everybody, listen to everything. I'm no exception."

Carly's shout was even more piercing the second time. "*Richard!*"

He grabbed Graden and pushed him toward the door with the gun barrel jammed against the back of his neck.

"When they thought you were dead, you had a chance. But now—"

"Shut up," Richard said as they emerged into the entry. "How many are there, Carly?"

"One car, four men," she said, peering through a small slit in the curtains. "Two are going around back. They all have guns."

Richard wrapped an arm around Graden's throat and moved the gun to his temple. "Get behind me, Carly."

"If you don't think they'll shoot me to get to you, then you have no idea who you're dealing with," Graden said.

"At least we'll go down knowing you went first, you piece of shit. Now open the door."

Graden hesitated, but then seemed to conclude that he was better off at the mercy of the men outside than at the mercy of his old friend.

Richard squinted into the sunlight as they stepped outside. There was an SUV parked sideways in the driveway and two men angling toward the front door with pistols in hand. The car Seeger had rented was close enough that the fake temporary tag was legible through the back window. It might as well have been in the next state.

"Drop your weapon!" one of the men ordered. They were spreading out, getting into positions where Graden's body would no longer offer protection.

"Drop it now!" the other one shouted, but his command was less a request than a diversion to allow his partner time to line up on Richard's head. There wasn't going to be a negotiation.

A shot rang out, and Graden pulled away, expecting the arm around his neck to go limp.

Instead, the back window of the SUV the men had arrived in shattered, and they both dove to the ground, their attention immediately refocused on the trees behind them. A second shot ricocheted off the asphalt only inches from the man to their right, and both scrambled for cover, shooting blindly behind them as they went.

Richard shoved Graden aside as Carly made a break for the passenger side of their car. She was already turning the key in the ignition when Richard jumped behind the wheel and slammed it into drive. The Chevy Aveo didn't have enough power to spin its tires but managed to put itself on two wheels as they sped around the circular driveway and headed toward the vehicle blocking their path.

"Go through the bushes to the right," Carly said. "I think we can make it."

He did as she said, holding his breath as the car bounced wildly through the dirt and the sound of gunfire intensified.

Carly twisted around in her seat to look through the back window just as a softball-sized hole appeared in the middle of it. She ducked involuntarily as the bullet passed through the vehicle and put a hole just below the rearview mirror Richard was staring into.

The still-parked SUV had steam coming from a punctured radiator, and Graden was running crouched back toward his front door. The men shooting at them had found cover, and Richard could no longer see either of them.

"Whoa!" Carly said, grabbing the dashboard as they came to the top of a small rise and the car almost left the ground. Richard kept shifting his attention from the approaching gate to the rearview mirror, and when the house was no longer visible, he slammed on the brakes.

A moment later, a badly limping Burt Seeger flopped into the back with a wide smile on his face and a sniper rifle in his hand.

"I love climbing trees and shooting at people," he said, lying across the seats. "God help me, I always have."

33

Baltimore, Maryland
May 6

"Don't run," Seeger warned as Carly threw open the car door and jumped out.

She slowed, trying to look natural as she started around the side of the ramshackle motel. Richard caught up just as she came around the front, pulling the brim of his baseball cap low over his eyes when they became visible from the lightly traveled street.

"Relax," he said. "It's going to be fine."

She didn't respond, instead fixating on a door midway down the building's façade. She knocked gently and tried to peek in the window, but the curtain was tucked tightly against the wall.

Probably no more than five seconds passed, but they seemed to creep by in slow motion. She knocked again, this time a little harder, and was about to rap on the glass when a muffled voice came from inside.

"Who is it?"

"It's us. Hurry."

The door came open a crack, and an eye peered out before it closed again and the chain came off. Carly rushed inside, kneeling on the stained carpet and gripping her daughter's frail shoulders. "Why did it take you so long to answer?"

"I was tired and I went to sleep. But you have to see what I found on the Internet! Come and—"

"I don't *care* about that stupid computer. When we knock, you need to come right to the door. You scared me to death."

"But, Mom! They—"

Carly threw her arms around Susie, muffling her protests while trying not to cry. When they'd given her an envelope containing an explanation of everything that had happened and told her to call Seeger's friend at the FBI if they didn't return, she'd just stared in horror. Leaving her there alone had been the hardest thing she'd ever done.

"I'm glad you're back," Susie said, clearly pandering. "I didn't want it to get dark."

Carly released her, and she ran over to grab her father's hand. "Come look at the computer. See what's on it!"

She led him to the bed, and he looked down at the memorial Website on the screen.

"People think we're dead!" Susie said. "They think that we went on Uncle Chris's plane and then it crashed! When we were on it! Why do they think something crazy like that?"

Seeger came through the door and closed it behind him, looking a lot worse for the wear. His leg had stiffened up badly in the car, and he was struggling just to hobble along at a normal pace.

"Are you OK?" Susie said, clearly alarmed.

"Oh, I'm fine, honey. I just hurt my leg a little."

"How?"

"Climbing a tree."

"You were not."

"I swear! In fact, in my day, I was a very fine tree climber."

She shook her head and pointed to the computer. "Come and see what I found! People think we crashed in a plane!"

"Susie," Richard said, sitting on the bed so he could look her directly in the eye. "I don't know why someone thinks we crashed on your Uncle Chris's plane, but we're going to call and tell them we're fine, OK?"

"When?" Susie whined. "'Cause all my friends think I'm never coming back now."

"Soon. We're going to do it soon so your friends aren't sad. But right now you have to go with Burt."

"Why? Aren't you coming?"

"Not yet. We have a few things we need to do."

"Why can't you do them from Burt's house? We could all stay there."

Richard managed to conjure a smile, hoping it didn't look as forced and desperate as it felt. In his peripheral vision, he saw Carly wipe surreptitiously at her eyes. "We'll be there soon. But your mom and I have some work to do."

The painful truth was that Susie was better off as far away from them as she could get. Seeger was a hell of a lot better equipped to protect her than they were.

"Are you going back home? Burt and I could—"

"No. We're trying to make you better. That's what we're working on."

"At the lab? But—"

"There are no 'buts,' Susie. Sometimes grown-ups have to do things that are hard to understand. Even for us."

Seeger held out a hand. "Come on, honey—we have to hurry and get to the house. Your parents have a lot to do, and the sooner they can get it done, the sooner they can come back."

* * *

Richard and Carly ate what remained of the pizza they'd left with Susie while daylight faded through the room's curtains. The local news was on the television, reporting from a world that they no longer seemed to inhabit. There was nothing at all about the gunfire at Chris Graden's house or them smashing through his front gate. It was like they didn't exist.

"How much money's left?" Richard asked. Carly was sitting on the bed surrounded by neat piles of cash she'd finished counting a few minutes before.

"Ten thousand and change."

They fell silent again, and he leaned back in his chair, listening to the old wood protest.

"Do you think she's going to be all right?" Carly said finally.

"She's going to be fine. Burt can look after her."

"That used to be our job."

He didn't respond.

"We have enough now, Richard—Chris confirmed that it's all true, and we have the photo of Mason. That's enough to at least go to the papers."

Again, he didn't answer.

"Isn't that what we want? To shine a light on them?"

He reached for the pizza box, but then thought better of it as his appetite abandoned him. "If we make all this public, they won't have any reason to keep coming after us. We might survive. But Susie won't."

"I don't understand. If the whole world knows what Mason's done, he'll have to talk. He'll have to tell how he did it."

"That's not the way it's going to work, Carly. Mason and the rest of them will run for the corners of the earth. There'll be a big bureaucratic investigation involving God knows how many countries, about half of which are hopelessly corrupt. And what if we do get them? Any company or university that Mason ever worked for will claim ownership, and the lawsuits will start flying. Then, when all that gets sorted out, the FDA will want to start controlled animal trials. And then there's the politics. Assuming a treatment ever does make its way to the marketplace, how long do you think it will take?"

"Longer than Susie has," she admitted quietly.

"Yeah."

Carly fell back on the dirty bedspread and pulled the laptop to her, scrolling down the screen. He took a seat next to her, looking at the pictures—her at the restaurant, him at the lab, parties for the kids. A different lifetime.

There was a place for people to make comments, and they read through them for a few moments.

"Kind of nice," she said, finally.

"Yeah. With the way our lives turned out, it's sometimes easy to forget the friends you make along the way. Who set up the site? Eric?"

She scrolled to the bottom, but there was nothing to indicate who was responsible, and there didn't seem to be any moderation. "Doesn't say."

Richard stared down at it for a moment and then sat up a little straighter against the headboard. "Go back up to the pictures."

"Why?"

"Just do it!"

He quickly scanned through them and then leapt off the bed. "Put the money in the duffel, Carly. We're getting out of here."

"What?" she said as he went to the front window and pulled the curtain slightly to the side. "What are you talking about?"

A late-model SUV came to a stop across the street, and four very serious-looking men got out and started toward the motel.

"Shit!"

"Richard," she said, starting to sound panicked as she scooped their money into the bag, "what's happening?"

He ran into the bathroom and checked the window, but it was probably only eight inches square. Even Susie wouldn't have been able to make it through.

"The Website," he said when he came out and went for the door leading to the adjoining room. Dead-bolted. "They're all photos from the Internet—nothing personal."

"So what?"

"Mason's people set it up! They're using IP addresses to track who's hitting the site, figuring we'd stumble on it sooner or later. When someone from a run-down motel not far from Chris's house pulled it up and then left it open, it was a good bet it was us."

"But..." Carly stammered as he ducked back into the bathroom in a futile attempt to find an escape route he'd missed. "Are they...are they out there?"

"Four of them," he said, coming out and dropping to the floor in order to examine the bed. It looked like a platform, but when he shoved the mattress back, he discovered the base wasn't solid. There was space between a set of wooden slats and the floor.

"Get in!"

"What are you talking about? We can't fit in there! It's not even a foot deep!"

He grabbed the duffel and wedged it near the headboard, then pushed her in after it. She managed to thread through the slats but got stuck trying to slide into the darkness beneath the section still covered with the mattress. He put a foot against her shoulder and heard her grunt in pain when he shoved her far enough to make room for himself. The creak of hinges penetrated the thin wall separating them from the room next door, and he immediately knew they would be coming from both directions— two armed men through each entrance.

He reached for the computer still on the bed, but then hesitated. They'd know it was here, and someone was undoubtedly monitoring the connection. If he severed it, they'd know the moment it happened.

"What are you doing?" Carly said in a harsh whisper. "Get in!"

Instead, he grabbed a marker off the top of the TV and used it to scrawl across the computer's screen.

The sound of creaking hinges was replaced by the quiet rattle of a hand on a doorknob, and he crammed himself in next to his wife before heaving the mattress back into position. The last edge was just falling into place when the muffled crack of the door bursting open filtered through.

He expelled the air from his lungs, feeling the mattress fall with his chest and taking quick, shallow breaths that he prayed wouldn't create visible movement. Footsteps pounded in the room, and he tried to mentally track the men's movements, his mind already starting to suffer from lack of oxygen.

Carly moved a hand against his leg, and he hoped that her size made her position more bearable. Not that it really mattered. It wouldn't take long for the carbon dioxide from their breath to build up and suffocate them.

"Bathroom's clear," he heard a voice say.

"Check the bed."

A sense of complete helplessness came over him as the mattress began to rise. He was dizzy from lack of air and crammed beneath a set of wooden slats. They wouldn't go down fighting. They'd go down like trapped animals.

Instead, darkness enveloped them again as the mattress dropped back onto his chest.

"Shit!" someone close to the bed said.

A more distant, lightly accented voice followed. "What is it?"

"The computer. Draman left a message written across the screen."

"What message?"

"It says, 'Nice try, asshole. Now I know what you look like.'"

Less than a second passed before the man with the accent started barking orders. "Pull back! Now! We're getting out of here."

There was an orderly retreat and the slam of a door, but Richard moved only enough to take hold of his wife's hand. The space was too confined to allow him to see his watch, so he didn't know how long they stayed like that. When the darkness turned gray and his oxygen-starved brain began creating flashes of reddish light on his retinas, he was force to shove the mattress back.

The men he half expected to still be there waiting were gone.

He rolled weakly onto his side, gulping the cool, fresh air, but his wife didn't move.

"Carly!" he said, pulling her to him. "Wake up! Please wake up."

She remained completely limp as he dragged her out of the bed frame and collapsed next to the nightstand.

"Carly!" he said again, shaking her. "You've got—"

Her eyes fluttered open, and a slow smile spread across her face. "I'd have bet against us on that one."

Satisfied that she was all right, he tucked a pillow under her head and staggered to the window.

"Are they…" she barely managed to get out. "Are they gone?"

"I think so. But not for long. Chris was telling the truth about these people. They've got a billion dollars and an army. We've got a few grand

and an old soldier who can barely make it up a set of stairs. Next time we won't be so lucky."

She pushed herself upright and propped her back against the edge of the bed. "We can't let them find us, Richard. Susie has a chance and so do the other kids. They can't win."

"We're not going to last another week alone," he said, his mind clearing as he continued to scan the parking lot. "But I've been thinking. What if we had our own army?"

34

Hagerstown, Maryland
May 7

Parsi Riju adjusted his earpiece and gazed out the SUV's window. It was nearly three in the morning, and the neatly tended street was still and dark. A serene mask hiding almost certain disaster.

There had been no time to learn the rhythms of the area—when the newspapers were delivered, when people went to work, possible insomniac dog walkers. A few hours ago, he'd been charging blindly into a Baltimore motel room, and now he was sitting in the middle of suburban America with an assault rifle in his lap.

A voice crackled over the radio. "In position."

He craned his neck, looking around him again before refocusing on the small home across the street. It was hard to put the architecture together with the former soldier who lived inside. It looked like an old woman's house. More evidence that it was better to die young.

He stepped out of the vehicle and slipped his weapon beneath his jacket before walking across the street.

"Moving," he said just loudly enough to be picked up by his throat mic.

His men, all completely invisible in the darkness, acknowledged the start of the operation.

Until now, the requests of the people he worked for—two men he knew only as Oleg and Karl—had been perfectly reasonable. Violent, of course, but meticulously planned and well compensated. But now things had changed. The stench of desperation was getting strong enough to make him wonder if it was time for his team to sever their lucrative relationship with those voices on the phone. It was hard to spend money from inside a prison cell and even harder from inside a coffin.

Riju stepped silently onto the porch, thankful for the thick hedges that threw it into complete blackness. He located the doorknob and pulled his tools from his pocket. Working entirely by feel, it took less than twenty seconds before the lock submitted. There was no deadbolt or alarm. What use would they be in this neighborhood?

"Open," he said quietly. "Cut power."

A moment later, the voice of one of the men covering the back came over the radio. "Power cut. We're ready."

"Use extreme caution. Seeger's old, but remember his service record."

He slipped on a pair of night vision goggles and turned the knob, entering with his rifle held at eye level. Two men appeared and slipped in behind him, one going for the stairs and the other for the kitchen.

They made no sound, but the house wasn't silent. There was a dull hum that got louder as Riju closed on the entrance to the basement. His finger tightened slightly on the trigger. No power should mean no sound.

The man he sent upstairs was already coming back down, signaling that he'd found no one.

Everything about this felt wrong.

"We're getting out of here," he said into his throat mic. "Exit through the—"

The lights suddenly came on, and Riju dove for the floor, ripping his night vision goggle off and crawling behind a floral-print sofa. When he looked over the arm, he saw his men finding similar cover wherever they could.

Nothing moved, and all he could hear was his own breathing over the incessant buzz from the basement. He scanned the room and spotted the light switches on the walls but knew they hadn't been flipped. The overheads weren't on—only lamps that could be easily toggled with remotes. It was obvious now that the hum was coming from a backup generator.

And where there were power and remotes…

"Move for the doors," he said. "Watch for booby traps. I repeat. Watch for traps."

He crept out from behind the couch, every muscle tense as he waited for the inevitable explosion that would engulf the house. Instead, a quiet whine became audible behind him.

He spun toward the sound, swinging his gun until the sights were fixed on a small, three-wheeled robot struggling across the carpet. A child's toy.

He kept his finger on the trigger as the robot stopped a few feet away and a camera boom on top tilted to look up at him. A moment later, a voice that he assumed belonged to Burt Seeger came over the tiny speakers.

"If my neighbors weren't a complete pain in the ass about noise I'd have packed the house with enough C4 to blow you into the next state. This is a gift, son. One soldier to another. But if I ever see you again, you'd better kill me. Because if you don't, I'll cut your head off and put it on your mother's fence post."

Riju shouldered his weapon and nodded. "Understood."

* * *

Burt Seeger leaned forward in his chair, deeply shaken for what he calculated was only the fifth time in his life.

What he'd said was a lie. If he'd had the time and material to set it up, pieces of his house would still be raining down on his neighbors' obsessively manicured lawns. He'd had to work with what he had—a backup generator, a bag of switches from Radio Shack, and a Web-controlled robot he'd bought for Susie.

Of course, it had been a given that they would eventually find him based on what he'd done at Chris Graden's house. But this wasn't eventually. It was less than twelve hours since he'd taken those shots. And in that time, they'd tracked down and mounted a very smooth operation against a forgotten special ops guy whose wife had been a patient of Richard Draman's more than a decade ago.

Seeger glanced back at the computer screen, looking at the frozen face of the man who had been in his living room. He was a pro—Seeger could smell them a mile away. If he and Susie had been there, they'd be dead. Neither one of them would have even known what happened.

He leaned back and stared at the dark ocean through the windows of his friend's beach house. His good old friend. How long until they sent someone here? An hour? Five? Sure as hell not ten.

He walked to the room where Susie was sleeping, her wrinkled face peeking out from beneath the comforter. Every day she seemed a little more tired. An old body slowly smothering a young soul.

He knelt next to her and tugged gently on the blanket. "Hey, Susie. Wake up."

Her eyes fluttered and finally opened. "Uncle Burt?"

"I've been thinking. It's too cold to be at the beach. We should go somewhere else."

"But all we do is move around. I want to stay here. I'm sleepy."

"I know you are, honey. I am too."

35

Upstate New York
May 10

Richard Draman scooped a few more leaves on the pile and settled into it again. He'd spent twenty-nine hours in that spot, and it was starting to feel depressingly like home. The ground beneath him was leveled and the rocks removed, a water bottle and a walkie-talkie hung from a branch above him, and Seeger's .22 rifle rested on a clean towel at his feet. Despite its low caliber, it looked like it meant business with a camouflage stock, homemade silencer, and deep black barrel.

Richard leaned forward and peered at the four-way stop through the foliage. Nothing.

The heavily wooded lots in the neighborhood were at least ten acres apiece, each hiding an opulent home sequestering an equally opulent family. It made for a sparse population base that translated into an average of twenty-four cars, three dog walkers, and seven joggers per day—each bringing a brief moment of panic followed by a long stretch of boredom.

Seeger had called that morning, and the more Richard tried not to dwell on the conversation, the more it consumed him. After men armed with assault rifles had infiltrated his home, Seeger had concluded that there was nowhere he could go that he and Susie would be safe. His only option was to buy a used RV and drive randomly around the country, staying on back roads and stopping in obscure campgrounds only long enough to sleep.

Not exactly the life Richard had pictured for his daughter, and one that would quickly prove too much for her.

The breeze that had been with him most of the day died, leaving him in silence. He'd never understood the cliché before, but it really was too quiet. Too much time to think about everything that could go wrong. About how desperation was rarely the foundation of good decisions.

Carly's static-ridden voice startled him out of a half doze. "He's coming! Do you read me? He's coming!"

Richard jumped to his feet and grabbed the walkie-talkie, feeling a jolt of adrenaline that Seeger had warned him would throw off his aim. "I read you."

"Don't miss, OK?"

He frowned and picked up the rifle, resting the barrel on a branch that he'd stripped of leaves. At military school, he'd wondered about the wisdom of teaching a bunch of juvenile misfits to use firearms, but it had been one of the few fun activities available, and he'd gotten pretty good. Of course, that was decades ago, and the targets had been meaningless and stationary.

Richard squeezed his eyes shut for a moment. What had Seeger said? Live in the moment during these kinds of things. Everything that had happened before didn't matter, and there probably wouldn't be a later.

Comforting.

After a few moments, the vehicle appeared—a black stretch limousine with heavily tinted windows. He allowed for the fact that it wouldn't come to a full stop at the sign and followed the leading edge of the rear tire in his scope, holding his breath and waiting until his heart was between beats.

There was the muffled crack of the gun, but beyond that, nothing changed. The limo accelerated through the crossing and disappeared from view just like all the cars before it.

Richard dropped the gun and ran through the trees, ducking branches as he zigzagged along a faint trail. His breathing got heavier and his speed slowed as he moved into less familiar territory, looking left to the road whenever the foliage thinned.

He was almost convinced that he'd missed when he spotted the limo riding its rim onto the gravel shoulder.

36

Near Fayetteville, West Virginia
May 10

Burt Seeger eased the RV through a deep rut, glancing behind him at Susie who had lost interest in the miniature stove and was now playing with a mechanical arm holding the television.

"Sit down, honey. You're going to fall."

"No I'm not. I have perfect balance," she said, opening a drawer and going through the drinking glasses cleverly secured in it. "That's what Mrs. Klein, my gym teacher, says. Perfect."

The twenty-five-foot vehicle was older than she was and smelled vaguely of mold, but she didn't seem to notice. There had been a little concern on her part when he'd sold his SUV to a used car dealer, but it had completely disappeared when their cab pulled into the driveway of the man selling the old camper. Not only was she certain it was the coolest thing ever, but it was also apparently totally rad.

He, on the other hand, saw it more as a necessary evil. Picking up pension checks was definitely out, so money was limited. And after what had happened at his home and the motel, staying in one place would be suicide.

The isolated dirt track narrowed, and Seeger rolled to a stop. They were ten hard miles from the nearest paved road and had turned off everything that could send an electronic signal. He'd feel more comfortable when there was a little more distance between them and Hagerstown, but they'd be safe for long enough to do what needed to be done.

160

"End of the line," he said, walking to the back of the RV.

Susie opened the door and watched him drag a large box toward it. After kicking the rusty stairs into position, he got out and bounced the crate down them with Susie trying her best to help.

"Step back, honey. You could get hurt."

"It's too heavy for you, and I'm not a baby."

"You're right," he said, keeping a close eye on her as he dropped the box the rest of the way to the ground and she lowered herself down the steps after it.

"Uh, Burt? Are we lost?"

"Of course not," he said, trying to stretch the kink out of his back.

"Where are we, then?"

"The woods."

"I know *that*," she said emphatically. "What woods?"

"You know. The one with trees and grass in it."

"You're being evasive."

"Evasive? Good word."

"Mom says it to dad sometimes."

"Well, what's *really* important is in the box."

"What is it?"

He held out a knife. "A little project. Why don't you open it?"

She took the knife and ran the blade over the tape.

"Be careful. It's sharp."

"I can open a box. I've done it lots of times before."

She seemed to have it well in hand, so he retreated, examining the dents and rust spots on the dingy white RV. Nothing that couldn't be fixed or obscured.

"It's paper and tape," she said, pulling out a roll of each.

"That's not all. Dig a little deeper."

She rummaged around and came up with a can of paint. "There must be fifty of these things in here! No wonder it's so heavy."

"And they're all blue. That's your favorite color isn't it?"

Her ancient face crinkled up for a moment, and she looked back at the RV. "No way! We're going to paint it?"

"We are indeed."

"Are you serious? We get to spray paint the whole thing blue?"

"You said you like blue, so we can't be driving around in a white one, can we?"

She yanked the top off the can and started for the vehicle with a mischievous look in her eye, but he caught her by the collar.

"Hold on there, young lady. Boring stuff first. We have to tape up all the chrome and glass. You want it to look good, don't you?"

She didn't seem completely certain, but dutifully grabbed some tape and padded toward the rear bumper. "I'll do the low stuff. You do the windows. But let's go fast. It's gonna get dark, and I don't want to do this my whole life. I want to paint!"

He watched her for a few moments, frowning when she crouched near the rear wheels. The pain caused by that simple act was visible on her face, and it scared him. He'd known some hard men in his life, but in many ways, this little girl was tougher than any of them. The fact that she was losing her ability to hide her fatigue and suffering meant that it was getting worse. Probably a lot worse.

"Hey, sweetie? You know what? I hate painting. I'll end up getting more on me than on the camper. Let's make a deal. If you let me tape, I'll let you paint."

The sun hit her fully in the face when she looked up at him, fading her skin to an ashy gray that he hadn't seen before. "Really?"

"Yeah. Otherwise I'll be blue for a week. Now why don't you go in and rest up for a while."

Watching her struggle up the stairs, he realized how dead he'd felt over the past few years. He'd become trapped in a house he'd always hated, unable to let go of the last part of a woman who would have been horrified at what he'd become. And now that he knew he could never go back, he found he didn't care. It had been long past time to let go of things that were gone.

Unfortunately, his newfound life was starting to look like it might not last all that long. The people coming after them would never stop—not of their own volition anyway. And being prey had a distinct disadvantage. A predator could make mistake after mistake. But the game was less forgiving for the hunted.

Richard's plan to level the playing field was an interesting one, and hopefully it would work. But in the extremely likely event that it didn't, he'd protect Susie until someone put a bullet in him. He owed her at least that much for rescuing him.

37

**Upstate New York
May 10**

Richard slowed when he came to the edge of a driveway cutting across his path, stepping from the trees and strolling along it toward the road. He made a show of checking the mailbox, but concentrated on his peripheral vision as the limousine stopped about twenty-five yards away.

The man who had been in the front passenger seat was frowning down at the damaged tire, and the driver was already headed toward the trunk. Richard wandered in their direction, trying to get his breathing fully under control and leafing casually through the letters he'd found.

"You guys all right?" he said as he approached. Despite his mouth being bone dry, his voice sounded reasonably natural.

"Just a flat," the man looking down at it said. "Not a big deal."

Both were as tall as he was, with expensive suits stretched across thickly muscled backs. Richard examined their waists, finding the bulge of a gun on both.

"I've got a jack and a lug wrench at my house if you need it."

"I think we're good, thanks," the man said, going back to help his companion with the spare and leaving the limo's front doors open and unprotected.

Right on cue, Carly came jogging up the other side of the road, limping slightly from the unhealed wound in her thigh. She was wrapped in formless sweats and a baseball hat in an effort to not attract the attention she did in her normal uniform of running shorts and a tank top. It seemed to work, because after a quick glance the two men went back to trying to free the spare.

She slowed to a walk, her footfalls going quiet as she abandoned the gravel shoulder in favor of asphalt. When she got within ten feet of the open driver's door, Richard started moving casually toward the passenger side. The bodyguards continued to ignore them, and he gave a subtle nod.

Carly dove through one door and Richard the other, ending up facing backward on his knees in the seat, clawing at the door handle. The bodyguards appeared from behind the trunk and ran at him, one already reaching into his jacket. The silver metal of a gun flashed in the sun, but it was too late—the doors slammed closed, and Carly found the lock button, sealing them in.

Outside, the two men were screaming unintelligible orders as they approached to within a few feet of the window with their guns thrust out in front of them.

According to Seeger, they'd be hesitant to shoot. Even in the unlikely event that the glass wasn't reinforced, a bullet could be deflected as it passed through, killing the man they'd been hired to protect. To Richard's ear, though, they didn't sound hesitant.

"What the hell do you think you're doing?"

It took a moment for Richard to tear his gaze from the gun barrel trained on him, but he finally managed to shift his focus to the man in the backseat.

In magazine and newspaper photos, Andreas Xander looked every bit the ninety-one years he reported, but in person, he looked a hell of a lot closer to the century mark.

His skin was gray and crisscrossed with broken blood vessels, falling from jutting cheekbones. The whites of his eyes had gone milky yellow and were rimmed in red as they flicked between his two captors.

"Tell them to lower their guns," Richard said, aiming the pistol Seeger had given him in the old man's general direction. "We don't usually do this kind of thing, and you don't want us any more nervous than we already are."

"What the hell's the matter with you two?" he said, reaching for the oxygen tank sitting next to him and increasing the flow to the tubes in his nose. "Are you a moron?"

Outside, one of the men was dialing a phone with his free hand. There wasn't much time.

"Answer my goddamn question!"

"What question?" Richard said.

This time Xander enunciated as though he were speaking to a small child. "Are. You. A. Moron?"

"I don't think you should go around insulting people holding you at gunpoint," Carly said.

Xander lifted an arm and they both jerked back a little, but he just pointed an arthritic finger toward the steering column. "The keys aren't in the ignition, and the tire's flat, you stupid hussy. Probably because you shot it out. What's the plan here? To just sit and wait for SWAT to blow your brains all over my upholstery?"

"Did you just call me a hussy?" Carly said. "Jesus Christ. How old *are* you?"

"Enough!" Richard said. "Look, we're sorry about this, Mr. Xander. I've tried to get in touch with you in a more conventional way, but I can't even get past your switchboard."

"Run," the old man said. "If you're gone by the time the police get here, I'll forget this ever happened."

"I'm Richard Draman, sir. I did biomedical research in the area of progeria. In fact, I—"

"Is it too much trouble for you people to pick up a newspaper every once in a while? Richard Draman died in a plane crash weeks ago."

"I wasn't on that plane, Mr. Xander. And neither was August Mason."

38

1,800 Miles East of Australia
May 10

Chris Graden had never been to this part of the island's compound, and he didn't know how to interpret the invitation. The garden was strikingly beautiful, with hanging palm trees and an indistinctly shaped pool with a greenish-gray bottom. As with all things Karl did, it was a triumphant combination of aesthetics and function—an outdoor sanctuary that would be completely invisible from above.

Graden followed the guard across the flagstones, aware of the cameras following their progress. The island's security was becoming as oppressive as it was obsessive. Who were the cameras there to watch? The watchers?

He wondered if Karl ever left. If he had a life somewhere or if he planned to spend the next millennium pulling the world's strings from the jungle.

They passed through a small gap in the trees, and the man leading him veered off, gesturing toward a table where Karl and Oleg were sitting.

"Please," Karl said, gesturing toward an empty chair. Graden took it, silently telling himself that he didn't have anything to worry about. Nothing that had happened with Richard and Carly was his fault. He'd faithfully played the role set out for him.

"Did you have a pleasant flight?"

The small talk seemed out of place coming from his lips. Perhaps intended to put him at ease, it had the opposite effect.

"I did, thank you."

"Then we'll proceed. I called you both here to discuss the Draman situation."

Karl's expression was passive, but there was something just beneath the surface. Rage.

"Obviously everyone at this table has underestimated their elusiveness and, admittedly, their luck. How this happened, I'm not sure. Chris, you've known them for years and were charged with making certain they considered you one of their closest friends. Oleg, you billed yourself as an intelligence mastermind—a man who would have no trouble with a situation like this one. But now we find ourselves in a very difficult position. Not only are the Dramans and their daughter still eluding us, but they've discovered more about our group than should have ever been possible. How did this happen?"

The question was clearly not rhetorical. Graden knew that he and the Russian were being asked to defend their actions. Perhaps their lives.

"My jet was used to try to get rid of them," Graden blurted before Oleg could speak. "But it wasn't my plan. And I held them at my house until our people came. The fact that they escaped has nothing to do with me. I'm not involved with who's sent and how competent they are."

"You did hold them there," Karl agreed. "According to our recordings, by telling them a great deal."

"That's not true! I didn't tell them anything useful—anything they didn't already know. I had to stall them. How else could I have done it?"

Karl nodded ambiguously and turned his attention to Oleg, who hadn't dared to interrupt but whose face had turned increasingly red at Graden's attempt to deflect blame.

"And yet they got away. Isn't that right, Oleg?"

"You understand the difficulties of finding reliable people who are sufficiently discreet," he said. "The men I sent were the only ones available, and there was no way to anticipate that they would have to deal with a former special forces sniper."

Another noncommittal nod from Karl. "It's difficult to argue against Chris's point, though, isn't it? Planning for the unexpected isn't what he was hired for. He was asked to keep them there until your people arrived, and he did that."

Graden relaxed enough that he dared pour himself a glass of water from the pitcher in the middle of the table. The heat and humidity were getting worse as the day went on, and his chair was the only one not shaded.

"Karl, I—"

"And by the time you tracked down this sniper and sent your men to deal with him, he was gone."

"We located his house within a few hours."

Karl shrugged. "How is that relevant? Too late is too late. Wouldn't you say that's true, Oleg?"

The Russian nodded reluctantly.

"I see this series of events as being brought about by a lack of thoroughness," Karl said, scooting back enough that he had a view of both men. "Chris, you didn't watch Richard Draman or Troy Chevalier closely enough. And Oleg, you weren't aware that the Dramans had gotten off the plane, and then you destroyed it to no purpose. You also allowed August to be tracked to Argentina, which puts me in the position of having to question *all* of our preparations up to this point."

He waved over the man who had escorted Graden across the garden, and he took a position next to the table.

"Chris, the work you've done for us has been very valuable. And, as you said, you're not an intelligence officer. Your sphere of influence is medical research, and with this one exception, you've covered that area competently."

Graden tried not to show his relief at what appeared to be a dismissal. As terrifying as the thought of death had always been, it was much more so now that it was no longer inevitable.

"But," Karl continued, "your involvement has been revealed, and we can't send you back. There could be questions that would be difficult to answer."

Graden's eyes widened a bit. Had his schedule been moved up? Was he going to be given the therapy?

The answer came when the man standing next to the table pulled a gun from his shoulder holster.

"No!" Graden shouted, jumping from his chair and holding a hand out. "You said this wasn't my fault! That I had done a good job for the group."

"And I meant that, Chris. But if there's anything we've learned from this, it's that even the smallest loose end can begin to unravel. Your sudden disappearance would just play into the story the Dramans can tell. My hands are tied."

The pain he expected to accompany the sound of the gun didn't materialize, and he had to look down at the red stain spreading across his chest before he comprehended what had happened. The tropical heat disappeared, as did the sound of the insects and birds. He looked up into the sky and squinted into the sun, watching it fade to black as he sank to the ground.

* * *

Oleg Nazarov maintained eye contact with Karl as two men materialized from the trees and carried away the piece of meat that had been Chris Graden.

"When Mason first told me about his breakthrough, I was skeptical," Karl said. "But his reputation preceded him, and the possibility that it could be used to create a therapy to reverse the aging process was too great to ignore. I set up a web of satellite labs in remote parts of the world, each working on a tiny piece of the puzzle. I paid government officials to provide human test subjects from their villages and prisons. I raised the three billion dollars it cost. And I controlled the impatience and frustration of the people I recruited while Mason's work stretched to nearly a quarter century. Some of the men who originally started down this road with me didn't live long enough to see him succeed. In fact, I almost didn't."

Nazarov looked on impassively, unsure where this was going. The trail of blood leading away from the table suggested that his life was hanging in the balance. Not particularly surprising, nor the first time. Involvement with Karl almost defined an all-or-nothing enterprise.

"I tell you this because I want to impress on you how far- reaching this is, Oleg."

"I understand."

"Do you? I hope so. I spoke with the group about you, and they were evenly split on how to proceed. For the first time, I had to cast the deciding vote."

Karl poured himself a glass of water while Nazarov stared at the still full one Chris Graden had left.

"I told them that it would be difficult to make a change at this point. That I have confidence in your ability to operate at a higher level than you have up to this point."

"Thank you," Nazarov said, wiping the sweat from his lip with a napkin.

"I understand that you joined us just as a number of difficult situations presented themselves, Oleg. But what *you* need to understand is that next time, the vote won't go in your favor."

39

Upstate New York
May 10

Richard watched Xander squint down at the eight-by-ten photo of August Mason as the guards outside continued to brandish their guns and shout. As long as he and Carly didn't make any sudden moves, they probably had a fifty-fifty chance of not getting their heads blown off. Until SWAT showed up, anyway.

"That's a hell of a story," Xander drawled between gurgling coughs. "Let me get this straight. August Mason is some kind of south-of-the-border Methuselah, and his little secret club is hot on your heels. Let me guess—in a flying saucer? I think I've got it. Are we through now?"

"What about Richard's driver's license?" Carly said, pointing to where it lay on the seat next to the old man. "That proves he's who he says he is."

"Do you have any idea how many cranks like you I've had to deal with over my lifetime?" He slapped the photo in his hand with more force than Richard thought he had in him. "Any six-year-old could get that license over the Internet in about a minute and a half. And as for the picture, I may not be as young as I used to be, but I have heard of Photoshop."

Richard wasn't surprised by the reaction and wondered for the thousandth time if this had been a huge mistake. Getting involved with Xander had a serious drawback—he was a ruthless, backstabbing, geriatric prick willing to do anything to escape the icy hands of death. But, from their standpoint, that was also his upside.

"I assume you have people who can check if the license is authentic and if Mason's photo has been altered. When they tell you they're genuine, my phone number is written on the back. In the meantime, if you could tell your bodyguards to put their guns down, we'll be on our way."

Carly pushed a button, and the back window next to Xander went down an inch. The old man ignored it, a glimmer of interest sparking in his wet eyes.

"That's it? No ransom? No demand that I tell your story on one of my television stations?"

"Actually, we'd prefer you keep this to yourself," Carly said. "Because of our daughter, we don't have time for the government to get involved."

"So you came to me instead?"

"We figured you'd be just as motivated as we are," Richard said. "And you're one of the few people in the world who can hold their own against a group this rich and powerful."

"You're very good," Xander said. "I'll give you that. Very convincing. But then, most insane people are."

"Do I really seem insane to you?"

He ignored the question. "So you think I should help two people who just carjacked me?"

"The upside for you is youth and possibly a patent on the most lucrative technology in history," Carly said. "The downside is that one of your assistants spends a few hours checking into our story and finds out it's bull."

"An interesting analysis. I'm ashamed to say it, but you two have piqued my curiosity."

With great effort, he rose to bring his mouth even with the crack in the window. "Put your guns down. They're leaving."

His guards did as they were told, and Carly gave her husband a worried glance before easing the driver's door open.

Neither of the two men moved as they got out, and Richard felt the knot in his stomach loosen a bit.

It didn't last long. A siren—maybe more than one—became audible in the distance and he froze for a moment, trying to calculate which of their planned escape routes would be best.

His moment of hesitation was all they needed. The man closest to him lunged, slamming into him hard enough to lift him three feet in the air before they came crashing down onto the road. The impact robbed him of his senses for a moment, but Carly's terrified voice finally brought him around.

"Don't hurt him. I'll shoot!"

His vision cleared as he was dragged to his feet by a powerful arm snaked around his neck. Carly had a gun aimed in his direction, but the barrel was shaking badly. The guard not using him as a human shield stood only a few feet away from her, his own pistol lined up with her temple.

"Quit screwing around!" Xander shouted from the limo. "Get 'em in the trunk before the cops get here."

40

**Upstate New York
May 12**

Richard walked to the window and looked out over Andreas Xander's spotlighted property, now suspecting that contacting the old man would one day top the lengthy list of his life's mistakes.

The window was unlocked, but they were on the third story with no way to climb down. And even if they could, they wouldn't make it ten steps toward the gate. Security was everything he would expect from one of the world's most controversial billionaires—mounted cameras, random patrols, dogs that seemed perpetually disappointed that there were no intruders to tear apart.

"Anything interesting?"

He turned toward Carly, who was sitting in one of the wingback chairs scattered around the room. As prisons went, it was a comfortable one—an opulent suite with a bathroom almost the size of the backyard of the home he doubted they would ever see again.

"If there were a lake, it would be full of sharks."

She was wearing a suede skirt and sweater selected from the expensive clothing that had been delivered shortly after they arrived. The sweater alone probably cost more than her entire wardrobe, and he realized how much he regretted that.

"Why don't you come and sit down, Richard? Try to relax."

"How the hell can I relax?" he said, snatching up the phone next to the bed. Dead. Just like every other time he'd checked. "We've been here two days and no one's said a word to us. What's Xander doing? Is he going to leave us here to rot until he finally keels over? This is kidnapping."

A wry smile spread across her face. "As opposed to shooting out someone's tire and holding a gun to their head?"

He ignored her. "I can't stay here any longer, Carly. We need to get in touch with—"

He caught himself before he said "Burt," looking around the room for the listening devices that he was sure were there. "We need to get in touch with Susie."

"I'm worried about her too, Richard. But she's in good hands. There's nothing you or I can do right now but sit here and wait. We're not dead, and we haven't been turned over to the police. That must mean something, right?"

"Don't give me that goddamn Zen crap," he said, finally losing the fight to stay in control.

She refused to take the bait. "Who would have thought that I'd end up the reasonable one?"

"Shit," he muttered and then let out a long breath. "I'm sorry, Carly. It's not you…"

"I know." She stood and crossed the room, pulling him close enough that her lips brushed his ear. "I'm afraid for her too. I'm afraid for all of us."

41

**Upstate New York
May 13**

Richard finished tucking his shirt in and went back to watching his wife blow her hair dry in a thick, white robe. How had he managed to find a woman like her? A woman who wasn't just smart and beautiful, but could stand unwavering in the face of a sick child, an obsessed husband, and now all this.

She turned off the dryer and faced him, smiling when she saw him staring. "What are you—"

The sound of a key in the door silenced her, and they both looked at the clock by the bed.

Their contact with the world outside that room had been governed by its illuminated numbers since they'd arrived. Breakfast had been delivered promptly at eight, as it always was, and lunch wasn't due for another hour and a half.

Carly pulled the robe tighter around her neck and took a position next to him, watching nervously as Andreas Xander rolled in.

"Not morning people, huh?"

The guard pushing his wheelchair retreated into the hallway and closed the door, leaving the three of them alone.

Richard straightened in an unsuccessful attempt to conjure a little confidence from his height advantage. "Why are you holding us here?"

"That seems like a stupid question for a man with your education."

177

"We haven't been able to talk to our daughter in three days. How long could it possibly take you to find out we're who we say we are? Like you said, a six-year-old could do it on the Internet in a minute and a half."

Carly squeezed his hand. "Calm down, Richard."

"You should listen to your wife. She's giving you good advice."

Xander didn't look any younger or stronger than the day they carjacked him, but he carried a menacing air that was magnified now that they were trapped on his playing field.

"So you know now," Carly said, her distaste for the man bleeding through her effort to hide it. "Isn't that right, Mr. Xander? You know who we are?"

"Oh, I know a great deal more than that. My people have gone through all the available information about the plane you were supposed to have gone down on, and they've retraced your steps in Argentina—"

"They were in Argentina?" Richard said. "Did they see him? Did they see Mason?"

Xander shook his head. "The house on that property burned to the ground the day after you were there. Everyone's gone, and the owner turned out to be a maze of bullshit offshore corporations."

"What about Chris?" Carly asked.

"He's dead."

"You mean he disappeared? They—"

"No, I mean he's dead. My people have seen the body. It's in a morgue in Eastern Europe."

"What happened to him?" Carly said. Her tone suggested that she hadn't yet been able to completely dismiss their friendship with Graden. It was easier to make the intellectual disconnect than the emotional one.

"The early talk from law enforcement is that he was developing designer narcotics with a group in Belarus and that it was a professional hit," Xander said, focusing on Richard. "Maybe you and Mason are involved too. It's a hell of a lot more likely than the story you fed me."

"What about the photo?" Richard said. "Have you had someone look at it?"

"Three different expert opinions and for once they all agree. They say it's genuine and taken where and when you said."

"What's the problem, then?" The cracks in Carly's carefully constructed patience were getting wider.

Xander shrugged his crooked shoulders. "The point of contention is whether or not it's Mason. Could just be someone who looks like him or someone you disguised to look like him."

"Why would we—" Richard started, but Xander talked over him.

"Mason's a fascinating guy. I have to admit that when he kept refusing to come to work for me I got pissed off and started looking into where he went when he disappeared back in the nineties. I figured he was off screwing little boys in Thailand or something."

"And was he?" Richard said, ignoring the fact that Xander had been looking for blackmail material.

"That's what's fascinating. I don't know. Despite all the money and effort I put into finding out, I came up blank. And that means someone was helping him stay underground. Someone more sophisticated than a bunch of gook pimps."

"They hid him while he was developing his treatment."

"I figured you'd say that."

"Why wouldn't he?" Carly said, the volume of her voice rising. "What more evidence do you need? We're wasting time. You have to help us. Please."

"It's OK," Richard said. "He's going to."

Xander tilted his head a bit to the side. "Am I?"

He nodded. "The way I see it, you have everything to gain by helping us and nothing to lose but a bunch of money and power that pretty soon you won't have much use for."

The old man tossed Richard the prepaid phone he'd been carrying when they carjacked him and then rapped on the door with arthritic knuckles. A moment later, a guard entered and wheeled him out.

By the time the door clicked shut, Richard was already dialing. It rang long enough that he started to feel nauseous, but finally a familiar voice came on.

"Hello?"

"Are you all right?" Richard blurted. "Is Susie OK?"

"We're both fine," Seeger said, a hint of suspicion audible in his voice. "I called yesterday, and someone I didn't recognize picked up. I thought you were dead."

"Not yet."

"What happened?"

"The plan worked right up to the part where they grabbed us," Richard said, moving the phone far enough from his ear that Carly could listen in. "They've been checking out our story, and we just got our cell back. Can you put Susie on?"

"She's asleep. I can wake her up, but she's exhausted. This has been really hard on her. She doesn't look that good, Richard. I'm not sure what to do."

Carly's expression turned a bit panicked.

"It's OK," Richard said, trying to keep his voice even. "Don't wake her up. You're giving her meds, right?"

"Hell yes, I am. Just like you told me."

"Then there's nothing else anyone can do. Just make sure she gets as much rest as she can."

"Maybe I should bring her there. Xander can protect her and she could settle into a routine."

Richard looked over at his wife. She chewed her lip nervously for a few moments before shaking her head. Obviously, she felt the same uncertainty about their host as he did.

"I'm not sure it's safe yet," he said. "We need you to keep her for a little longer."

42

**1,800 Miles East of Australia
May 14**

Oleg Nazarov gave the steel and bronze sculpture a wide berth. It had always struck him as a bit grotesque, but after not sleeping for more than forty-eight hours it was vaguely threatening.

He had completely lost the luxuries of prioritization and delegation—he had to personally scrutinize every piece of evidence. Nothing was irrelevant, and he couldn't trust the judgment of others knowing that the next mistake would probably be his last. It was vividly clear that the only reason he wasn't floating along the sea floor with Chris Graden was that it would be impractical to replace him when things were unraveling so quickly.

"You bring me good news?" Karl said as the Russian approached. "You've found them?"

"No. I've come to tell you that someone is looking into our organization."

"I don't understand. We already know that the Dramans—"

"It's not the Dramans. Questions are being asked about the offshore charities and accounts we've used to transfer money as well as about Chris Graden's death. We also have reports of unidentified men going through the ashes of Mason's house in Argentina."

"Who?" Karl said. His voice was even and calm, a monotone that was so much more intimidating than the flashes of anger and frustration he'd displayed over the past weeks. So much more inhuman. "Is it the soldier? Seeger? He would have contacts—"

"No. This is at a level far higher than he would have ever operated," Nazarov said, trying to find the courage to say aloud what he'd discovered. "It appears that the Dramans found a way to contact Andreas Xander."

The deathlike façade that Karl had managed to regain slipped slightly. His face flushed and the muscle in his jaw twitched visibly. "Xander? Are you certain?"

Nazarov nodded. "I discovered his involvement less than an hour ago."

In truth, it had been a bit longer than that. The old bastard was doing nothing at all to hide his involvement, but there was little reason to tell Karl this. Nazarov knew that his usefulness was under constant scrutiny and that he couldn't afford to pass up an opportunity to demonstrate competence.

"And have you made an assessment of the threat he poses to us?"

"It's significant. He has almost limitless resources that he can use without our overriding concern about maintaining anonymity. And he has so little time left, that we have to assume he will use those resources without reservation."

"Then we need to get to him."

Nazarov let out a long, quiet breath. "It would be extremely difficult. The security on his estate rivals—perhaps even exceeds—your security here. Short of aerial bombing or gas, I'm not sure what we can do to penetrate it."

"He has to leave it sometime."

"He drives in a heavily armed motorcade, but I agree that it's our best opportunity. Having said that, there is no way to do this subtly. If we succeed—or even if we fail—it will be on every channel of every television in the world."

"And if we do nothing?" Karl said. "What happens to our anonymity then?"

"Xander systematically dismantles it."

"Then we have no choice. We'll deal with consequences later."

"I'll start working on a plan immediately," Nazarov said with a respectful bow of the head.

"And the Dramans?"

"With Xander dead, they'll be more or less defenseless. Putting an end to that problem should be a simple matter."

"Will it? Will it really, Oleg? Are you telling me that one day you'll walk in here with an issue resolved instead of another disaster you weren't able to prevent?"

Karl's meticulously constructed serenity continued to crumble, displaying a glimpse of the man inside—something that made even the old KGB man want to step back.

Containing the Dramans had been feasible—likely even. But Nazarov knew that his ability to control Xander was nonexistent, and his ability to get to the old man was, at best, limited. It was time to start planning for the likelihood of future failures. And how he was going to survive them.

43

North of Baltimore, Maryland
May 14

Richard and Carly slid to their respective sides of the SUV's back seat and peered out. In front of them, a man with an assault rifle was waving Xander's limousine through the gate protecting Chris Graden's driveway.

They followed, watching the level of activity increase as they got closer to the house. Cars were parked haphazardly at the edges of the asphalt, people were darting purposefully around the grounds, equipment was being unloaded from trucks. They were forced to stop a good fifty yards from the portico, but Xander's chauffeur was more determined, easing across the grass behind a man walking with what looked like a small satellite dish.

"Mr. Xander would like you to join him," their driver said, toggling a switch that unlocked the rear doors.

They stepped out and started toward the old man as he was lowered to the ground.

The front door of the house was wide open, and the police tape that had once blocked it was now fluttering in the breeze. Above, men armed with rifles sat on the sills of the upper windows, watching the chaos below through dark sunglasses.

Xander seemed oddly energized. He brushed off the man behind him and used his withered arms to propel his chair in their direction.

"What do you think?"

"Isn't this a crime scene?" Richard responded. "Is it legal for us to be here?"

"Legal?" he said, a coughing laugh causing his eyes to excrete something approximating tears. "People like me don't really have to worry about legal."

Richard saw his wife's expression darken, and he interjected before she could start an argument about social justice or something equally unproductive. "Who are all these people, Mr. Xander?"

"Mostly former cops. I've always liked cops. They tend to be a flexible lot. And then there are all the acronyms you'd expect—people I hired away from the FBI, CIA, and NSA. Handy people to have around and, as you've noticed, well connected with the locals."

"Having the police in your pocket is all very nice," Carly said. "But what about the people Chris worked for?"

"What about them?"

"Isn't it possible that they're watching? That they know we're here?"

"If they've got a problem, they should come and see how their army does against mine. They're not up against a goddamn cook and a biologist anymore."

It was obvious that the statement wasn't intended as an insult—that would imply that they were actually worth insulting. It was more of a dismissal.

"Andreas!"

A fit-looking man in his early fifties appeared on the front porch, and Xander started wheeling toward him. Richard followed, but then stopped when his cell phone rang. He glanced down at it, immediately recognizing the number Burt Seeger was using.

"Hello?"

"Daddy!"

A tightness in his chest that he hadn't realized was there dissolved at the sound of his daughter's voice. Seeger was right, though. She sounded tired. Weak.

"How are you, sweetheart? Are you having fun?"

"Sure! We were at the beach, but not for very long, and now—"

"Susie!" he heard Seeger say. "What did we talk about?"

"Oh. Sorry. I forgot. I'm not supposed to say where we're going. But it's going to be super cool. Are you coming to meet us?"

Carly was leaning into the phone, listening. "We'll try, honey."

"Mom! Do you know what we did yesterday? We went and saw—"

"Susie!" Seeger cautioned again.

"Come on!" she said in an exasperated voice. "This secret stuff is going too far!"

They both smiled. She'd always had a mind of her own, and they encouraged her to use it. The downside was that it made her accustomed to understanding what was going on around her. They'd never been "because I said so" parents. Until now.

"How are you feeling?" Carly said.

Susie's annoyance grew. How she was feeling tied with math as her least favorite subject. "I feel fine."

It was a lie that no one but them would pick up on. There was a certain resonance missing from her voice—the sound of it seemed to wander, even when she was angry.

"We went today and watched some kids play on a—"

There was a jostling sound and Seeger's voice came on. "Sorry. Obviously, we haven't quite worked out what we're supposed to be saying and what we're not."

"Oh, come on," came their daughter's muffled voice. "I can't say *anything*. You said I can't even talk about the weather!"

"That's about the only thing you *didn't* talk about," Seeger said. "We're going to practice some more tonight because you just got a D minus in talking on the phone. Now say good-bye. It's time for your nap."

"But we just—"

"We had an agreement, Susie. We'd watch the kids, but then you'd give me a two-hour nap."

"I didn't sign anything."

"Go."

"Good-bye!" she shouted, and they heard her footsteps fade away.

"Sorry," Carly said into the phone. "She can be kind of a handful sometimes."

"That's the way kids are supposed to be. Don't worry. I'll get her trained on the phone thing."

"How are you doing?" Richard said. "Are you all right? Are you safe?"

"We're fine for the time being. How about you? Are you making any progress?"

Richard saw Carly take a nervous look around her and guessed that she was feeling about their situation the same way he was. Xander seemed to be a little out of control. It was as though he was courting a confrontation with Mason's people—the final defiant act of a man watching the last of his vitality and power spin down the drain.

"Things are a little weird right now," Richard said. "Would you mind keeping her a little longer?"

Over the phone, he heard a door creak and imagined Seeger walking outside. But that's all he could do: imagine. They had no idea where he and Susie were or what they were doing. No idea if a mistake had been made that Mason's people could use. It amplified their sense of powerlessness to a level that was almost unbearable.

"I'm getting a little worried," Seeger said, lowering his voice. "We're having to move around a lot, and I think it's too much for her. Plus, she misses both of you. It's hard for a kid her age to be separated from her parents."

Carly's eyes started to well up, and Richard put an arm around her.

"I'm afraid," Seeger continued. "I'm afraid I'm going to do something—or not do something—that's going to hurt her."

"There's nothing more we could do for her."

"You're an expert—you know what to look for if she's..." His voice faded for a moment. "You could keep her in one place. Calm things down."

Richard stepped out of the way of a man carrying a box full of papers and computer disks. "I don't think I'd use the world 'calm' to describe our situation."

"We trust you," Carly managed to get out. "And we don't hold you responsible. Just a little longer, OK?"

"OK. Fine."

"Just keep her resting as much as you can. And make sure she takes her meds."

"About that. We're running out of some of them."

"Carly gave you copies of all the prescriptions. Not all pharmacies stock some of them, so you might have to call ahead. But you won't have any problems."

"All right. Look, I've got to go. We've already been here too long. We'll try to give you a call tomorrow, but don't worry if we don't. I'm not sure we'll have a signal."

44

North of Baltimore, Maryland
May 14

Chris Graden's normally immaculate house had taken a serious beating from Xander's men. Disassembled phones and lamps were dangling from their cords, heating grates had been tossed carelessly on priceless rugs, and most of the furniture was overturned. Richard wasn't sure what they were looking for, but it if it was there, he was willing to bet it would be found.

They tracked down Xander in an enormous room that Chris opened only for large parties. He was tapping nervously on the arm of his wheelchair as he spoke to the man who had called out to him on the porch earlier.

"Richard! Carly!" Xander said when he spotted them by the door. "Come here. I want you to meet someone."

They did as they were told, and he pointed to the man in front of him. "This is Bill Garrison, a Harvard boy I stole from the bureau to run my security. This investigation is his baby."

"Nice to meet you," he said, shaking hands with both of them. His demeanor seemed strangely serene when compared to Xander, who seemed even more agitated than when they'd arrived.

"How's your daughter doing?" the old man asked as he leaned back in his wheelchair and stared directly at them. His tone didn't suggest concern for her well-being so much as concern that there was something in his universe that he didn't control.

"Fine," Carly responded.

"You should bring her to my house. She'll be safe there."

"Yeah, that'd probably be a good idea," Richard said, feigning enthusiasm for the plan.

"Tell us where she is and Bill can send a team to pick her up."

"That's OK," Carly interjected. "We can have the person she's with bring her."

Xander fell silent, obviously calculating whether he should push.

"Did you find anything?" Carly asked before he could decide.

"It was definitely bugged, but the hardware's been removed," Garrison responded. "You can't erase all traces of it, though. Also, we found repairs—very careful ones—of the bullet impacts you described from last time you were here. Other than that, there isn't much."

In Richard's mind, it was a wild understatement. Despite all the people, the place felt empty. Dead. Memories of the good times they'd had there were twisted and grotesque now.

"Don't worry, though," Garrison continued. "I'm just getting warmed up—taking the obvious paths first. What we've learned so far is that whoever we're up against is incredibly thorough, careful, and well financed—even by Andreas's standards."

"Finally, a worthy opponent," Xander said.

Garrison seemed a bit more apprehensive. "I prefer them not to be this worthy."

"Do you think they know we're here?" Carly said.

"It wouldn't surprise me. What we can be certain of is that they've noticed they're being investigated. We were following Mason's money through his maze of bogus charities and offshore corporations when someone started collapsing it all. They're pulling back, trying to slam the door on anything that could be used to track them."

"Is it going to work?" Richard asked.

"Hell no, it's not going to work," Xander responded angrily. "When Bill gets his teeth into something, he doesn't let go."

Garrison acknowledged the compliment with a respectful nod. "It's going to be tough to penetrate it all. Particularly when the people in this room are the only ones who have the big picture—"

"And that's the way it's going to stay," Xander said. "One leak and we're going to have every government hack and tabloid reporter on the planet parked on my lawn. As long as no one knows, we've got room to maneuver."

By that, Richard assumed the old man meant that he was free to do whatever he wanted—like ransacking a crime scene and carting off evidence. Or worse. The desperation that made Xander such a valuable ally also made him dangerous. He was a cornered animal, and they were standing way too close.

"Dr. Draman," Garrison said, "in order to make this drug, I assume they'd have to have some kind of a lab or production facility. Is that right?"

Richard nodded.

"Could you write me up a description of what that facility might be like? What kind of equipment it would have in it, what kind of materials they'd be using?"

"I'd need to think about it."

"Then think about it," Xander said. "But we need a list by eight o' clock tonight. Do you understand? Eight o' clock."

Xander watched as one of his security men led the Dramans out, waiting until they were out of earshot before turning back to Garrison. "Have you found their daughter yet?"

He shook his head. "We know she's with a retired soldier named Burt Seeger. He has a fair amount of intelligence training, though, and he's being very careful."

"I don't want to hear excuses, Bill. Find her. If things don't go our way, I need to have something the people we're looking for want. Something I can bargain away."

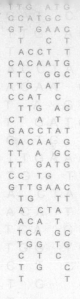

45

Upstate New York
May 17

Richard settled a little deeper into the backseat of the SUV as it trailed Xander's limo through light highway traffic. It had been three days since Chris Graden's house was ransacked, and they'd spent all of it confined to Xander's compound.

The inactivity was slowly driving him crazy—there was nothing to keep his mind occupied other than staring distractedly at the pages of books he'd found in the basement library or wandering aimlessly around the grounds. Carly had taken over the cooking from Xander's overwhelmed personal chef and was now leading the team that prepared three meals a day for the ever-expanding security force stationed on the grounds. At least it kept her from spending her days dwelling on their daughter, Mason, and everything else. Like he did.

"How did you think Susie sounded when we talked to her this morning?" Carly said in a tone that suggested she wasn't sure she wanted to hear the answer.

"I think she sounded fine," he lied.

Carly lowered her voice to the point that the men in the front seat wouldn't be able to hear over the road noise. "Do you think we're making a mistake not having him bring her to us?"

Richard put a hand in hers and squeezed gently. "I miss her too. But we've talked about this."

At first, the army that Xander had amassed was reassuring. But it was becoming increasingly clear that the old man was taunting Mason and his people. That he was looking for a fight.

Better to keep Susie as far away as possible and hope that if Mason managed to get to them, he would lose interest in her. She was no threat to him or anyone else.

"But what if she gets sick?" Carly said. "What if we're not there?"

"Gets sick" was the euphemism that had evolved for "dies." Like all euphemisms, though, it had lost the power to hide its meaning after too many years of use.

"I wish I had an answer, Carly. But I don't."

They fell silent as they swept through the gate of a private airport and came to a stop in front of a jet with Xander's corporate logo on the tail. As they climbed out of the SUV, the old man was already rising into the plane on a hydraulic lift. Two guards rode along, facing outward with hands hidden suggestively in their jackets.

"Richard, Carly!" Xander said, waving as they climbed into the plane. "Back here."

His wheelchair had been secured behind a small table, and they took the seats across from him.

"How've y'all been doing? We making you comfortable? I hear Carly's been cooking up a storm." He seemed even more manic than he had that day at Chris's house. It was clear that he was feeding off his competition with Mason, but his increased energy came off as dangerous—the blinding glow of a light bulb right before it exploded.

He opened a folder lying on the table and spread out six large photographs. August Mason was there, but Richard didn't recognize the people in the other five.

"Who are they?" Carly said.

"Wealthy, powerful men who have died since around the time Mason reappeared, but whose bodies have never been recovered."

"That seems like a lot," Richard said.

"It's more than a lot. It's a freakishly high number," Xander said, an arrogant smile threatening to split his chapped lips. "Based on history, the probability of all these men disappearing is more than a million to one. And I doubt that's all of the people involved. There are probably more still in their natural state."

"Natural state?" Richard said as the plane began to accelerate up the runway.

"People who are involved but haven't been treated yet. Like Chris Graden. It's not easy to orchestrate these deaths, and they're already pushing it with the number they've done."

Carly tapped the table next to the photos. "So you found these people? Is that where we're going?"

"Even better," he said, pressing a button on the wall that released the clamps securing his wheelchair. "Now enjoy the flight."

They both twisted around in their seats, watching him roll up the aisle and disappear through a curtain near the front. When Richard finally faced forward again, the anger was clearly visible in his wife's face.

"We're in the air, and he still won't tell us where we're going," she said.

"He likes to be in control."

"This goes beyond control, Richard. Haven't you noticed? He isn't outraged by these people. He doesn't care that they tried to kill us or Susie, that they're keeping a drug that could save millions—maybe billions of people—to themselves. It seems like the only thing he thinks Mason's done wrong is not include him in their little cabal."

Richard didn't respond. He'd known from the beginning that they were making a deal with the devil, but what choice did they have? The only thing that mattered was giving Susie a chance to grow up.

"Do you ever wonder what he's going to do with it?" Carly continued.

"Use it, I would think."

"Yeah. But after that. Will he build a company around selling it and become the richest man in the world? Or will he keep it under lock and key?"

Richard leaned his head back and let out a long breath. "I don't know, Carly. I just don't know."

46

West of Boise, Idaho
May 17

His watch read one in the morning, but Richard Draman didn't even know what time zone they were in anymore. He and Carly had been ushered off the jet and into yet another black SUV that had immediately accelerated onto a maze of unfamiliar back roads. As usual, the men in the front seat refused to answer even the most innocuous question.

He and Carly matched the silence of their escorts, watching the dark blur of trees on the side of the road and reading street signs for clues to their location. Beyond the vaguely reassuring fact that they were in English, there was little to be learned.

A distant glow became visible through the windshield, and he quickly identified its source—a biomedical research campus similar to the ones he'd spent most of his adult life in.

"What is that?" Carly asked as they sped toward it.

Richard silently mouthed the response along with the driver. "I wouldn't know, ma'am."

The man inside the tiny guardhouse was definitely familiar. One of the guards who handled the dogs on the estate? One of the snipers who had been sitting in the windows of Chris Graden's house?

They weaved through the brick and glass buildings, finally stopping in front of one at the back. Bill Garrison was standing out front, waiting patiently for Xander's driver to complete the complex process of extricating his boss from the vehicle.

195

Richard and Carly took the hint and stepped cautiously from the SUV, looking around them at the spotlight-created shadows and trying not to imagine what might be waiting in them.

"It's good to see you both again," Garrison said as they approached. Behind him, Xander was being wheeled into the building's heavily guarded lobby.

"What is this place?" Richard said as they were led inside.

"Let's go on up, Doc. You're gonna like this."

Xander had staked out a corner in the tiny elevator, and they squeezed in next to him as Garrison inserted a key above the buttons.

They rose to the top floor where the doors opened directly into a laboratory that made his own research facility look like it was put together with stuff found at Kmart.

"This is it?" Richard said. "You found it already? The place where they're making the drug?"

"I told you Bill was a miracle worker," Xander said.

Garrison seemed uncomfortable with praise. "It really wasn't as hard as you'd imagine. We just followed the sales of the equipment on the list you gave us. This kind of machinery generally goes to well-known—or at least well-documented—companies. All I had to do was focus on ones that didn't fit the bill."

Richard looked back at the closed elevator doors and then at the cameras angling down at them from the ceiling. Was someone watching? Did Xander even care?

"How did you get access?" Carly asked.

"They don't own the building," Garrison said. "They probably decided that buying real estate in the U.S. left too much of a paper trail. Easier just to rent."

"So who *does* own the building?"

A broad smile spread across Xander's face, stretching the loose skin into something grotesque. "As of this morning, I do."

A walkie-talkie hanging from the side of his wheelchair crackled to life, and he picked it up.

"We've got two SUVs coming our way at high speed," a voice said.

Xander rolled his eyes in feigned impatience. "It seems we have a leak."

Garrison nodded serenely. "Unavoidable. Nothing to be done."

"Nothing to be done? We can get the hell out of here," Richard said. "Look, we've come up against these people before. They don't play around."

"And I do?" Xander snapped, spinning his chair and starting toward the covered windows. "Come!"

They did as they were told, but when Xander toggled a switch that opened the shades, Richard pushed his wife behind him. It was difficult to see through the glass into the relative darkness of the parking area, but anyone outside would be able to see them as though they were standing on stage. And as well equipped as this lab was, bulletproof glass generally wasn't an option.

Garrison dimmed the lights, and the scene below sharpened. For the moment, everything was as still as a photograph—just empty streets and silent buildings.

The sound of racing engines and squealing tires came first, followed by two black SUVs that looked almost identical to the one they'd arrived in.

"This is crazy," Richard said as they skidded to a stop in front of the building. "We've got to get—"

"Shut up," Xander responded as four men jumped from the lead vehicle and three more from the other. They were wearing street clothes, but all had assault rifles hanging across their chests on short straps.

Carly grabbed him by the shirt and pulled him back from the glass just as Xander rolled toward it.

"Light 'em up," he said into the walkie-talkie.

A moment later, the two SUVs and the men who had arrived in them were covered in tiny red dots. They didn't even bother to aim their weapons, instead raising their hands and remaining completely motionless as they squinted into the shadows that had worried Richard when they arrived.

"Should we take them out?" came the voice over the radio.

Xander turned his chair and looked back at them. "What do *you* think, Carly? It probably wouldn't be a bad idea. At least some of those guys are probably involved in tracking down your daughter. Should we get rid of them?"

"You mean murder them?" she said. "You can't do that."

"No?" he said, seeming to enjoy her horror and confusion. "I doubt they'll have the same reservations when they finally catch up with little Susie."

She didn't answer, and he affected disappointment at her weakness before speaking into the walkie-talkie again. "Just hold 'em 'til we're done. Then set 'em loose to do whatever they want."

The implication was clear and obviously intended. If anything happened to Susie, it would be their fault. Of course, the idea that he based his decision on their wishes was laughable. More likely, he wasn't confident enough in his above-the-law status to order the deaths of seven human beings while sitting in a lab he'd broken into.

Xander's men separated themselves from the shadows, and their shouts were audible through the glass, though too muffled to be understood. Their captives dropped their weapons and fell to their knees with their hands behind their heads. Xander was clearly disappointed in the orderliness of the scene. Deep down, he'd probably hoped for something more visceral. Something that would run a jolt of omnipotence through his failing body.

"Do you want them questioned?" Garrison asked.

"No," the old man responded. "They don't know anything."

"How can you be sure?" Richard said.

"Because Mason isn't stupid enough to tell a bunch of hired muscle something we could use," he responded and then pointed back into the lab. "Now quit talking, get a marker, and put an X on everything you want. There'll be a truck here in ten minutes."

47

**1,800 Miles East of Australia
May 17**

The waterfall had a perfection of flow that suggested a human hand in its design. Oleg Nazarov stood before it, staring at the sun's reflection and letting the crash of it fill his ears. Karl was staring at the water too, but he remained silent and opaque.

"Why wasn't the lab shut down and moved weeks ago?" he said, finally.

Nazarov's heart felt hollow in his chest, as though it knew he didn't have much more time. Before agreeing to subordinate himself to the group, he had wielded enormous influence—near omnipotence in his small corner of the world. Now he was nothing.

"Our manpower is extremely limited. I'm trying to make everything top priority, but obviously that's impossible."

"What could be more of a priority than the lab?" Karl's voice cut through the sound of the falling water with surprising ease.

"Mason and the others—ensuring that they aren't discovered and captured."

Nazarov shared Karl's distaste for excuses, and he was loath to give them. But in his current situation, it seemed wise to overcome that bias. The truth in this case was that he had been outsmarted. He'd taken Xander's reluctance to hide his activities as bravado—a dying man trying to wield the last of his power. And that was undoubtedly partly the case. But it had also lulled Nazarov into carelessness about watching for less overt activities—such as the sale of the building that housed the lab to a company carefully designed to look like an unremarkable real estate investment group.

Karl opened his mouth to speak but seemed to lose his thought. Sweat beaded on his forehead. Or maybe it was just the mist.

"What did he get from the lab?" Karl said.

"Everything. Computers, equipment, files. And the refrigeration unit."

Karl seemed to want to lash out. He looked around him with awkward, jerky movements, clenching and unclenching his fists. "Projected damage?"

"They'll get into the refrigerator and find some of the components for the therapy stored there. I spoke with Mason, and he says there's little they can learn from them."

"And the therapy itself? Can they access that?"

In what had been yet another stroke of devastating luck, a dose had recently been completed for one of the group scheduled for transition. It too was contained in that refrigerator.

"It's in a separate protective case that's all but impenetrable."

"All but?"

"There are no certainties, Karl. But we're taking steps to further reduce the chance that they can penetrate the container."

"The computers?"

"Everything is heavily encrypted. I'm told by our technical people that it would take even America's National Security Agency years to crack."

48

**Upstate New York
May 18**

"Could we shorten this counter so it doesn't go all the way to the wall?" Richard Draman said.

The contractor ran a finger along the blueprints spread out on a piece of drywall and nodded. "No problem. They told me if you want a solid gold statue of yourself twelve feet high, you get it."

"Let's start with the counter, and I'll think about the statue."

"Right on," he said, trudging off to check the progress of a group of men tearing plaster from the ceiling of Xander's cathedral of an attic.

"Wow. Maybe I should have brought my hard hat."

Richard turned and saw his wife approaching with his lunch on a tray. "Amazing, isn't it? In a week, I'll have a facility that I would have killed for at the Progeria Project. And it all came from a wave of Xander's hand."

"His private jets and security and mansions didn't really make that much of an impression on me," she said, shaking her head in amazement. "But getting contractors to show up on time and work? That's power."

Richard laughed and took the tray, setting it down next to the blueprints.

"You don't do that very often anymore," she said.

"What?"

"Laugh."

"I thought that there wasn't a lot to laugh about. But now I think maybe I was wrong."

"Could this really be it?" she said, looking around at the chaos. "Could this attic be where you find a way to help Susie and the other kids?"

"It's hard not to let yourself start to—"

He cut himself off when one of Xander's security men strode through the door and motioned to them. "Could you both come with me, please?"

"Where?" Richard said. "I'm a little tied up here, and I haven't eaten all day."

"Xander's orders," the man said. It was a phrase that was starting to come up as often as "I wouldn't know," and it was just as ironclad. People acted as though God spoke directly through the old man and displayed what seemed to be honest confusion when Richard questioned his periodic decrees.

There was no point in fighting it, so Richard followed his wife toward the door. As she passed the guard, he nodded respectfully. "Lunch today, ma'am…that was the best chili I've ever had. And I'm from Texas."

49

**Upstate New York
May 18**

Richard and Carly had become accustomed to chasing Xander's limo in one of the many black SUVs used by his protection detail, but now the protocol had changed radically. In addition to the driver and the man in the passenger seat, there were now two machine-gun-toting guards in a third row of seats behind them. Just as obvious was the fact that their motorcade had grown to be nearly a block long.

"I don't think the president has this kind of security," Carly said as the lead vehicle blocked an intersection so they could maintain their speed as they passed through.

"There's no way Mason doesn't know about Xander. It's not like he goes out of his way to keep a low profile."

"He's stupid and arrogant," she said, not caring that her criticism would be reported back to the old man—assuming he wasn't listening already.

Richard squeezed her hand. "We didn't come to him for subtlety, Carly. Sometimes you just have to reach for the biggest hammer."

"Maybe. But it'd be nice to have some say over what it hits."

He sighed quietly. She was right, but it was hard to complain too much. Did Xander have a psychotic compulsion for tempting the gods? Sure. But there was also no denying that his methods had provided them the contents of Mason's lab, the identities of some of the members of his group, and an impenetrable fortress to live in. Where would they be without the old bastard? Probably dead, with Mason's assassins hot on Susie's heels.

"Carly, I think we just have to be gra—"

The flash came first, followed by a wave of sound that seemed to suck the air from his lungs. Richard tried to throw himself protectively over his wife, but was hurled backward when the SUV slammed over a curb.

His head hit the side window hard enough to crack the glass, and he saw the two men behind them stand up through the sunroof with their guns as he tried to shake off the pain and refocus his vision.

Carly didn't seem to notice any of it. She just stared blankly through the spider-webbed side window as the SUV accelerated. When his head had cleared enough for him to maintain his balance, he twisted around to see what she was looking at.

Xander's limo had flipped over in the middle of the street and was spinning slowly on its roof. Flames billowed through it, sending a column of black, oily smoke into the sky as the people inside were engulfed.

"Get down!" he heard someone yell, and he pushed Carly back into the seat. Her body convulsed as she sobbed beneath him, and he gently stroked her hair, concentrating on trying to breathe.

It was over. Xander was dead, and in a few minutes, they probably would be too.

Susie's last hope was on fire.

50

1,800 Miles East of Australia
May 18

Oleg Nazarov monitored Karl's expression as he watched the video of Xander's limousine being destroyed by the explosives planted beneath a manhole cover.

"What about the Dramans?" he said, the tension that had been growing so visibly in him subsiding somewhat.

"We aren't certain. Our hope was that they would be in the limousine, but based on the escape tactics deployed by the rest of the motorcade, we now believe that they were in the vehicle behind."

"You didn't plan for this? That they might travel in separate vehicles?"

"I was aware of the possibility, but with no intelligence, there was nothing to be done. This operation was focused on Xander, and it appears to have been a success. If he is indeed dead, the Dramans will be vulnerable again."

"*If* he's dead?" Karl said, pointing to the flames on the screen. "You think he could have survived that?"

"I'd feel better if our people saw the body," Nazarov responded, knowing that he couldn't afford another mistake. "We're watching Xander's house to see if the Dramans return, and our people in law enforcement and the media are continuing to watch for any attempt by the Dramans to make contact. But there's been nothing so far."

"What about Mason and the others?"

"We're nearly finished sterilizing everything. They've all been moved, their identities changed, and their assets laundered. Within the week, our original organization will have virtually ceased to exist."

"Virtually?"

Nazarov took a seat unbidden and again failed to think of a way to soften the impact of what he had to say. "The exception is you and this island. Those are the last unaltered links to our former structure."

Karl's expression darkened predictably, but it had less effect than it normally would. As angry as he would be over having to abandon everything he'd built there, Nazarov was even more pleased. The island was inescapable—a universe created and controlled by one man. The alternate location that Nazarov had selected was much more conducive to a hasty retreat on his part should it become necessary.

"On a more positive note," Nazarov continued, "Susie Draman may have surfaced. Someone called in an order for medications under her prescription to a pharmacy in Kansas."

Karl turned to the video again. It had looped back and he was temporarily mesmerized by the image of Xander's car being lifted into the air. "Do we have people on site?"

"We do. We're also tied into the store's computer system and surveillance cameras. Even if someone other than Burt Seeger fills the prescription, we'll know real-time when they're scanned and we'll be able to track the person who takes possession of them."

Karl nodded slowly, fixing his gaze on Nazarov. "This is the last piece, Oleg. With her, we gain control of her parents. It's an opportunity you can't afford to miss."

"Yes, sir. I understand."

51

**Upstate New York
May 18**

Richard kept his arms around his wife as the SUV pulled up to a concrete box of a building centered in a sea of empty asphalt. The area was ringed by an electric fence, and steel posts had been set into the ground to make it impossible for a vehicle to approach quickly or directly. Beyond the fence was a flat, treeless landscape that allowed the patrolling guards an unobstructed view in all directions.

Their driver jumped out and opened the back door, but Richard didn't move. He had no idea where they were or why. Xander wasn't a man who left a great deal to chance or the discretion of others, so it seemed that he'd have given orders as to what was to happen to them if he was killed. Were they just a complication now? Something that could muddle his legacy? What was inside that building? A crematorium? A wet cement foundation that would become their final resting place?

"Sir?" the man prompted.

Richard finally stepped out, gently pulling his wife along with him. She made it to the curb but then sank down onto it and put her head in her hands.

"Honey?" he said, his fear of Xander's men suddenly eclipsed by concern for his wife. He'd never seen her like this. She'd sobbed for almost a half an hour after Xander's death, finally slipping into a near catatonic state as they made their way here.

"Sir?" the man prompted again, and Richard spun toward him. "Could you just give us a fucking minute?"

The force of his tone surprised everyone within earshot, and the man retreated to a heavy steel door set into the building, scanning the horizon while he waited.

"Carly? Are you OK?"

"I never had any hope," she said.

"What?"

"That's my secret. You always thought it was strength, or Zen, or whatever. But it wasn't. I knew you'd never cure her. Everyone did."

He knelt next to her, and she took his hand. "It wasn't that I didn't believe in you, Richard. But it was impossible. The years go by so fast, and the disease…" Her voice faded for a moment. "It was too much for you. For anyone. But then I saw Mason, and for the first time I thought Susie could have a future. I let myself imagine her growing up. Going to her wedding. Having grandchildren."

Richard just nodded, unsure what else to do. He knew what hope could do to a person. If there was anything in life he really understood, it was that.

52

Upstate New York
May 18

The lobby of the building housed two well-armed men wearing body armor and another sitting behind a bank of monitors. Richard and Carly were led past them to a heavy door that opened automatically when they got close.

Despite the comfortable familiarity of the steel counters, sinks, and gleaming lab equipment they found inside, Richard felt a jolt of adrenaline when the door clanged shut behind them. The lack of windows, the sense of powerlessness, the loss of hope, all started to close in on him.

"It's about goddamn time."

The voice sounded hollow as it bounced around the room but not so hollow as to be from beyond the grave. They both stood frozen as Andreas Xander rolled out from behind a row of file cabinets.

"Don't look so surprised," he said, the familiar psychotic glee audible in his voice. "They're gonna to have to do a hell of a lot better than that if they want to kill me. This isn't amateur hour anymore."

Richard glanced over at his wife, whose mouth was actually hanging open as she tried to process what she was seeing.

"Who was in the car?" she finally managed to get out.

"A decoy. I got a few of 'em," he said, his lips stretching over stained teeth in what passed for a grin. "I suppose they'll want raises now."

To him it was just another victory over his enemies—another thing he could use to transform the reflection he saw in the mirror into the young, powerful figure he once was. The people who had died for him in that car—their families and friends—meant nothing.

"This is the best we could do on short notice," he said, waving a hand around the room. "It's defensible if those idiots working for Mason manage to find it, and it has everything you need to tide you over until we can get the lab at the compound done."

Richard put a hand on his wife's back, keeping her close as he examined the mix of new instruments and equipment plundered from Mason's lab. It wasn't over. He still had time. Susie still had time.

"Where are the computers?"

"India," Xander replied. "We've got the best people in the world on it, but I'm being told that they're going to be tough to crack. Maybe a week, maybe a month. Maybe never."

Richard reached out to open the refrigerator they'd taken but then hesitated and looked back at Xander.

"Go ahead, Doc."

Inside he found neat rows of vials and test tubes, all labeled with numbers that he suspected tracked to those inaccessible computer files.

Xander pointed a bony finger at a steel box on the bottom shelf. "You wouldn't believe what we went through to get into that thing."

Richard opened it, struggling with the weight of a solid steel lid that was almost an inch thick.

"It had an incredibly intricate locking system and three separate explosive charges designed to incinerate its contents if it was improperly accessed."

"So this is special," Richard said, reaching out and running a finger over the smooth glass of the vial inside. "They didn't want anyone to get to it."

"That's the goddamn understatement of the century. We tracked down the guy who made the box, and guess what? He just happened to die in a house fire twelve hours before we got to him. All the plans were gone, and his assistant was found in some field with a bullet in his head. They didn't even bother to try to make that one look like an accident. It's a miracle our people cracked it without having the thing blow up in their faces. One in a hundred chance."

Carly was beside him, staring down into the box, mesmerized by the gleam of the tiny vial. "Could that be it?"

"I don't know," Richard said. "Maybe."

"How long for you to find out?" Xander asked. "How long before I can take it?"

Richard glanced over at the old man, but turned away before their eyes could meet. He already knew what he would see—or more precisely, what he wouldn't see. There would be no memory of Susie and the other children, no thought of what this could mean for the world. Xander was a cold, empty universe unto himself.

"I have no idea," Richard said finally. "We don't know anything about it. How does it work? Is this one dose or a thousand? How's it administered—all at once or over the course of a year? Is it complete as is or only one of ten components? Hell, is it a decoy? Could they have let you find it on purpose?"

"That's why you're here, isn't it, Doc? To answer those questions."

"Yeah."

"You'll be safe here until you can be moved back to the house. We can't have you going back and forth, though. It's too dangerous."

"OK."

"Whatever you need, you get," Xander said. "Do you understand what I'm saying? A million dollars, ten million, a hundred million. It's all the same to me. The only thing that matters is getting this done and getting it done fast."

Xander turned and began wheeling toward the door. "Come on, Carly, you can ride with me. We need to get back before those bastards find out they screwed up."

"I'll stay here with Richard."

He stopped but didn't turn. "I had to promise the men that I'd bring you with me. If you aren't there to cook, I might have a mutiny on my hands."

While his syntax had a calculated politeness, his tone carried the real message: "I have your wife, and I expect results."

They were in no position to negotiate, so Richard forced a smile. "You don't want to be stuck here sleeping on the floor."

He leaned forward to kiss her, but she bobbed her head left at the last moment, bringing her lips close to his ear. "Whatever happens, no one could have done more to help Susie and the other kids. No one."

He watched her follow Xander through the door and continued standing there for a long time after they were gone, ignoring the security cameras tracking him from the ceiling.

He could almost feel the vial radiating behind him. But radiating what? A future for Susie? For men like Xander? For all of humanity?

It was impossible to consider something that powerful without regressing into thoughts of good and evil.

But which one was it?

53

Wichita, Kansas
May 20

The plan was to be in and out quick—ten minutes. Fifteen, tops.

That had been five hours ago.

Burt Seeger reached for his coffee but then decided that he'd already had too much. His jitters were bad enough without feeding them.

The Walmart across the street was clearly visible through the windows of the McDonald's, and he watched the afternoon sun glint off the sea of cars in the parking lot. His eyesight and memory weren't what they once were, making it even more difficult to identify telltale patterns in the comings and goings of hundreds—maybe thousands—of customers.

The people he was up against weren't going to pull a big surveillance van into the middle of the lot and let loose a bunch of steroid addicts with earpieces. They'd be more subtle than that. They'd be invisible.

And so there he was, sitting in the middle of American suburbia feeling like he was staring into the entrance of an Afghan slot canyon.

He pulled a cell phone from his pocket and dialed, hearing a familiar voice pick up almost immediately.

"Hello?"

"Hey, Susie. Everything OK?"

"Where *are* you? What, did you go to the Walmart in France?"

He managed a smile, but it faded quickly. Being forced to leave a sick eight-year-old girl alone in a rusting RV didn't do much for his mood.

"They told me the medicine I ordered was in, but it's not," he lied.

"You should have let me come. I know the names of all of them, you know. And not just the brand names. I know the scientific names. I can even spell them. I could have helped."

"I know you could have. But it won't be long now. Are you playing the new video game we got?"

"No. I got tired, so I thought I'd wait."

He chewed unconsciously on his thumbnail. She'd begged him to buy it—swearing that she'd never tell her mother that he let her play a game involving a buxom heroine blowing the heads off walking corpses.

Most of the time she was still the enthusiastic little girl he'd carried in from his driveway a month before. But sometimes—usually when she thought no one was paying attention—she seemed to fade.

"Maybe we can have a go when I get back. Now, you remember where the library is, right? Where I showed you, down the street?"

"I don't have to remember, Burt. I mean, I can see it out the window."

"OK, good. If you don't hear from me in one hour, I want you to go there and call your parents. Tell them to come and pick you up."

"What do you mean?" she said, the exaggerated fear of abandonment that all kids her age suffered from rising in her voice. "What are you doing? You're going to leave?"

No, he thought. *I'm going to die.*

Despite what the parenting Websites he'd been reading said, though, this was probably an instance where honesty wasn't the best policy.

"Of course I'm not going to leave, sweetie. But it could be that in order to make sure you stay safe, I have to go somewhere else."

"Why would you have to go somewhere else? Did I do something? I didn't mean to. I—"

"Calm down, Susie. You didn't do anything. Most likely, I'll see you in just a little while. What's our motto?"

"I don't—"

"Come on. What is it?"

"Always have a plan B."

"That's right. Now I want you to set the timer on the watch I left you. One hour. Do you understand?"

54

Wichita, Kansas
May 20

Burt Seeger took a circuitous route, working his way three blocks north before crossing to the Walmart side of the street. The sidewalk was depressingly empty—walking was an increasingly lost art in America, and it made him far more obvious than he would have liked.

He took a path behind a series of shops bordering one side of the center's parking lot, staying close to the battered fence that ran along the back and occasionally ducking behind a Dumpster to see if he was being followed.

Nothing.

But then, he really wouldn't expect to see anything. They'd just watch him and wait until he led them back to Susie before they made a move. The fact that he'd called in Susie's prescription created a link. Admittedly a tenuous one, but a link nonetheless.

He came to the end of the series of shops and peeked through a gap in the fence. Close up, the Walmart didn't look any more sinister than it had from a distance. Average people towing average kids and normal grocery bags.

Despite that, he wanted nothing more than to just walk away. It wasn't an option, though. Susie needed her meds, and this was the only way to get them.

Seeger was about to climb over the fence when he noticed a ladder running up the back of a pizza shop. The roof was flat, ringed by a wall

215

that looked to be in the range of three feet high. A good vantage point to take one last look before diving in headfirst.

He ascended the ladder quickly, but ducked back down when his head cleared the top.

His heart rate surged—not necessarily a good thing at his age—but the adrenaline still did the job it always had. His surroundings came into clearer focus, the noises around him separated and sharpened, the aches and pains he'd become so used to disappeared.

After a quick look to confirm no one was approaching from below, he eased himself upward again, stopping when his eyes cleared the ledge.

The man was on the far side of the roof, sitting cross-legged in front of a bank of small monitors. He was wearing tan slacks and a white button-down shirt that accentuated the V of his back and contrasted dark, East Indian skin. The headset resting on his black military-cut hair was wired directly into a console to his right.

Seeger couldn't be absolutely sure it was the man who had led the team that broke into his house, but the resemblance was a hell of a lot more than superficial.

He eased himself up another rung, trying unsuccessfully to find a plausible explanation for what he saw. A cop on a stakeout who just happened to be of Indian descent? The director of an independent foreign film about the American shopper?

Not likely.

The sun was in his face, which normally would have been a disadvantage, but in this case, it would keep his shadow behind him. The surface of the roof looked like rubber and would absorb the sound of his footsteps if he could avoid the gravel strewn across it.

But even with all that and the element of surprise, what were his chances? There was a time that he wouldn't have thought twice about an intel-gathering opportunity like this one, but that time was more than a quarter century past. Was it worth the risk?

He fished a knife from his pocket and flipped it open with his thumb. The blade was only three inches long and not really designed for the task at hand, but it was quiet and sharp and would have to do.

Swinging a leg onto the roof, he crept silently forward, pausing when the man ducked down to study the monitors that Seeger could now see were tied into Walmart's security cameras. The images changed rhythmically—the registers, the refrigeration section—with one exception: the feed from the pharmacy was constant.

With only a few feet to go, the wind kicked up behind him, and he was forced to lunge, worried that the man would smell the obnoxious pineapple-scented shampoo that Susie had so carefully selected for him.

Seeger yanked out the cord connecting the headset and immediately threw his weight left, anticipating the elbow coming around as the man twisted his body into a defensive position.

The years had robbed him of even more speed than he thought, and he got clipped hard enough to cause him to lose his balance and fall toward the edge of the low wall behind him.

The man drove a hand into Seeger's chest, doubling the force of gravity pulling him toward the brick barrier. He let his knees collapse and managed to take the impact across his shoulder blades instead of his lower spine as the man had planned. The flash of pain was accompanied by a crackling sound that he assumed was shattering bone.

Surprisingly, his right arm still worked, and he threw it forward, fixating on the face less than two feet away. There was no fear or anger in it, just calculation and unwavering determination. It wasn't the fanatics he worried about. It was the cold sons of bitches like this one. They were the ones who would kill you.

The man swung a fist in a flawlessly timed arc, but Seeger ignored it, focusing on keeping his hand moving feebly forward. He managed to swivel his head away at the last moment, avoiding the full impact of the blow but still sprawling to the ground beneath a now out-of-focus sky.

Stepping forward, the Indian started to press his advantage, but then he slapped a hand to his neck and pulled it back wet with blood. Seeger wasn't surprised by his confusion. One of the many obsessions he carried with him from the military was the painstaking maintenance of his gear.

What the knife concealed in his palm lacked in size, it made up for with its meticulously honed edge. The man hadn't felt it slice across his carotid artery.

The assassin's blood spurted powerfully with the beat of his heart, shattering his professional calm. He ignored the life flowing out of him and grabbed Seeger by the shirt, pulling him up and slamming him against the edge of the wall again.

The blade fell from his hand, and he grabbed for the gun stuffed in the back of his pants, abandoning all hope of doing this quietly or learning something useful.

Lining up for a kill shot obviously wasn't going to happen, and he was forced to aim lower, hoping that a .357 round to the thigh would slow the man down enough for the blood loss to take effect.

The Indian seemed almost clairvoyant, grabbing his wrist and hammering it into the sharp edge of the brick until the weapon went cartwheeling thirty feet to the ground.

Seeger knew that if he didn't do something quickly, he'd end up lying next to it with his brains leaking all over the asphalt.

He kicked uselessly at the man's legs, trying to hook a foot around one of them as he was leaned out into the open air. It was no use. He was going over.

Seeger thought of Susie and her parents. Of his wife. And of the many friends who'd gone before him. He was suddenly overcome by the sensation that they were watching and he reached out, grabbing the Indian's chin and the back of his head in a maneuver that once would have neatly snapped his neck. He twisted as hard as he could, but the years and repeated blows to his back had taken too much out of him. All he could hope for now was that the effort didn't look pathetic to his imaginary audience.

As expected, the satisfying crack he so wanted to hear didn't materialize. What he hadn't anticipated, though, was that as the Indian's head turned, the gash in his neck opened into a gaping hole. The pulsing flow of blood intensified, spraying across his face and chest, burning his eyes and leaving the metallic taste of iron in his mouth.

Feeling a sudden glimmer of hope, Seeger gripped tighter, keeping the wound open as his one-way trip to the parking lot started to feel a bit less inevitable.

The Indian's expression became increasingly vague, and a hard shove finally toppled him onto the gravel and tar roof. Seeger scooped up the knife and dropped a knee onto the man's chest as he fought weakly to get up.

"Who the hell are you?"

The Indian clamped a hand to his neck again in a futile effort to stop what was left of him from pouring out onto the roof.

"Nobody," he choked.

"Who do you work for?" Seeger pressed. "There's no point in not telling me now, son."

The man's hand dropped away from his wound, and he turned his blood-soaked face toward the sky.

"*Who do you work for?*"

But he didn't speak again. The force of the bleeding subsided, and his gaze turned fixed, leaving Seeger to lurch toward the ladder. There was no way the dead man's team could have missed the battle on the rooftop. They would be coming.

He grabbed the rails and pressed his feet to the sides, sliding down fast enough that his bad leg nearly collapsed when it contacted the ground. He took a few steps back the way he'd come, but then stopped when he saw an armed man sprinting up what he'd hoped to use as an escape route. Seeger turned, but before he could even start in the other direction, he spotted a man rolling over the top of the fence in front of him and dropping nimbly to the ground.

He reached reflexively for his pistol, remembering it wasn't there just as both men lined up their weapons.

"Drop it!" one of them yelled.

It looked like he'd used up what was left of his luck on the rooftop. This time he was dead. Not in Afghanistan or Somalia or Iraq. At the Walmart.

There was no point in being taken alive, so he crouched and ran at the rickety fence, aiming for a badly damaged section as silencer-muffled shots filled his ears.

Anticipating the bullet impacts, he stumbled and hit the fence backward. The rotted wood gave way, and as he fell through he saw one of the men drop to the ground and the other take cover behind a Dumpster. Seeger was tumbling across the tall grass of the adjacent lot when he realized why he was still alive. They weren't shooting at him. They were shooting at each other.

The breathy thump of gunshots weren't slowing, and he leapt to his feet, sprinting as best he could for the road. It wouldn't be long before the battle behind him was decided and the winner started looking for a new target.

* * *

Seeger stayed close to the building, examining the splotchy blue RV that contained Susie Draman. A quick check of his watch suggested that she would be heading to the library to call her parents in exactly ten minutes.

Activity around the vehicle looked completely natural, and he hoped that it wasn't just a carefully orchestrated illusion—that the men at the Walmart really had been too preoccupied to track him. Hope, though, wasn't something he normally liked to rely on.

He dialed a number into a prepaid cell and held it to his ear, retreating a little farther into the shadows.

"Hello?"

"Let me talk to the doc."

"One moment."

Richard's voice sounded a bit panicked when it came on. "Why are you calling? We weren't supposed to talk until tonight. Is Susie all right? What—"

"Calm down," Seeger said. "Susie's fine. But I can't get her meds."

"Why not?"

"Because there are people all over the store."

"How—"

"My guess is that they're tied into the pharmacy computer systems. And damn near everything else as near as I can tell."

A few seconds went by before Richard spoke again. "How soon can you get here?"

"There's more, Richard. I'm pretty sure one of them was the man who showed up at my house—Mason's goon. But there was also someone here who's definitely *not* on Mason's team."

The list of people with the resources to track confidential prescriptions at national chains was fairly short, making the implication obvious: Andreas Xander.

"How soon?" Richard repeated.

"Did you know that Xander was going to have men here?"

"No, but he's been concerned about Susie. He thinks she'd be safer at the compound."

It was almost certain that the dusty old bastard was listening, but Seeger didn't care anymore. "Really, Richard? Andreas Xander's wringing his hands over the welfare of an eight-year-old girl he's never met? Exactly how likely do you think that is?"

"It doesn't really matter, does it? If you can't get her the meds she needs, then you have to bring her here. How soon?"

"Reasonably? A few days."

There was another long pause over the line. "How about unreasonably?"

55

Alberta, Canada
May 22

"Be careful, you idiot!"

The men barely managed to keep Xander's wheelchair from falling, and they paused to regain their footing before carrying him the rest of the way up the icy steps.

The burst of adrenaline he once would have felt—the racing of the heart, the sensation of wet heat in his palms—was replaced by an increasingly familiar constriction in his chest. He looked behind him to the degree his stiff neck would allow, lingering for a moment on the jagged slope of the stairs, the armed guards strategically positioned on the endless landscape, and at the darkness that he had come to fear.

The wind that had buffeted his helicopter the entire way to this empty corner of Canada began to gust again, penetrating his thick parka and then seeming to continue right through him.

It hadn't always been so. He'd started his working life at the age of fourteen, delivering ice in a horse-drawn cart. Nothing could touch him then—not the cold, not the backbreaking labor, not the sixteen-hour days.

Now he was at the mercy of everything—a sudden fright, a momentary loss of balance, an insignificant piece of food lodged in the disintegrating muscles of his throat. All he had built over the better part of a century, all he had become was slipping from him to a generation of men—and now even women—who wouldn't have endured so much as a few hours of his childhood. Privileged fools who had everything handed to them.

"Go," he said after his men set his chair down in front of the house's open front door. He listened to them retreat while his eyes adjusted to the glow coming from inside. It was a modest home by his standards, six thousand square feet of log and stone surrounded by a thousand acres of meticulously fenced pine forest.

It had taken an army of forensic accountants, but a moment of carelessness had finally been uncovered in a bank transfer done by one of the wealthy men who had disappeared over the last decade. And the unraveling of that seemingly insignificant error had led him to this place.

Xander used gloved hands to propel his wheelchair through the door, the relative warmth of the interior registering against his skin but refusing to penetrate any farther.

"Andreas!" Bill Garrison called, starting toward him from the far end of the foyer. "I hope you didn't have too much turbulence coming in."

"What have you found?" Xander said, uninterested in small talk. There was no more time.

"As near as we can tell, the house was abandoned weeks ago. It's a hell of a lot easier for them to cut connections than it is for us to make them."

The detached, businesslike demeanor that Xander had always respected in Garrison now infuriated him. He was the only one other than the Dramans who knew what was at stake, but he treated it no differently than any investigation he'd done before—just another job to pay the mortgage on his suburban home and the tuition for children who used college to escape work.

He was still young enough that his mortality was still just an occasional flash on a distant horizon. It would be years before he really understood what was at stake. What it was like to rot from within.

"We talked to people in the closest town and found a woman who worked here a few years ago. She said it was owned by an unmarried male in his mid thirties. We showed her pictures of the men we've identified digitally regressed to about that age, and she tentatively identified one of them as being him."

"Tentatively?"

"The regression algorithms aren't perfect, but I'm confident it's him."

"So what?" Xander said, trying to control a surge of the hopelessness he had managed to shake off after coming to know Richard Draman. "Where does that get us?"

"Probably nowhere," Garrison admitted. "These people have been perfecting their ability to disappear for a long time now, and they've gotten damn good at it."

"So this is nothing but another dead end?"

Letting his anger surface wasn't the release it had once been, now serving only to help obscure his exhaustion and fear. "We can't afford to always be one step behind these people, Bill."

"I'm not sure what to tell you. I'm doing everything I can."

Xander pointed to the open door. "You and your people get out. We're leaving."

Garrison nodded and started back up the hallway while Xander sat motionless, fixating on a potted tree dying of neglect in the corner.

Richard Draman had been working for five days on the materials they'd taken from August Mason's lab, and every time they spoke, it was the same story with different phrasing. Inconclusive. Making progress. Moving in the right direction. All words that Xander had come to recognize as the platitudes of people who had no idea what they were doing.

It was time to admit that it could be ten years before Draman discovered anything useful and even longer before Garrison got close enough to one of these people to capture them. Time that Xander's doctors all agreed he didn't have.

He propelled himself down the hallway, looking for answers in the belongings of a man who had beat death, who had cut the last thing that tied him to the ordinary people milling about in the streets leading their useless lives. A man who knew what it was like to feel his strength flood back to him.

People began appearing in the hallway, careful to avert their eyes as they passed on their way to the front door. By the time Garrison materialized, the house had descended into complete silence.

"I'll be outside if you need anything, Andreas."

Xander continued to stare blankly at the fading tree, momentarily lost in the past. When he heard the door close behind him, he rolled toward a small table and laid a sealed envelope on it.

The address consisted of two words scrawled in his own shaky hand.

The Immortalists.

56

Upstate New York
May 22

Richard Draman pulled away from the microscope and looked up at the cameras bolted to the ceiling. For the better part of a week, he'd been a full-time resident of the temporary lab Xander had sealed him up in—allowed only a few short conversations with Carly and Susie. A subtle reminder that his life was no longer his own. That they existed only to carry out the old man's wishes.

He went back to the microscope, knowing that it was critical to maintain the appearance of deciphering August Mason's life's work. That's all it was at this point, though—a pageant designed to convince an increasingly desperate Andreas Xander that immortality, and not death, waited for him just around the corner.

The vial they'd found contained various viruses and bacteria, some of which he could identify and others that he couldn't. Their function was clear, though—to invade cells and deposit tiny strands of genetic material that would transform the subject's genome in a way never intended by nature.

But how? What sections of DNA were targeted? From what creatures were the replacement strands taken or were they entirely engineered? How would the patient's immune system react to the carrier germs? Those were just a few of the thousand questions he hadn't been able to answer.

The bottom line was that it was hopeless. Even with an army of the top people, it would take them years to understand what Mason had done—

maybe decades. But he didn't have years, or even months. The carriers in the serum were starting to die. It seemed likely that this dose had been created for someone specific and that long-term storage hadn't been the goal.

Based on his best estimate, the serum would lose enough of its potency to be ineffective in another week. Seven days and it would be over. For everyone.

Richard stood, trying to move naturally beneath the cameras. He opened the refrigerator and used a key hanging around his neck to pull the vial from a strongbox inside.

His hand shook as he put it in a centrifuge that contained an identical vial quietly planted there that morning. Since his arrival, he'd spent more time studying the security procedures than he had Mason's elixir. He'd eaten lunches with the guards, charted their shift changes, calculated every camera angle.

There were a number of places in the lab that the monitors outside couldn't display—the most useful being the centrifuge he was now standing in front of. Richard pressed a button, gave it a brief spin, and then removed the decoy vial, returning it to the lockbox in the refrigerator after putting a small drop on a slide. He didn't allow himself to look at the door, but listened intently, half expecting the guards to burst in, aware of his deception.

But there was nothing. Just the incessant hum of the ventilation system.

By the time he returned to his microscope, the shaking in his hands had worsened significantly, and the sweat had turned frigid across his back.

It was more than just fear. The brush of his clothes against his skin was starting to feel like sandpaper, and the cramps in his stomach were becoming powerful enough to cause him to jerk forward a few inches when they struck.

The men watching him weren't stupid, and it seemed unlikely that he could fake a situation dire enough to cause them to disregard their orders to keep him there, so about an hour ago, he'd poisoned himself.

It had been a bit more complicated than he'd thought. In college, no classes had been offered on how to make yourself look like you're going to die without actually crossing the line into reality. When the room started to turn vaguely liquid, he wondered if he'd pushed too far. It was his one chance, though, and a little indigestion wasn't going to convince Xander's minions to defy his godlike wishes.

Richard's first attempt to stand produced no result at all, and for a moment, he felt panic overcome his growing nausea. He closed his eyes and saw his daughter—her birth as a healthy baby, the first signs of her disease. Her unwavering belief in him.

His second attempt was more successful, and he lurched across the room toward the centrifuge, starting to fall a few feet short of it but managing to catch himself on the counter. Reaching up in a way calculated to look like he was steadying himself, he managed to get a sweaty palm around the vial containing Mason's serum before he slid to the floor.

A moment later, the door behind him was thrown open, and he rolled onto his side, letting his lab coat fall across him as he slid the delicate vial into the pocket of his jeans.

"Doc! Are you all right?"

Richard looked into the face of the man hovering over him. Behind, another guard had his gun out and was looking intently around the room for danger.

"No."

"What's wrong? What happened?"

"I was—" Richard started, but a wave of cramps forced him into the fetal position. He didn't know what dying felt like, but he was pretty sure this was it. He'd taken too much.

"I was handling a dangerous chemical earlier," he said through short gasps. "I dropped some, but I didn't think any got on me..."

"It's poisonous?" the man said. "Are you telling me you've been poisoned?"

Richard nodded weakly. "You need to get me to a hospital."

The man's expression turned from one of alarm to one of uncertainty. "There are people out there trying to kill you, Doc. Mr. Xander made it clear that—"

Richard clamped a hand over the man's muscular forearm. "If I don't get to a hospital now, their job will be done for them."

57

1,800 Miles East of Australia
May 22

The heat and steepness of the slope finally became too much, and Oleg Nazarov was forced to stop. The bugs he'd been barely keeping ahead of immediately swarmed, and he struggled not to suck them in with every ragged breath. Above, the jungle canopy shut out the sky and reverberated with the light rain that had enveloped the island for the last two days.

"Are you all right, sir?"

The security guard sent to escort him on his hike had stopped at a respectful distance, the only sweat visible on him a dark outline beneath his shoulder holster. He peered into the jungle, keeping up the halfhearted appearance that he was there to protect Nazarov when they both knew he was there to watch him.

The Russian put his hands on his hips and bent at the waist, losing himself for a moment in memories of his early days at the KGB. He'd always been the strongest and fastest—able to continue on tirelessly after the other recruits gave up. The instructors had acted unimpressed while quietly designating him as someone with a future.

The past was something that had never interested him, but he found himself thinking about it more and more as he got older. His victories and defeats. His regrets. In some ways, those long-dead images were beginning to feel more tangible than his future.

"Sir?" the security man prompted. "We should turn around now. We're getting close to a restricted area."

Nazarov didn't immediately respond, instead watching the guard in his peripheral vision. He was typical: mid thirties, seemingly chiseled from stone. Like he himself had once been.

"All right. Just let me rest for another moment."

He nodded and looked back the way they'd come, undoubtedly anxious to end the tedium of marching through the jungle at an old man's pace. Nazarov's attention fell to the rock that had inspired him to stop. It was about eight inches long and shaped like a blunt arrowhead.

When the younger man had turned fully away, Nazarov scooped it up and strode toward him, covering the distance as quickly as he could without allowing his footsteps to sound unnaturally rushed.

He thought the kill would be simple and clean, but at the last moment, his victim craned his neck. "Are you read—"

He threw up a tattooed arm, but it was too late. The point of the rock came down just above the right side of his forehead, crushing the bone and penetrating his brain.

He didn't immediately fall, instead standing frozen, the blood running thick into his eye and then fanning out across his damp cheek.

Nazarov unsnapped the shoulder holster and relieved him of his gun as he sank. Allies could be so much more dangerous than enemies—an important lesson that would be this young man's last. One that he himself was now forced to act on.

There was a long and perfectly legitimate list of reasons for his failure to resolve the Draman issue. But Karl—and indeed he himself—were not men interested in reasons. One performed or one did not. And for the first time in his life, Nazarov found himself in the latter category.

He had been backed into making guarantees that his plan to capture Susie Draman would succeed, and a few hours ago it became clear that things had once again not gone according to plan. It was, as the Americans were so fond of saying, his third strike.

Nazarov dragged the body into the jungle and then continued up the trail. The area ahead was restricted for a reason—it contained the island's hangar and airstrip. Something Nazarov very much needed to avail himself of.

58

**Upstate New York
May 22**

The air coming through the open back window felt as though it were slashing through the skin on his face, but it was something to focus on— something to keep him from throwing up.

"You gonna make it, Doc?" the driver said, staring at him in the rear- view mirror while his partner spoke urgently into a phone.

Richard didn't respond, trying unsuccessfully to determine who the man in the passenger seat was talking to and what he was saying.

Beyond their headlights and the headlights of a chase vehicle fifty feet behind, there was nothing but darkness. Richard hung an arm on the win- dowsill, using it to keep himself upright enough that he could see out. His stomach cramped and he bit down hard, barely managing to hold down its contents. Next time, he knew, he wouldn't be so lucky.

The easily described landmark he was hoping for hadn't materialized. The terrain rolled monotonously, carpeted with wild grass and bordered by a wire fence gleaming in the circle of light they were generating. No trees, no houses. No nothing.

"Doc? We're not too far from the hospital. No more than twenty min- utes. Hold on for me, OK?"

Richard wasn't sure which one of the men had spoken, but he registered for the first time emotion in the voice. Not concern for him as much as fear for themselves. Andreas Xander wouldn't be happy if the man he was count- ing on to conjure him a future expired in the backseat of one of his Yukons.

"Doc?"

The lights reflected off a sign ahead, and Richard squinted through watering eyes at it. As they drew nearer, the white numbers grew in prominence. He leaned farther out the window, ignoring the increasing force of the wind lashing him.

It was a mile marker. Number forty-eight.

"Stop the car," Richard said, his voice carrying more force than he expected. He was running out of time. And so was Susie.

"What?" the man in the passenger seat said. "Take it easy, Doc. We're not fa—"

Richard grabbed the handle and pulled it, unlatching the door.

"Shit!" he heard the driver yell. They were probably traveling close to eighty, and Richard was in no condition to anticipate the effect of the sudden deceleration. The door swung outward with his arm still hanging through the open window dragging him toward the speeding asphalt below.

His mind couldn't react fast enough to follow what was happening, and he didn't fully grasp that he hadn't fallen until the vehicle had come to a complete stop. When he glanced back, he saw that the man in the passenger seat was on his knees with a hand tangled in his lab coat.

Richard swung a foot out of the vehicle and stretched his arms behind him, slipping out of the coat and stumbling across the gravel shoulder toward the scrub brush beyond. He heard a door being thrown open behind him, but he kept going, not dropping to his knees until he had escaped the lights of the chase vehicle that had skidded to a stop behind them.

His stomach cramped again, and this time he let his dinner flood out into the bush in front of him. The man who had kept him from falling from the car was hovering about fifteen feet back.

"Doc, we can't stay here. We've got to get going."

Richard signaled for him to keep his distance and turned away again, convulsing uncontrollably for a few moments before managing to look back. There were four men in all, and with the exception of the one directly behind him, all were focused on the surrounding darkness and the army it might contain.

The way he'd seen it in his mind, he'd had more distance, more darkness, and the cover of his lab coat. But none of that was going to happen. There would never be another chance.

When the man behind him briefly turned his attention to his companions, Richard pulled the vial from his pocket and tucked it beneath the branches of the bush in front of him. He was brushing some dirt toward it when he was grabbed from behind.

"All right, Doc. That's it."

He fought weakly, certain that he'd been found out, but no one made a move for the vial, and he felt himself being dragged toward the car.

"Shit, man. Relax, would you? We're gonna get you to the hospital and everything's gonna be fine, OK?"

59

1,800 Miles East of Australia
May 23

Oleg Nazarov considered ducking into the jungle and creeping up on the hangar from behind, but almost immediately discarded the idea. Those types of operations were long behind him. What little fitness he had left was solely the result of his fondness for young women. Hardly sufficient preparation.

What he did have—all he had—was the illusion of authority. And so that's what would be used.

He increased his pace as the edge of the hangar came into view, trying to dig the details of flying from the fog of his memory. It had been almost a quarter century since he'd piloted a plane, and as he recalled, his ability had been only barely above average. None of that mattered, though. He preferred to hang his future on those questionable skills than Karl's mercy.

The hangar bay door was open, and Nazarov entered, his eyes struggling to adjust to the lower level of light. There was only a single plane inside, a small Lear similar to one he'd owned in the mid nineties. He regretted now sitting in the back drinking vodka while his pilots chauffeured him around the world, but he was confident he had gleaned enough to get into the air. Landing was something he could worry about later.

He continued forward cautiously, looking for security but finding none. It seemed too easy, and he moved a hand closer to the stolen gun tucked into his waistband.

"Hello?"

Nothing. Just the sound of the rain on the roof and the distant calls of tropical birds.

"Is anyone here?" he said a bit louder, continuing toward the open hatch of the Lear.

Again, nothing.

He started up the steps thinking that his luck might have finally changed, but that illusion disappeared when he entered the cabin.

"Oleg. I was starting to think you'd lost your way."

Karl was sitting in the seat at the back, his hands resting on the table in front of him.

Nazarov reached for his gun, but then felt the barrel of a pistol make contact with his temple. He'd let Karl distract him from the man pressed against the wall next to the hatch. An amateur's mistake.

His weapon was taken from him and tossed out into the hangar. The clack of it skittering across the concrete floor sounded very much like his last hope disintegrating.

"I was out hiking," he said, stammering perceptibly. "The man I was with fell. He…"

"I completely understand," Karl said, standing and motioning toward the hatch. "We appreciate you coming here to try to find help. Unfortunately, it's too late. My understanding is that he's dead."

Nazarov descended the steps obediently, finding that the security people so conspicuously missing when he arrived were everywhere now. They watched silently as Karl came alongside him and angled toward the open hangar door.

It had been a plan born entirely of desperation, Nazarov recognized now. The idea that he would just stroll onto Karl's plane, taxi it to the runway, and take off unchallenged seemed almost laughable. And even if he had succeeded—where could he have gone that would be beyond the group's reach?

They walked in silence, turning onto a steep trail that led toward the coast. "It's my understanding that Burt Seeger wasn't acquired at the pharmacy and that he killed one of our men," Karl said finally.

"That's correct."

"I also understand that Xander had people there."

Nazarov was having a hard time holding the pace Karl's newfound youth allowed him, and he struggled to speak evenly. "We dealt with the body and haven't had to do anything to cover up the gunfight. Xander used his influence to deal with that for us. The public will never know any of it happened."

"Yes, but *I* know."

Silence once again descended on them, lasting until they exited the jungle onto a flat expanse of stone. Karl walked straight to the edge and looked down the hundred meters to the ocean. The sun reflected off the water, contrasting deep blue with frothing white as it impacted the cliffs. Under other circumstances, it would have been startlingly beautiful.

"Do you know how Seeger knew your men were waiting for him?"

"It's impossible that he saw any of them," Nazarov said, not quite coming up alongside Karl. The height and the chaos of the waves only added to his sense of dread.

"All evidence to the contrary, Oleg."

"It was a perfect operation. I can show you. It was meticulously planned. It was —"

Karl reached into his pocket and held out an envelope.

"What is this?" Nazarov said, accepting it and looking down on the shaky scrawl across the front.

The Immortalists.

He unfolded the sheet of paper it contained and began reading, the words draining what little strength he had left.

"Xander left it at our property in Canada yesterday," Karl said.

"Yesterday? But how—"

"The car you destroyed was a decoy. Xander is still alive. Still dismantling our networks. Still in possession of the contents of Mason's lab."

"He won't find any of our people. I've—"

"You've done what?" Karl shouted. "What is it exactly that you've done for us, Oleg?"

"Xander's health is deteriorating," Nazarov responded. "He's dying. He may not last the month."

"Or he may live for another decade," Karl said. "We didn't bring you in so that we could hope our problems die of natural causes."

Nazarov took another step away from the precipice, spotting two armed men hovering at the edge of the jungle. "These things were beyond my control. They—"

"I know," Karl said, plucking the letter from his hand and holding it up. "But with this in my possession, I have to wonder what purpose you serve."

Nazarov waited for the security men to pull their guns, but they just stood there. Watching.

He was so focused on them, he didn't see Karl's foot swing toward his knee. The joint, already weakened by arthritis, broke easily, and Nazarov screamed as his leg collapsed beneath him. Pain consumed his mind, blurring the image of Karl as he moved behind him.

"I had hoped for more from you," he said, threading an arm around Nazarov's neck. The Russian clawed uselessly at the damp stone beneath him as he was dragged backward.

Lack of oxygen and panic weakened him, but he didn't allow himself to stop fighting. He managed to get hold of Karl's ankle as he felt himself being spun to face the cliff. His legs dangled over it, buffeted by the salty wind coming up from the water.

The pressure around his neck disappeared, and he gasped for air as Karl began prying his fingers from his ankle. Nazarov heard one of his fingers snap, but this time he didn't feel anything. His mind had reached its limit and couldn't process any more.

He went for a tiny sapling growing from a crack in the rock, missing it by less than a centimeter. A moment later, everything faded away—the tropical heat, Karl, gravity. He was floating, spinning, surrounded by the roar of the ocean.

Karl leaned out over the precipice and watched the waves pound Oleg's mangled body, finally dislodging it from the boulders and pulling it under. The letter had fallen to the ground, and he picked it up, tucking it carefully back into his pocket.

It was time to end this.

60

**Upstate New York
May 24**

Burt Seeger took a few more steps forward, shielded his eyes from the rising sun, and examined the rolling rural highway. It probably never got much traffic, but at this time of morning, it was nothing more than an empty black ribbon cutting through grass and scrub.

The stillness and silence were comforting in that anyone approaching would be obvious, but nerve-racking in that their presence was as obvious as the proverbial sore thumb.

He turned east and paused, watching Susie trudge along in her stocking cap and Flintstones parka. A pair of oversized sunglasses perched precariously on her nose, serving the dual purpose of disguising her tragically memorable features and keeping the glare down as she continued her search of the bushes.

It was good to see her out of the musty RV and in the sunshine where children belonged. She slept more and more as the weeks went on, and she got dead still when she did. It was probably nothing more than the deep sleep that was one of the many wonders of youth, but it scared the hell out of him. He was up no less than ten times a night checking on her.

"How're you coming along?" he called.

She looked up from the ground and shook her head. "I've found four rusty cans and a dirty old pack of cigarettes."

"You might be getting a little far from the road. Come back in a little and stay sharp. It's a contest, you know. Who's going to find it first?"

"What are you going to give me if I win?"

"I don't know. What are you going to give me if *I* win?"

"You're not gonna!" she said, adjusting her trajectory and nudging a particularly dense bush with her toe.

They'd been about a hundred and fifty miles away when he'd gotten a call from Richard that lasted probably less than ten seconds—just a rough location, what to look for, and instructions on how to contact him when they found it. Seeger wondered if there would be anyone to contact, though. Richard sounded like he had one foot in the grave and the other on a sheet of ice.

He started forward again, walking in a zigzag pattern five feet wide, focusing tired eyes on the ground. While it was true that he still hadn't figured out how to get Susie's medication and he was just one old man pitted against what looked like an army of mercenaries and intelligence operatives, he believed Andreas Xander to be no different than the men they were running from. And, as it turned out, Richard felt the same way. The young scientist wasn't as naïve as he seemed.

But it was more than that. Seeger just didn't want to give her up. The life he'd led before seemed so distant now—the purposeless days, the loneliness. He didn't want to go back to that. Ever.

"Gross!"

He turned and spotted Susie fifty feet away, using a stick to poke at something on the ground.

"What is it?" he said, running toward her as best his leg would allow. "Did you find something?"

She nodded, the disgust etched into her ancient face. "I think this is where Dad threw up."

"Great job!" Seeger said, dropping to his knees and feeling around in the grass. "I knew those eagle eyes of yours would come in handy."

"Does this mean we're going to live with Mom and Dad now? That's what you said, right? That we're going to go stay with them?"

"I'm not sure; we'll have to talk to your father."

"But you said—"

"I know what I said, Susie, but what we need to do now is keep looking, OK?"

Her lower lip quivered for a moment, but then she eased herself to her knees and began digging around in the shrub next to him.

Less than fifteen seconds passed before she came up with a small glass vial. "Is this it?"

Seeger grabbed it and stared down at the sun filtering through the cloudy fluid inside. He put a hand out and helped Susie to her feet. "You beat me. You win the grand prize! But first, let's get the heck out of here."

They hurried back to the RV, and she locked the door behind them as he dialed his cell and started the engine.

When the hospital receptionist answered, he gave the fictitious name Richard had told him to use. A moment later he was connected.

"Hello?"

"You sound better," Seeger said. "What—"

"Did you get it?"

Richard's voice was weak, but the mix of emotions was still clearly audible. Relief. Fear. Uncertainty.

"Yeah. What's in it? Is it what I think it is?" Seeger said, speaking quietly. Susie had slipped into bed and appeared to be asleep already.

"I hope so."

"What do you mean, you—"

"Do you still have syringes?"

"A few. Richard, what—"

"I want you to inject Susie with the contents of the vial."

"You just told me that you're not sure what it is."

"We don't have time to argue, Burt. I've got four of Xander's men sitting right outside my door."

"Bullshit. You're asking me to shoot something into her that you're not sure about? How much? What's it going to do?"

"All of it. And I don't know."

Seeger lowered his voice even further. "What the hell do you mean, you don't know? What if it kills her?"

Silence.

"Jesus Christ, Richard. I'm not going to do it. I—"

"There's no choice, Burt. You've been with her long enough now. Long enough to see what's happening."

"Do you understand what you're asking me to do? You're not the one with the needle. You're not the one who would have to stand here and watch her…" He couldn't finish the sentence.

"This is my decision, Burt. If something happens to her, it's my fault, not yours."

61

**Upstate New York
May 24**

"I can't believe you did this to yourself. You're usually so careful."

Carly dabbed a cool cloth on his forehead as he sank deeper into the pillows. The hospital had released him that morning to an ambulance that had brought him back to Xander's compound in a motorcade that now appeared to include air support.

"Richard? Are you in there? Are you OK?"

He forced a weak smile. In a way, he'd never been happier to see anyone in his life. But in another way he was terrified—of her, of being back in the luxurious prison Xander had created for them. Of what he'd done.

He squeezed her hand with what little strength he'd regained. "I'm just a little tired and sore. I'll be fine."

"Come on. I know you. It's more than just—"

He put a finger to her mouth and pulled her close enough that the listening devices they assumed covered the room couldn't pick up his voice. "We need to talk."

"What's going on? You're starting to—"

The phone on the nightstand began to ring, and he nearly knocked her off the bed grabbing for it.

"Hello?"

"I called when I got into town like you said. But someone I didn't recognize picked up."

Burt Seeger's voice, following the script they'd created on what Richard prayed had been an untapped hospital line.

"I had an accident at the lab and had to go to the hospital. I'm OK now, though. You can bring her in."

As planned, there was a long silence over the phone. Richard slid off the bed and hobbled to the window as his wife looked on. The fear was so deeply etched in her face that he had to turn away, gazing out over the well-lit property and the security people patrolling it.

"I'm not so sure," Seeger said finally.

"What?"

"How do I know you haven't been compromised?"

"Look, I'm at Xander's house right now. We can send some of his people to meet—"

"How would I know they're his people? How would I know they weren't the men who came to my house to kill me?"

"We don't have time to screw around," Richard said, affecting just a touch of anger. "Susie needs her medications, and you're telling me you can't get them. Would I be asking you to bring her if it wasn't safe?"

"No offense, Doc, but you don't seem all that tough to me. A few bamboo shoots under your nails and who knows what they could get you to say."

"Goddamnit, she's my daughter! You're going to do whatever the hell I tell you."

Carly came up beside him, fear now turning to terror. He shot her a reassuring glance, but she barely noticed.

"Here's what I'm going to do," Seeger said. "I'm going to get me and Susie to a safe distance, and then I'm gonna call you back. At that point, we can figure out how you're going to convince me everything's OK."

"No way. We—"

"The plan's not negotiable, Doc. That's the way it's going to be."

Richard let out a long, frustrated breath that sounded surprisingly convincing. "If anything happens to her..." He let his voice fade for a moment. "How is she?"

"Not so good. She's sick—running a fever a little over a hundred and one."

That wasn't on the script, and Richard felt his mouth go dry. He tried to tell himself that it was to be expected—that her immune system was attacking the serum's carrier germs—but it didn't help.

"I put her in a cool shower, and I'm giving her aspirin," Seeger said. "That seems to be controlling it. For now."

"If you have *any* reason to think she's getting worse, you call me immediately. Any time day or night. Do you understand? Or I'll come out there and track you down myself."

"I'll be in touch."

The line went dead, and Richard stared down at the phone in his hand.

"What's going on?" Carly whispered. "What's wrong?"

He turned on the television, and they stood directly in front of the speakers, letting the sound mask their conversation.

"I have something to say to you. But I need to you stay calm and speak very quietly."

"What?" she said, terror now becoming to panic. "Is something wrong with Susie? Where is—"

"Just listen to me, OK? You need to be quiet and listen."

She took a deep breath and nodded.

"I poisoned myself on purpose to get out of the lab. I stole the serum and left it by the side of the road for Burt."

"I don't understand."

"He injected Susie with it."

She blinked a few times, obviously having a hard time processing what she'd heard. "You figured out how it works? Already? Oh my God, is it going to—"

A brief shake of his head silenced her.

"I was never going to figure it out, Carly. And in another week, whatever's in that vial would have deteriorated to the point of being unusable."

"What do you mean, 'whatever's in that vial'? You don't know what you gave our daughter?"

He didn't answer, just standing there watching the blood drain from his wife's face.

"Tell me!" she said, the volume of her voice rising dangerously. "Is that what you did? Is it?"

"There was no choice, Carly—"

"But you said that that vial could be anything. It could be incomplete or a thousand doses. It could have been left there on purpose so Xander would find it. What if that's what they did? What if they left it there? What if it's…"

Her eyes seemed to lose focus, and he reached for her, thinking for a moment she was going to pass out. Instead, she jerked back and pushed him away. "You didn't say anything. You didn't ask me. That se—"

He clamped a hand over her mouth, but she wasn't going to be so easily silenced. A hard shove almost toppled him in his weakened state, but he kept his grip on her and managed to spin her onto the bed, landing his superior weight on top of her.

"Carly—" he said as she tried to squirm out from beneath him.

After a few seconds, she resigned herself to the fact that she couldn't escape and went still, turning her head to stare at the wall.

"What about her?" she said when he removed his hand. "Did you ask her?"

In a way, he was he was glad she wouldn't look at him. The betrayal and horror in her eyes made it hard for him to breathe. He'd gambled everything—his wife, his daughter. In the end, maybe even his own sanity.

The sound of a hand on the doorknob was quickly followed by the door to the room being thrown open. Richard pushed himself off his wife and struggled to his feet, grabbing hold of a piece of furniture to help him support his weight. "What the hell's going on? What do you want?"

"Come with us," one of the men who entered said.

"I just got out of the hospital," Richard said, trying to buy time. Had they heard? Did they have video cameras that allowed them to read lips?

The lead guard strode across the room and grabbed his arm, pulling him toward the door. His companion took a similar hold of Carly, but she didn't seem to notice as she was dragged from the bed and into the hallway.

62

Upstate New York
May 24

Richard hadn't known this wing of the house even existed. Based on the length of the stairs they'd just descended, the endless corridor they were walking down was deep underground—cut off from everything above. No sound got through, and the air had a stale, recycled feel to it.

He glanced back at the men following them and at Carly, whose daze had deepened to a state bordering on catatonia. He knew what she was going through—that her soul was being consumed by the same thing his had been for so long: visions of the day Susie wasn't with them anymore.

They passed through a set of doors at the end of the hallway and found themselves in what could have been the intensive care unit at the Mayo Clinic. The walls were an unblemished white, the equipment was state-of-the-art, and everything smelled vaguely of antiseptic. There was one important difference, though. Everything was centered on one bed.

The security guards took up positions on either side of the door as he and Carly continued unbidden toward the facility's lone patient. When they got within ten feet, Xander flicked a hand at the man taking his blood pressure, and he scurried from the room.

"You both look like shit."

Richard was too nervous to respond, and Carly gave no indication that she'd even heard.

The pillow propped behind the old man was the only thing keeping him upright, and his normal pallor had become a near translucence, as though he was starting to disappear. Next to him, a heart monitor beeped out an alarmingly erratic rhythm.

"My doctor tells me that I've had another cardiac episode. He says it was minor, but we both know that nothing at my age is minor. The next one isn't far off, and it'll most likely kill me."

He moved a bruised arm with difficulty, pointing to a shelf next to the bed. Richard hadn't noticed the metal box, but immediately recognized it.

"I want you to give me the serum."

"What?" Richard said. "No."

"I'm not asking you. I'm telling you."

Richard felt his mouth go dry as he grasped for excuses. "I…it could kill you. We don't even know what it is."

Not exactly true. It was saline with a few inert additives to make it match the appearance of Mason's concoction.

"Yeah, it might kill me. But I figure not taking it will *definitely* kill me."

"What about our daughter?" Carly said, suddenly coming back to life. Her voice sounded strangely far away. "What about all the other people it could help?"

Her words cut both ways, though Richard couldn't discern whether it was intentional. His logic had been exactly the same as Xander's when he'd decided to give Susie the serum. He'd never even considered the other children or the rest of the world when the moment came.

"I spent millions getting my hands on that goddamn vial," Xander said. "And I gave your husband every chance to study it. But he's gotten nowhere. Your daughter and all those other people are going to die because *he* failed. Not because I did."

"You've had your life," Carly said. "What makes you think you deserve another one?"

Xander's chapped lips curled into a barely perceptible smile, and he motioned to one of the men standing by the door.

"I hoped we could keep this civil, but I guess I didn't really expect it." The guard stopped a few feet away and aimed a gun at Carly's head.

"Wait!" Richard said. Carly didn't react at all. She just stared down in disgust at the dying man in front of her.

"Wait for what, Richard? Everything that happens from now on is up to you. It always was."

"You win, Andreas. Tell him to lower the gun."

Xander nodded, and the man returned to his position near the entrance.

Richard tore the wrapper off a syringe and opened the box, carefully sucking the useless fluid from the vial.

"I assume you understand the precarious situation you're in," Xander said, closing his eyes when the needle penetrated, trying to feel inviolable laws of nature being reversed inside his withered body. "The world thinks you're dead. And the few people out there who know the truth are committed to making the world right."

"Your point?" Richard said, disposing of the syringe and pressing a cotton ball against Xander's shoulder.

"My point is that if I ever thought my health wasn't your primary concern, you wouldn't be much use to me, would you? I mean, there would be no reason for me not to have my people march you right out our front gate. No money, no transportation, no identification. Just the clothes on your back. How long do you think you'd last?"

"What happens if I do everything I can but you still die?"

"The exact same thing. So, for your own sake, I'd suggest you don't let that happen."

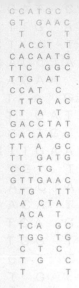

63

Upstate New York
May 25

Richard looked at the clock next to the bed for the hundredth time that night and then went back to staring at the dark ceiling: 2:38 a.m.

Carly was lying next to him, though she'd scooted as far to her edge as possible. Her breathing lacked the deep rhythm he'd come to know over the years, suggesting that she too was awake.

They'd barely spoken since he'd told her what he did. After he gave Xander the fake serum, she'd disappeared to start dinner for the men imprisoning them there—for the man who had just put a gun to her head. The kitchen had always been a place of sanctuary for her. Somewhere she could think or just lose herself. When she'd finally returned at ten thirty, she showered and climbed into bed without a word.

He, on the other hand, had spent the day trying to put order to the partially built lab in Xander's attic. Much of the equipment was still in boxes, and wires still hung uselessly from the walls, but the workers and their tools were nowhere to be found. Now that the old man believed he'd used the only dose of the serum, he'd lost all interest in how it worked or if it could be mass-produced. Richard had assumed that some provision would be made for discovering the secrets of the most valuable—and potentially profitable—product in the world. But on reflection, he shouldn't have been surprised. Men like Xander pursued money and power not because they needed it but to set themselves apart from the rest of humanity. If everyone lived forever, the value of immortality would be badly diluted.

And so he was allowed to continue to putter around in the lab under the constant scrutiny of the security cameras, but the truth was that his only purpose now was to usher Xander down the path to godhood.

Richard let his head loll to the right and watched the side of his wife's face in the dim glow of the clock. He was conjuring the courage to touch her, to try one more time to explain, when the phone on the nightstand rang.

A powerful surge of adrenaline was followed by an equally powerful wave of nausea as he grabbed for it.

"Hello?"

"She's got a rash all over her, and her temperature hit a hundred and three an hour ago," Burt Seeger said by way of greeting.

Carly leaned into him, though he suspected the physical contact was nothing more than a by-product of her trying to hear.

"Can she keep down fluids?"

"I don't know; I can't get any into her. She won't wake up, Richard. I need to take her to a hospital."

"No," he said, knowing that the first thing they'd do would be to give her antibiotics and antivirals that would kill the carrier germs. "No doctors. No hospitals."

"I know you're supposed to be some kind of genius, but I've watched young guys who could run thirty miles without breaking a sweat get dehydrated and die over the course of a few hours. She's—"

"*No hospitals*," Richard said, barely managing to get in enough air speak. It felt like someone was piling weights on his chest. "Do you understand me? Put her in cool water, and when she wakes up give her—"

"I've done that, Richard. At the very least, she needs an IV. I—"

"Then get her one."

"Where? At the 7-Eleven?"

"You're a resourceful guy."

"Fuck you," he said, veering well off their script. "I'm bringing her in. You know how to take care of her."

"No. You can't ever bring her here. Ever."

He half expected the line to be disconnected by the men he knew were listening, but it didn't happen. Xander had undoubtedly told them to get all the information they could on Susie.

"This is bullshit," Seeger said, his voice shaking audibly. "You aren't here watching this. You aren't the one who's going to be digging a hole for her in some field when she dies. I've already been through this, Richard. I'm not doing it again."

"You need to—" Richard started, but Seeger cut him off.

"Put Carly on. I want to talk to her. Now."

He tilted the phone in her direction, unsure what she was going to say.

"You need to do exactly what Richard tells you."

There was a long silence before Seeger responded. "Fine. She's your kid."

The line went dead, and Richard put the handset back in its cradle. When he turned to his wife, she reached up and caressed his cheek.

"I wasn't ready," she whispered, tears barely visible in the gloom. "It's funny, isn't it? You spend years preparing for it, seeing what the other parents go through, telling yourself that one day something…irreversible will happen. But when the time comes, it doesn't mean anything."

His throat had constricted to the point that he didn't think he could speak, so he just wrapped his arms around her.

"What's going to happen to her, Richard? Is she going to be all right?"

The truth was that his hope was beginning to fade. Susie just wasn't strong enough to handle a process this violent. The germ invasion was only the first step. If she managed to get through it, the next step would be surviving the stress of her body going full tilt to repair the damage done by her disease. He couldn't help comparing the pale, overweight scientist August Mason had been when he disappeared with the tan athlete he'd become when he returned to the world. Had that transformation been necessary to meet physical demands of the treatment?

"I don't know," he said so quietly that even he barely heard. "I just don't know."

She lay on her side, pulling him down with her. "I suppose she has as good a chance as we do. It would be funny, wouldn't it? If she lives forever and neither of us make it to forty? I wouldn't care. She deserves that."

"We all deserve that."

A short, bitter laugh escaped her. "Xander will never let us go. He's going to listen to that call, and he's going to notice he's not getting younger. Eventually, he'll figure out what you've done. He's an evil man, Richard. I truly believe that. But he's not stupid."

"Then maybe we should leave."

Another laugh, just as humorless as the first. "Do you know many how men he has here?"

"No."

"I do. I feed them. Forty-eight, plus dogs. And there's not one of them that would give a second thought to killing both of us if Xander gave the order."

"What if I told you I had a plan?" Richard said. "Something I was working on in the lab today."

"Are you serious?"

"I don't want to oversell it. The chances of it working are probably somewhere between slim and none."

"I have to see her again, Richard. Even if it's just to say good-bye, I have to see her again."

"Then you're in?"

She nodded. "I always have been."

64

Upstate New York
May 26

Xander was out of bed and back in his wheelchair, though still reliant on an IV and oxygen bottle. He drooped sideways slightly, one hand seemingly paralyzed and lying palm up on the blanket covering his legs.

Richard approached quietly, unsure if he was asleep. The old man seemed incredibly small in the expanse of the bedroom, as though he were a piece of furniture that had been set out to be discarded.

"I don't feel younger," Xander said, opening red-rimmed eyes.

"I wouldn't expect you to. If anything, the amount of energy this is going to take will probably make you feel worse. Besides, it's only been two days. The kinds of genetic changes we're talking about will take time."

Richard went to a medical cabinet disguised as a wardrobe and took out a syringe. "Have you been feeling abnormally tired?"

"What the hell are you talking about?" Xander said, but his voice didn't carry the weight it had even a week ago. It wouldn't be long now—a day, a month. And Richard had no doubt that the vindictive bastard was being honest about the orders he'd left.

"How about abnormal joint pain," Richard said, preparing the syringe. "That's something else I'd expect to see."

Xander thought about it. "My knees have been keeping me awake at night. And my back…"

254

Richard nodded sagely. It was something he'd learned from working with cancer patients: desperation made people highly susceptible to the power of suggestion.

"What's that?" Xander said, nodding toward the needle.

"I'm just going to take a little blood."

"What for?"

In truth, he was concerned that Xander would lock him out of the lab, and he couldn't allow that. Not yet.

"I'm looking for increased cell renewal and hormonal changes—anything that could indicate that the aging process is reversing and give me an idea of how quickly. Because of your physical condition, it makes sense to try to anticipate the process and any problems it might cause you."

Xander stared at him as he tried to find a useable vein. "How's your daughter?"

It was a question he was prepared for. In fact, he was surprised it hadn't come sooner. "She's ill."

"Is she going to die?"

The direct wording was obviously calculated to crack Richard's defenses, but it wasn't going to be that easy. "Someday, Andreas. Just like the rest of us."

65

**Upstate New York
May 27**

Richard pretended to gaze at Xander's blood sample through the microscope, but he was actually concentrating on the clock in his peripheral vision. The second hand had just swept past noon, and if Carly was anything, it was punctual. She'd spent half her life standing by the door waiting impatiently for him and Susie to find shoes and wallets, finish video games and book chapters, or tap in the last line of an e-mail.

She finally entered at nearly one minute past the hour, his lunch neatly arranged on a tray. Roast beef sandwiches and fries, if he correctly remembered the schedule posted next to the kitchen.

She seemed particularly beautiful that day—the dark hair skimming across her forehead, the immaculate chef's jacket and wool slacks. In truth, she looked like she always did when she was working, but his realization that this could be their last day together amplified everything he loved in her.

She set the tray down on a plywood countertop and gave him her customary peck on the lips. Today, though, he slid his arms inside her open jacket and pulled her close, kissing her again as he slipped a small vial into her back pocket.

"What is it?" she whispered when their lips separated.

"Put it in the stew tonight. But be careful. Use rubber gloves and then throw them away."

They hadn't talked about the specifics of his plan—the heightened security had made the risks outweigh the benefits. Even at that moment, he wasn't certain the people watching couldn't hear, and he tried to pull away.

"That's it?" she said clinging to him and shooting a nervous glance at one of the cameras trained on them. "You're going to drug them?"

"Carly…" he cautioned, making another subtle attempt to pull away. She held fast.

"Don't you think I've thought about that standing around all day making their food? It won't work. The guards eat in shifts. If you drug them, the people who haven't eaten yet are going to notice everyone passing out."

"Look, just—" he started, but she cut him off.

"And some don't eat at all, Richard. They bring their own food. Or they don't get around to it for hours because of where they're posted."

The door to the lab was suddenly thrown open, and one of Xander's men strode in.

"You both need to get back to work," he said. "Now."

66

Upstate New York
May 27

Carly had brought the untouched beef stew on the counter next to him forty-five minutes ago. That meant everyone who was going to eat had— the last shift would just be finishing up now.

He'd told her to be at the base of the stairs leading to the half-finished lab at seven sharp, and he started cleaning up his slides—making sure to follow the routine the cameras had grown accustomed to.

He was almost finished when one of the guards assigned to watch him appeared in the doorway. He had his hand clamped around Carly's upper arm, and she was trying to keep her face passive, but it was clear that she was terrified.

"Xander wants to see you," he said.

Richard tried to act naturally, smiling with studied weakness as end-less worst-case scenarios flickered across his mind. "I…I'm not feeling well. I don't think I have all those toxins out of my system. Could you tell him that I need a little time? Usually it goes away—"

"Mr. Xander doesn't wait for people. People wait for him. Now let's move."

The man released Carly and started back toward the stairs, motioning for them to follow. She reached out and took Richard's hand, squeezing it tightly as they obediently followed. What choice did they have?

"How did dinner go?" Richard asked, keeping his tone as light as he could manage.

"Fine," she replied. "The stew's just like you wanted."

When they got to the steep staircase leading to the house's third floor, the man in front of them stopped short. The passage was narrow and poorly lit, plummeting into shadow before it took a hard right midway through.

"What is it?" Richard said, leaning subtly forward to better see the guard's enigmatic expression. "Are you all right?"

His thick brow knitted, and he blinked a few times before jerking his head awkwardly in Richard's direction. "What…what are you asking that for?"

They descended quickly, emerging into a wide hallway that they followed in a direction that Richard had never been. His wife's hand felt slick in his and he squeezed a little tighter, trying to be reassuring but knowing that the gesture was hollow.

At the end of the hall, the guard threw open a door and took a position next to it, pointing them into an expansive study.

The walls were full of well-dusted books, and an unlit fireplace large enough to walk into soared directly in front of them. A single leather chair made up half a conversation pit, and there were still indentions in the carpet where the matching chair had once been.

The door to their right opened, and Xander rolled in, parking his wheelchair just over those marks as a man Richard didn't recognize took a place in the chair. He was probably mid thirties, with dark hair and a blue suit that gave the impression of antiseptic fastidiousness.

"This is my new associate, Karl," Xander said. "Karl, Richard and Carly Draman."

"It's a pleasure to finally meet you," he said with a light accent that Richard couldn't quite place. "I must say that Dr. Mason and I were beginning to wonder if this day would ever come."

Richard stiffened at the mention of Mason and released his wife's hand, staring intently at Karl as the man casually crossed his legs.

"The answer to the question forming in your mind is yes," he said. "In fact, I was the very first human to take the therapy. I had just turned eighty-nine at the time."

Richard glanced at his wife and assumed that her stunned expression was reflected on his own face. The photo of Mason had been staggering, but it was nothing compared to physically standing in front of this man. There were no signs at all that he had once been nearing the edge of human longevity. He could go anywhere, do anything. No one would look twice.

"I'm told that the contents of the vial we recovered actually *was* a complete dose," Xander said. "Apparently, I should either be dead or it should be beginning to take effect by now. Any thoughts on what could have gone wrong?"

Richard dragged his attention from Karl to face the old man but found himself mute.

"Don't understand the question, Richard? Let me make it easier. You got out of the car on the way to the hospital after you poisoned yourself. Any chance you left something behind out there?"

A lengthy inventory of lies and diversions ran through Richard's mind, but all sounded ridiculous, even to him. "I think you already know the answer to that, Andreas."

"Where is she?" Karl said. "Where is your daughter?"

"I don't know."

"And even if we did," Carly broke in, "we would never tell you."

"Ah, yes," he said. "The love of a parent. I'm told that there is no psychological force quite as strong—not even the instinct for one's own survival. It doesn't matter though. We have a photograph of the vehicle they're in from an ATM camera near the pharmacy where Burt Seeger attempted to fill your daughter's prescriptions. I'd be very surprised if it takes our combined forces more than a few more days to locate them."

"Why?" Carly said, taking a step toward them before Richard grabbed her arm.

"Why what?" Karl responded.

"Why not just manufacture it? Sell it? You'd make billions."

"Because it would be the end of society as we know it. I don't suppose it's lost on you that the stupider and more useless people are, the more prolifically they breed. Can you imagine every welfare mother, every criminal, every dim or genetically diseased person having access to this? What would stop them from spilling out endless streams of children while the elite have one or two children per century?"

"There could be regulation—"

Xander laughed more loudly than Richard thought possible. He had lost the starring role in this particular drama and obviously wanted it back.

"Regulation? You think the government's going to tell anybody they can't have this? That they can't have as many children as they want? Hell no. They're going to hand it out to everyone, and they're going to use it to consolidate their power. Can you imagine? The same entrenched politician elected over and over again for centuries?" He pointed to Richard. "And your field wouldn't fare any better. A bunch of tenured old professors who ran out of ideas eighty years ago locked into their positions and preventing the rise of anything that shakes tradition."

"He's exactly right," Karl said calmly. "You'd have tens of millions of people psychologically unprepared for this step in human evolution, living mundane lives, doing tedious jobs, watching television, having children. Forever. Not out of any sense of purpose or an effort to make a contribution, but because they're afraid to die."

"And you're not?" Richard said.

He shrugged. "The practical problems with immortality are far greater than you can imagine. The beneficiaries of this therapy must be extremely intelligent, flexible—"

"So a bunch of rich, arrogant murderers like you?" Carly said, "What about Mother Teresa? Or Picasso? Why do *you* get to choose?"

"Someone has to," Xander said.

"But not you," Carly pointed out. "You weren't good enough. *They* didn't choose you. We did."

"Not entirely true," Karl interjected. "Andreas's health is poorer than we would normally accept."

"The therapy could kill him," Richard said to no one in particular, thinking of his daughter fighting for her life in the back of Seeger's RV.

"It's quite possible," Karl said. "Likely, even."

"I thought people might become twisted if they lived forever," Carly said. "But I was wrong. You start out that way."

Richard actually let out a short laugh.

"You think this is funny?" Xander said, obviously expecting more groveling and terror than he was getting.

"I've never heard so much bullshit in my life," Richard said. "Don't give me all this crap about the fabric of society. You don't give a rat's ass about contributing—all you want to do is spend the next five hundred years hoarding wealth and power. If I were choosing, *you* would be the ones excluded. I'd rather have ten welfare mothers than either one of you."

"Then it's fortunate it isn't up to you, isn't it?" Karl said.

Xander had clearly heard enough, and he hit a button on his wheelchair. A muffled buzz drifted in through the closed door behind them. "You shouldn't have turned on me, Richard. You didn't just kill yourself—you killed your wife and daughter."

"Nice try, Andreas, but I'm not stupid. We were dead anyway."

The door opened behind them and the guard entered, a gun hanging loosely from his hand.

Xander pointed a bony finger in their direction. "Get rid of them."

67

Near Madison, Wisconsin
May 27

The air was warm and still as Burt Seeger hobbled down the RV's steps carrying a collapsible wheelchair. He unfolded it next to a picnic table, pausing every few seconds to look around at the activity in the surrounding sites.

He'd parked as close to the center of the campground as he could, making it nearly impossible for an assault team to get to him without being noticed by his new neighbors, many of whom tended to stay up all night drinking.

Susie was still in the RV, sprawled across the bed with two sleeping bags piled on top of her. The IV he'd cobbled together had done its job rehydrating her, and she woke up a few times a day now, always hungry and always cold. He'd bring her favorite—mac and cheese—and get a few spoonfuls into her mouth before she lost consciousness again. There was no recognition in her eyes anymore. Maybe her brain had been damaged by what he'd given her. Maybe he'd destroyed what made her who she was.

Seeger went back up the steps and pulled the sleeping bags off her, immediately adding a down parka and stocking cap to the fleece tracksuit that had failed so miserably to keep her warm. She felt almost weightless as he carried her down the stairs and eased her gently into the wheelchair.

The sun dispersed the clouds hanging on the horizon as he pushed her onto a path that led into the rolling grassland that surrounded the campsite. He knew she should be in bed, but it was so hard to see her lying in the musty old vehicle day after day.

There was a soft crunch behind him, and he spun, reaching for the gun in his jacket before realizing it was just a young couple out for a jog.

"Sorry! Didn't mean to scare you," the girl said, her polite smile turning a little sad when she looked down at Susie.

He watched them recede, cursing himself. They'd made it to within twenty feet before he'd realized they were there. The older he got, the deafer he got, and the more he found himself lost in his own mind. It was only a matter of time before his luck ran out. One day very soon they'd find him. And it would be over before he even knew it had started.

The quality of the trail deteriorated, and Susie slumped right as the chair got hung up in a set of rocky ruts. Her eyes fluttered open, and he pointed to a squirrel standing on its hind legs watching them.

"Look who's come out to say hello," he said, carefully propping her back upright.

A week ago, her ancient face would have been transformed by child-like wonder. Today she just clawed clumsily at the snaps on her jacket, not bothering to lift her gaze from the ground.

He touched her forehead, and it felt hot, but not the burning heat of the fever she'd been running. Maybe the fresh air and sun had finally driven away the chills that had been plaguing her.

"Let's leave the coat on a little longer, sweetheart. We'll start with taking your hat off and see how that goes."

He pulled the knit cap from her head and was about to stuff it in his pocket when he froze. The sweat broke across his lip, and he wiped it away as he stared down at the top of her head. It was an illusion, he told himself—a combination of old eyes and angled sunlight.

Seeger wasn't sure how long it took him to muster the courage to reach out and run a hand across her scalp, but when he did, he discovered it wasn't a mirage. It was real.

He laughed out loud, tears welling up in his eyes as he caressed the downy fuzz of sprouting hair where before there had been nothing.

68

**Upstate New York
May 27**

"I told you to get rid of them!" Xander said.

The guard just stood there, pistol dangling uselessly from his hand. The sound of a muffled gunshot drifted through the open door, but he didn't react other than to squint back toward the hallway as though he were trying to catch a glimpse of the bullet.

Richard didn't know how long the confusion would last, and he lunged, slamming him against a wall and grabbing for his gun hand. He heard Carly yelp in surprise, but she regained her composure quickly, getting hold of the man's other hand and sinking her teeth into his wrist.

He let out a strangled wail and collapsed to the ground, releasing the gun and putting his arms protectively in front of his face. Richard grabbed the weapon and swung it in the direction of Karl and Xander.

But they were gone.

"What the hell's wrong with him?" Carly said as the powerfully built man cowered in the corner.

Richard pulled her into the hallway. "I'll explain later."

They ran back the way they'd come, listening to the shouts of people in other parts of the house mingle with the sound of gunfire and howling dogs. He slowed when they neared the stairs leading to the ground floor, putting a cautionary hand out and peering down at the entry hall. A man with a blond crew cut had taken cover behind a flipped table and was crying inconsolably as he watched the escalating chaos over his pistol sights.

"You!" someone behind them shouted, and they spun in the direction of the voice.

The man was running at them full speed, and Richard pulled his wife into an empty room. She slammed the door behind them and tried to twist the lock knob but was a fraction too slow. It flew open with the sound of cracking wood, and she sprawled backward, pedaling her feet on the polished floor in an effort to get away. Richard managed to get hold of a floor lamp, and he swung it like a baseball bat at the man charging into the room, catching him square in the face.

The force of the blow lifted him off the ground and he landed hard on his back. Richard stood over him with the lamp raised, but the man lay motionless, blood gushing from his nose and a lip held on only by a narrow flap of skin.

Carly crawled to the door and shoved it closed, putting her back against it as a gunfight erupted downstairs. "What the hell did you do?"

"Acid," Richard responded, edging toward the window and looking outside. Directly below them a Doberman was chasing its tail while two others lay motionless in the grass. Their handler, who apparently had let them get into his leftover stew, was perched in the branches of a pine tree.

"LSD? You had me put LSD in the food?"

He nodded, watching Xander's security force continue to disintegrate. "Like you said, tranquilizing them wouldn't work—the later shifts would notice and some of them don't eat. I needed something that didn't have an obvious onset and that would keep the people who didn't get a dose busy."

"LSD," she repeated, a hint of admiration in her voice. "I would have never thought of that."

She got on all fours and opened the door just enough to peek out. The gunfire downstairs had gone silent, but the shouts and screams hadn't.

"So what's the plan? Are we going to climb out the window? It's pretty far, but—"

"You've never dropped acid have you, Carly?"

"No."

"Well, I have, and I don't think we want to be climbing down the side of the building with a bunch of tripping mercenaries below us."

"Why am I suddenly getting the feeling you haven't fully thought this through?"

"The guards' reaction was too unpredictable to work out anything detailed. But we've got a chance. All we have to do is walk out of here."

"Excuse me?"

"Don't look at anybody, don't make any sudden moves. Just walk."

"That's your plan? We just leave?"

He didn't answer, instead pulling the broken door open and heading back into the hallway. She started to run to catch up, but he waved a hand behind him, and she slowed to a more or less natural gait.

"Richard," she said in a hoarse whisper. "We can't just—"

He put a finger to his lips, silencing her. "No talking."

The alarm began to sound just as they started down the stairs, but he kept going, ignoring its deafening wail and the men faced off below.

"There's someone at the bottom," Carly said quietly.

The man was lying on the marble floor, his face covered with his hands. Richard kept moving, slipping the gun he'd taken from his waistband. If the man noticed them stepping over him, he gave no indication.

They'd almost made it to the front door when a shot sounded behind them and exploded into the plaster to their left.

"Freeze!"

The man stumbled forward and fired another round, obviously having trouble aiming. This one shredded the edge of a portrait depicting Xander in much younger days.

Richard lined up his own pistol and fired back, but his military school had wisely drawn the line at training its misfit students on concealable weapons. The shot went wide.

He abandoned his effort to keep them invisible and started to run, dragging his wife along behind. They came out into an enormous circular driveway and charged toward a black SUV parked at its edge. Carly yanked the passenger door open and jumped in, sliding over the console into the driver's seat. "The keys are in it! Get in!"

The sound of a window breaking above caused Richard to duck involuntarily. A moment later, a man bounced off the vehicle's front fender and hit the pavement hard enough to collapse the right side of his head.

Richard looked down at him—at the lifeless eyes half open, at the blood matting his hair. The other reason he'd chosen LSD was that it was impossible to overdose on. He hadn't wanted to kill anyone.

"Richard! What are you doing?" Carly shouted as she started the SUV's engine. "Get in the damn car!"

The man who had shot at them inside the house finally made it to the driveway and this time took careful aim. Richard tensed as he pulled the trigger, but instead of an earsplitting crack, there was a quiet click.

"Richard!" Carly shouted again, and he jumped in. The door nearly slammed on his legs when she floored the vehicle through an elaborate flowerbed and aimed it at the iron gate leading to the road.

"Air bags!" Richard shouted, and she spun the wheel, drifting the vehicle one hundred and eighty degrees. She threw it in reverse and sped backward toward the gate, wrenching it from the stone fence with a deafening crash and a shower of sparks.

Richard turned in the seat as she launched the SUV up the road, looking through the spider-webbed rear windshield at a black sedan squealing away from the curb and accelerating in their direction.

"Go! Go!" he shouted. "They're coming after us!"

But the sedan took a hard right and disappeared through the demolished gate—probably in answer to an SOS from Karl and Xander.

Richard gripped the seat as Carly swung the vehicle onto a wider, less secluded road. No one followed, and within a few minutes they were mixing with other cars, passing pedestrians, barns, and tractors. The real world. He'd almost forgotten it existed.

69

**Central Laos
Seven Years Later**

The woman's voice rose to a near screech, her words coming in a desperate, unintelligible flood. Richard Draman sat down on a stool fashioned from a tree stump and signaled for calm as he formed the sentence "He's going to be fine" in the local language.

A familiar expression of confusion appeared on the woman's face for a moment as she attempted to decipher what he'd said, and then she returned to her panicked diatribe.

He leaned back against the grass wall of the hut and looked down at the infant lying on a blanket spread out on the floor. The infection wasn't serious, but his mother's fear was understandable. In this part of the world, Monday's mild fever often deteriorated into Friday's funeral.

"OK, OK," he said, enunciating carefully, as though that would somehow make her understand English. "Just wait here for a second."

He walked to the door and looked down at a teenage girl lying in the shade of a flowering tree. Seven years of unlicensed doctoring in rural Laos and he could still barely communicate on the level of a two-year-old.

"A little help?"

She raised herself up on her elbows and frowned at him, dark hair falling across a round face marked by just a few pimples. "Mom says you're using me as a crutch. She says I shouldn't reward that kind of behavior."

He thumbed to his ancient Range Rover. "It's a long walk home, Susie."

She considered his point for a moment and then stood, slapping dust from the plaid skirt and white blouse that was the uniform at her school.

She was a beautiful girl but didn't seem to notice. After growing up with the pitying and shocked stares of nearly everyone she came in contact with, she would have been grateful for simple anonymity—something hard to come by for a five-foot-nine-inch white girl living in the Laotian countryside.

Susie bowed politely when she entered the hut, her easy smile soothing the woman noticeably.

"Tell her that her son's going to be fine."

Susie translated in what people assured him was perfect Lao, and he held out a small bottle of pills. "She needs to crush one of these up in his food every day. And he needs to take them all—even if he's feeling better before they're done."

When Susie finished explaining, the woman grabbed his hand, shaking it violently and continuing to talk in rapid-fire Lao.

"She says she has some nice silk she's woven. Or a chicken. You get your pick."

"What do you think?"

"I'd go for chicken tonight. Mom could make that really spicy pepper sauce."

"Yeah…the pepper sauce is good, isn't it?"

His medical fee squawked loudly as he shoved its wicker cage in the back of the Range Rover. One of the beers rolling around on the floorboard caught his eye, and he popped it open, taking a grateful swig of the hot liquid.

"Can I drive, Dad?"

He shook his head. "Remember what happened last time?"

"That was a freak accident. You can't hold that against me." She pointed to the can in his hand. "Drinking and driving kills."

He thought about it for a moment and then climbed reluctantly into the passenger seat. A moment later, they were fishtailing off in a cloud of dust.

"Just because we live in the third world doesn't mean we have to drive like we're from here, Susie."

"What are you talking about? I *am* from here."

He didn't respond, instead taking another pull on his beer. It was essentially true. While he was little more than a trapped tourist, she had lived half her life in Laos.

There was no reason to believe that Karl and August Mason would ever give up trying to track them down, and they'd needed to get permanently lost. Where better than the mountains of Southeast Asia?

Of course, he and Carly had considered going to the authorities, but quickly decided against it. Even if they had been able to find a government agency that Mason's people couldn't influence, where would it have left Susie? At best, word would get out, and she'd become a reluctant celebrity with something everyone wanted. At worst, she'd become a guinea pig, an unwilling religious figure, or a lightning rod for jealousy and hate. Maybe all of the above.

After everything she'd endured, she deserved a normal life. Or at least as normal as he could provide.

"When are we going to go back, Dad?"

"What do you mean? Back where?"

"To America."

"I don't know."

"What about Europe?"

He turned in his seat to face her. "Why the sudden interest?"

"I don't know. I've never seen any of it. You tell stories, and I watch movies, but that's different."

"We'll plan a trip."

She knew a lie when she heard one, and he watched her expression turn sullen. She was growing up so fast. They wouldn't be able to put off what he and Carly had dubbed "the talk" for much longer, though he still wasn't sure what they were going to say.

The truth was that he didn't know what was going to happen to her. It was possible that Mason's serum did nothing but cure her progeria. In that case, she would grow old and die just like everyone else.

On the other hand, she might just continue to mature normally until she was thirty or so and then stop and stay that age forever.

He didn't have the equipment to look deeply into her altered genome, but based on what tests he had been able to do, she was in no way an ordinary girl anymore. In fact, there were probably significant enough genetic changes to make the average taxonomist consider categorizing her as a subspecies. At this point, he didn't even know if she'd be able to have viable children with an unaltered male.

And that's why "the talk" always seemed like something for tomorrow. He suspected that discussions starting with "your mother and I aren't sure you're technically human, and there are a bunch of incredibly powerful men who will hunt you until the end of time" rarely ended well.

Richard settled back in his seat and went to work on his beer again, remaining quiet as Susie's driving became increasingly reckless. She had every reason to be angry.

Thirty minutes of silence later, they pulled up to the old French colonial house he'd purchased when they'd arrived in the country. The roof was bowed, the paint was peeling, and there was no electricity. On the other hand, the breeze blew through the open windows year-round, and flowering coffee plants still covered the hills surrounding it.

It wasn't really how he'd pictured his life turning out, but in many ways, it was better. He lived in one of the most beautiful places in the world, his daughter was healthy, his family was intact, and he helped people every day. One at a time, of course, but there was a certain pleasure in it that couldn't be duplicated in a lab.

Susie leapt to the ground, and he jogged up behind her as they went through the house's open front door. Carly and Burt Seeger were sitting on a bench in the shabby grandeur of the foyer when they entered. Richard had convinced the old soldier to escape with them, and he'd quickly become just another part of the family. Susie started calling him Grandpa when she was nine, and at some point Carly had started calling him Dad. It just seemed natural.

Richard's eyes adjusted to the shadow of the room, and he suddenly could see the fear in their faces. He grabbed Susie by the shoulder, dragging the surprised girl back toward the door.

"Too late," an unfamiliar voice said.

Three white men emerged from the arch leading to the kitchen. The two carrying assault rifles took up positions at the edges of the room while the third walked unsteadily to its center. He was probably in his mid thirties, but pale and completely bald. His thin frame was noticeably bowed, and he leaned heavily on a cane for support.

"It's been a long time," he said. "I believe the last time we saw each other, you had just given my men a massive dose of LSD."

Richard's breath caught in his chest, and he pulled Susie the rest of the way behind him.

"I'm sorry," Seeger said, as Carly patted his hand. "I've gotten so goddamn old."

"It's OK," Richard replied. "It's not your fault."

"What's going on, Daddy? Who are these people?"

"Don't worry about it, honey. This doesn't have anything to do with you."

Xander locked his eyes on her, squinting through the gloom at her unlined face. "She doesn't know? You haven't told her any of it?"

"Nothing," Carly said. "So there's no reason for you to hurt her."

Xander waved a hand dismissively and eased himself into a chair. "You're hard people to track down. My compliments."

Richard looked at the two armed men and then behind him at Susie. She was scared, but also curious. She remembered her former life, her disease, her old last name. She'd always known there was something they weren't telling her.

"There aren't many of us left," Xander said. "Ironic, isn't it? Karl was the first to get cancer. In his kidney. They removed it, but the cancer came back in his bones, and that was the end of him. Then the others started getting it. Some survived the first, even the second bout, but remission never lasted long. When they discovered it in Mason, it was in his pancreas. He didn't last three months."

"And you?" Richard said.

"Lungs. Funny, huh? Never smoked a day in my life. They say I'm going to live. This time."

Xander motioned to his security men, and they filed out the door, leaving them alone. "Mason thought he had the cancer problem beat. Turns out he was wrong."

Seeger's attention moved to a rifle hanging on the wall, and Xander immediately noticed.

"Make a move, old man. I guarantee you won't get three feet."

"Everyone just relax," Richard said. "What do you want, Andreas?"

"What do I want? You know goddamn well what I want." He pointed to Susie. "She's next, you know. Maybe not this year. But next year or the year after that. You'll watch her die in agony. Just like I watched the others."

"Daddy?"

"It's OK, honey," he said.

"Your father's lying to you, Susie. He's been lying to you all along. It's not OK."

"Shut up!" Richard said.

"Spare me the drama," Xander responded. "I'm here to offer you a chance to save her. You're a brilliant scientist with a background in cancer research. You know the therapy exists, and I can get you all of Mason's data. You can figure this thing out and still keep everything quiet."

"Why keep it quiet?" Richard said. "Seems like you'd do whatever you had to in order to stay alive. If there's anything I remember about you, it's that."

The familiar anger flashed in Xander's young eyes, but he managed to control it. "I don't suppose there's any reason at this point for me to bullshit you, Richard. In order to maintain our anonymity and power base, we've been forced to do things that...let's just say they wouldn't be appreciated. I've got a long life to live, and I'd rather not spend it in prison."

"So I should save you?"

Xander shook his head and pointed to Susie. "You should save her."

EPILOGUE

Near Munich, Germany
25 Years Later

"Your meeting with the architects doing the expansion of the genetics lab has been moved to three, and I've rescheduled your interview with *Time* magazine for after."

Richard Draman tapped his temple with an index finger. "No problem, Greta. I've got it all in my head."

His secretary scowled in a way that only Germans could—a veritable treatise on his inefficiency and absentmindedness. And she was probably right. She usually was.

"One last thing," she said. "Your wife called and said she'll be a few minutes late for lunch. Traffic, apparently."

Richard gave her the thumbs-up, prompting another scowl before she turned on her heels and marched out of his expansive office. He reached for his keyboard with the intention of finally getting around to the overdue budget reports, but instead opened an encrypted photo of Susie, Carly, and Burt Seeger. It had been taken the day they left Laos on Xander's private jet. Almost twenty-five years ago now.

Susie stared out from the screen with a mix of excitement and apprehension, everything in her life having just been turned upside down. She'd eventually travel the globe and collect the experiences of ten lifetimes over the course of just a few years.

A fight with melanoma at eighteen had hardly slowed her down. She'd even found time to fall in love with the son of a South African

diplomat—a wonderful kid who had stuck with her until she finally suc-
cumbed to leukemia at the age of twenty-two. Seeger had followed a
year later, and though he normally didn't believe in such things, Richard
suspected it was from a broken heart.

His gaze shifted to Carly, but it was hard now to put the woman in the
photo together with his wife. Xander's surgeons had altered their appear-
ances before creating elaborate new identities for them. And then, of
course, there were the years.

He spun his chair to face the glass wall behind his desk and looked out
on the grass-covered research campus below.

Xander hadn't been as durable as he'd given himself credit for, dying
a few months after he'd created the Cancer Venture and installed Richard
as its director. Strangely, that was less an end than a beginning. He'd left
not only *his* money to the Venture, but the money that he had inherited
from his group of would-be immortals. Richard now controlled billions of
research dollars and was the driving force in the world's still unsuccessful
quest to cure cancer.

He heard the door behind him open, and a moment later Carly leaned
over the back of his chair and wrapped her arms around him.

"You left before I woke up this morning," she said.

"Couldn't sleep."

"It's always that way, isn't it? You always get so melancholy on your
birthday. You know what they say. Seventy is the new fifty."

"Is that really what they say?"

"As far as you know."

He smiled and ran a hand slowly along her arm. "Do you ever wonder, Carly?"

"Wonder about what?"

"What it would be like to be young again?"

He watched her reflection in the glass as she considered the question.
"Never."